FOR ALL OF YOU

FROM ALL OF US

Peter Davis

Bill Panzer

Acknowledgments

First and foremost, I would like to thank Bill Panzer and Peter Davis for allowing me to go on this grand adventure with *Highlander*; it has been an amazing experience. I would also like to thank everyone listed on pages ix–x. This book could not have been created without their generosity of time and spirit.

And special thanks to (alphabetically):

Dennis Berry and Richard Martin for being such gracious hosts and allowing me to inhabit their sets
Laura Brennan for being the goddess of photographs
Richard Cook for sharing his photographs and his art
Marc Goldstein for sharing his storyboard art
Ken Gord for being Ken Gord
Tracy Hillman, Don Paonessa, Rainmaker Digital Pictures, Post Modern Sound, and all the folks in postproduction for their hospitality
Kari Hobson for keeping me supplied with videotapes
Gillian Horvath for the introduction
Donna Lettow for being my guide through the slide morass and for keeping the episode guide on the path of righteousness
Florence Mayeur for being my guardian angel in France

And personal thanks to:

Beth Barter for, among other things, thinking driving in Paris was a good idea
Betsy Mitchell for her patience and her humor
The High Lonesome for the music

HIGHLANDER™

THE COMPLETE WATCHER'S GUIDE

BY
MAUREEN RUSSELL

ASPECT®

WARNER BOOKS

A Time Warner Company

All photos courtesy of Davis Panzer Productions, Inc., except where indicated.
Photo on page 62 courtesy of Richard Cook.
Postproduction photos on pages 142, 143, and 145 courtesy of Rainmaker Digital Imaging.
Storyboard art on pages 54–55 courtesy of Marc Goldstein.

Warner Books, Inc., 1271 Avenue of the Americas, New York, NY 10020

Visit our Web site at http://warnerbooks.com

A Time Warner Company

Printed in the United States of America
First Printing: September 1998
10 9 8 7 6 5 4 3 2

Library of Congress Cataloging-in-Publication Data

Russell, Maureen.
    Highlander : the complete watcher's guide / Maureen Russell.
        p.   cm.
    ISBN 0-446-67435-4
    1. Highlander (Television program)   I. Title.
PN1992.77.H53R87   1998   98-17609
791.45'72—dc21   CIP

Cover design by Don Puckey
Book design and text composition by H. Roberts Design

Enter the World of
Highlander

Roger Daltrey, on his Immortal role as Hugh Fitzcairn: "I'm the leprechaun of *Highlander*."

David Abramowitz, head writer: "I think the core of our show is about honor and integrity, the sense of spirituality, and humanity. That's what I hope I bring to the show . . . along with some kick-ass action and a little bit of romance."

Director Dennis Berry, responsible for such popular episodes as "Archangel"and "The Samurai": "I try to add a dimension of madness to the surreal *Highlander* dream."

Production designer Steve Geaghan, credited with giving the show its distinctive look: "In the *Highlander* world you could turn a corner and run into something completely different. The look of the show was gritty and dark and very stylish."

Fight choreographer F. Braun McAsh, sword master and expert on bladed weapons: "The fights have to tell a story, they are there to further the plot, they are there to tell things about the characters."

Producer Ken Gord: "I don't actually do anything myself. I just make sure that it gets done."

A postproduction wizard who wishes to remain anonymous: "We could tell you our secrets, but then we'd have to kill you."

HIGHLANDER™
THE COMPLETE WATCHER'S GUIDE

Contents

The Players of This Piece

(Alphabetically)

David Abramowitz as creative consultant
Tom Archer as "Sparky"
Roger Bellon as composer
Dennis Berry as director
Chester Bialowas as effects editor
Laura Brennan as script coordinator
Jim Byrnes as Joe Dawson
Richard Cook as art director
Roger Daltrey as Hugh Fitzcairn
Peter Davis as executive producer
Anthony De Longis as Otavio Consone
Joe Fisher as communications director, Rainmaker Digital Pictures
Steve Geaghan as production designer
Chantal Giuliani as production designer
Marc Goldstein as storyboardist
Ken Gord as producer
Elizabeth Gracen as Amanda
Tony Gronick as sound supervisor
Gerard Hameline as director
Ken Hayward as digital compositor
Tracy Hillman as postproduction supervisor
Gillian Horvath as associate creative consultant
David Houle as president, Post Modern Sound
Peter Hudson as James Horton
Stan Kirsch as Richie Ryan
Donna Lettow as associate creative consultant
Charles Lyall as production manager

F. Braun McAsh as sword master
Katie McFadden as operations manager, Gastown Post
Christina McQuarrie as costume designer
Stein Myhrstad as editor
Bill Panzer as executive producer
Don Paonessa as creative consultant, postproduction
Adrian Paul as Duncan MacLeod
Valentine Pelka as Kronos
Stephen Pepper as digital compositor
Rex Raglan as production designer
Vince Renaud as lead mixer
Darryl Smith as operations supervisor, Gastown Post
David Tynan as executive script consultant
Peter Wingfield as Methos
Amy Zoll as production assistant and house archaeologist

THE COMPLETE WATCHER'S GUIDE

CHAPTER ONE

Beginnings
"He was born. . . ."

Denis Leroy, Executive Producer (Head of Production)

*W*e meet at Gaumont in Paris. The offices are an impressive array of metal and glass. —M.R.

I am Denis Leroy. I am head of production for Gaumont Television. Gaumont, as you may know, is one of the feature production companies and feature distribution companies in France and in Europe. Gaumont opened this television branch five years ago, and one of the first projects we developed was *Highlander: The Series*.

Gaumont's president, Christian Charret, had formerly worked with Christophe Lambert, who was the lead in the feature. I think that's how the connection got done at the very beginning. Bill Panzer and Peter Davis had the underlying rights from the feature, and Christophe somehow made the link between what he knew was a Davis-Panzer project and what he knew was a potential for Gaumont Television.

I traveled to Vancouver, at the start, to meet people and find out how we would set up the production because we had made the joint decision to shoot the series in Canada and Europe for coproduction reasons. There was also a legitimate and very creative reason for doing so. Because of the flashbacks and the history of our characters, it was natural to use the locations and the talent in Europe and Northern America.

And we have set up this logistically efficient cooperation between the Paris segment, the Vancouver segment, and the L.A. segment. I supervise the shift between Canada and France as well as the overall production budgeting and planning. And my job is production-oriented. I make sure that whatever we plan will be shot on time, on schedule, and on budget. I am in charge of meeting the various people who collaborate on the show. I take part in the approval process for the directors and key talent such as directors of photography and editors.

I have been doing this for many episodes, over a hundred. It's been fun. I know what happened at the very beginning. We were all on the same level and we had the same kind of motivation to make it work. It was not only business; there was a part of us at stake there, too, to make it a success. So we kept working and doing our best.

When I look back at it, now, I have no regrets. I think it has been fun all the time. It's incredible when you start mixing various continents and countries. The combination of personalities and talents is just incredible. And I think you learn a lot from that. British actors, French and Canadian directors, American writers, Canadian writers—it is such a cocktail of talent that you have to learn something from it. It's different from the usual way.

What do you think you've learned?

I think I learned how complex the communication process can be in various countries. But I also learned how to solve it by addressing the right issues at the right time and also by learning how to combine talent and procedures between various countries. Basically, a camera is a camera, whether it's a Canadian camera, a French camera, or an American camera. But the people behind it sometimes react differently or have a different approach or a different style, and this is where you have to make sure that everybody connects with the right spirit and the right style.

And people tend to think this is one of the toughest shows, because we move to so many locations. In France, we never go back to a studio. We keep running from one practical location to another almost every day with the exception of the barge. Given the transportation problem that you probably experienced in this city, you can imagine how many hours are spent in moving. And sometimes, when we want to find a new and different location, we have to pack all our trucks and the whole circus and drive one or two hours away from Paris and settle down in a castle for a couple of days. This makes it a tough task. But after a few days the crew understands the requirements of the show. Every show is somehow a different environment. I think that's very motivating. Basically, you don't have time to get bored. It's tiring, but never boring.

CHAPTER TWO

The Writers

"Dear Murdering Bastards . . ."

*T*his book will follow the creation of a show from start to finish. That is, it all begins with the writers, their concepts, ideas, and scripts. When the script is approved, it goes to the set, where the show is created, produced, and made into film. The film is then sent to postproduction, where episodes are cut, polished, and made ready to air.

We meet the story department in Los Angeles. Story has the best toys and treats. —M.R.

David Abramowitz, Creative Consultant

I am David Abramowitz. I am creative consultant. I am the head writer on the show. If this were an American-based show, I would be an executive producer. What do I do? I am in charge of all the writing. I help steer the ship, creatively, spiritually, emotionally. I'm the last typewriter. I'm the arbiter of most arguments. Bill [Panzer] and I have kind of creative control over the show. We fight sometimes. Sometimes we agree. And it's a kind of give-and-take between the two of us.

We have a wonderful staff now. And I've had a wonderful staff of people over the years and they provide lots of ideas. I don't care where the ideas come from, just as long as they come. And even if they come from me, I'm not sure where they come from. They're out there and they happen if you get lucky. Some ideas are better than others are.

Do you have any favorite ideas or episodes?

I like a lot of different episodes for a lot of different reasons. **"Legacy"** I like because everybody is wonderful in it. The characters are wonderful. It plays great. It's a wonderful action-adventure story. I loved Rebecca and I love Amanda and I love the stuff between Mac and Amanda. It wasn't a tremendously spiritually deep episode, but it was great fun and a good piece.

I loved **"The Valkyrie"** because it posed an inherent moral question as to whether it was all right to kill one today to save a hundred tomorrow. That, I thought, was a great question. I loved **"Little Tin God"** because it asked some very, very good questions. It dealt with man's relationship to God.

There was an episode called **"Warmonger"** that I liked for the question it basically asked, which was How long do you have to keep a promise? And what's the difference between honor and vanity? Which is a major point that we play in the show.

I loved **"The Samurai"** because I loved the idea of the way that MacLeod got his katana. And that was a show about honor.

Many of your shows are about honor.

I think the core of our show is about honor and integrity, the sense of spirituality and humanity. That's what I hope I bring to the show along with some kick-ass action and a little bit of romance.

I had a conversation with Steve Geaghan once, whom I respect tremendously, who said that after a conversation with me, he understood what *Highlander* was—which was a Talmudic discussion with ass-kicking. I thought that was a great definition of what *Highlander* was.

There was an episode called "**Brothers in Arms**" where Charlie died. I liked that one because I thought it was a great story. It was vivid emotionally and it was wonderful. I loved "**Armageddon**" because Jim Byrnes gave an incredible performance, which was heartbreaking. And I loved that.

I loved "**Duende**." I loved the way it was directed. I love the feel. "**Duende**" was a flamenco, a dance that tells a story about betrayal, passion, and vengeance. If you look at "**Duende**," it's like that. I thought the flashback was great. I thought the fight between Anthony De Longis and Adrian was wonderful. And, basically, "**Duende**" happened because Anthony came in with that style of fighting and said, "Can we do something regarding this?" And I said, "Absolutely." And we put something together, and he starred in it.

Another episode that I liked when we did it is "**Studies in Light**." "**Studies in Light**" marked a turn for us. I remember sitting there and saying, "I would like to do an episode

about a nihilistic Immortal." I thought it would be interesting to explore an emotional and mental construct rather than another bad guy. For me, that was the beginning of recognizing that we could build stories about intriguing characters, not just evil characters.

"**Blind Faith**" I liked. It didn't turn out as well as I would have liked, but the question I love: whether redemption is possible.

There are a lot of episodes that I left out, like "**Deliverance**" and "**Something Wicked**." And I loved "**Comes a Horseman**." There are lots that I am really proud of. Some I love for the great production values. Some I love because magic was created on the screen. And some I love because there is some spiritual or intellectual content that I think is really valuable.

Have there been any episodes that disappointed you?

I still love them, they are my children, but, yes, some have disappointed. Most of the time when I dislike an episode it's because I thought it was better on the page. Sometimes some of the scripts aren't particularly good. You think they're good, and then in hindsight, you realize you didn't spend enough time. I think what happened with **"Richard Redstone"** was that everyone was so exhausted and so high from doing **"Comes a Horseman"** and the hundredth show that the thought was, "How can we possibly follow this with something equally dramatic?" So we went for a comedy and a bit of a spoof, and it didn't really work. I was disappointed in it.

What else didn't I like? **"The Zone."** We have difficulty doing episodes where there are no Immortals. We always have. I think one of the problems with that is unless there is life-and-death jeopardy to MacLeod it is hard to keep the dramatic tension going. In our universe the only people who have greater powers are MacLeod and his fellow Immortals. So it becomes difficult for me as a writer and difficult for us as a group of writers. This is probably my failing, that I couldn't make it work better.

Everyone must ask about the Immortal sword battles.

It's in the core of the show. It's inherent within the universe. We have been accused of being a very violent show, and I don't think that we are. And I think that we work very hard at having MacLeod not take pleasure in causing death. I think he would certainly rather live and let live, but circumstances create themselves where he has to act. It's kind of like someone going to war. Sane people don't like to kill other people, and neither does MacLeod.

I think, overall, the reason that I love *Highlander* is because there are very few shows on television where I can play out the intellectual discussions that go on in my head. The best thing about the business for me has been the writers. I really love writers. When I got started in this business, there were four or five older writers, and at the end of the day, six o'clock, a bottle of vodka would come out and guys would just sit around and they'd talk. And they'd talk about their philosophy on life and they'd talk about the nature of good and evil and they'd talk about morals and ethics and they'd talk about all kinds of things. That's the best part of the business. And that's the best part of the show for me. Being able to talk about those kinds of things in a forum that I think is fun.

As you may know, everyone raves about you.

I think they're overstating. The truth is that you're never as good as they think you are and you're never as bad as they think you are. My history is such that I work as a cantor, which means I am a singer of prayers in a Jewish synagogue. I take a Torah class, which is basically a Bible study group. And the man who leads the group is a Jungian analyst as well as a Talmudic scholar and a rabbi, so it gives me great opportunities to look at the very questions that we pose in *Highlander*.

What does someone who is five thousand years old think of God? And what is God to him? When MacLeod was asked, "Do you believe in God?" his answer was "Sometimes." I think MacLeod's philosophy would be close to mine, which is, it doesn't matter whether you believe in God or not, what matters is that you live your life as though you do.

Speaking of five thousand years old . . . what about Methos?

Methos is an extremely complex character. He's great fun to write, and he's wonderfully acted by Peter Wingfield. You can write the most wonderful character in the world, and if someone doesn't understand the character and believe the character, the audience is not going to. But Peter

does; he believes the character, and he's happy to be the character. It is interesting. Methos has lived; he has been good and evil. He has seen civilizations rise and fall. He has been through vanity and has been through his God trip and has probably been through a time in his life when people thought he was a god. He is a little more closed than the other characters are. And I think that's good, because mystery is important. But we know what he was and we know that he changed. And we know that Methos' greatest ability is the ability to survive. That's what he does; he survives. So in looking at Methos, I think the most important thing to him is that "I am." Because I think that he's seen so much morality and ethics be situational and changing according to the times that he believes that the only true agenda for him is that he keep living. I believe that he would like to do the right thing, most of the time. I think what is very telling about Methos is in **"Chivalry,"** when he takes Kristin's head. And he says, "I was born before the age of chivalry." In many ways he is the ultimate feminist, because it doesn't matter to him. A sword is a sword and a head is a head.

What about Joe Dawson?

I love Joe. How can you not love Joe? Because I love Jim Byrnes. Jim's soul plays through Joe Dawson. It was interesting; in the beginning with Joe, the Dawson we wrote was a totally different character and it didn't work as well as it could. So we came up with the idea of the blues bar, which was a perfect place for him and gave us opportunities to hear his music. He's a human guy; he's a real mensch, Jim. There are no illusions. There is strength but not a tremendous amount of vanity.

He was incredible in **"Armageddon."** And we talked to him. I called him before and I said, "Jim, how do you feel about this?" Because I would never do anything that would make him uncomfortable as a human being. But he was actually excited to do it. He was really into it, up for it, going for it. He's come to terms with his life and who he is. I can think of no one I would rather hang out with, to tell you the truth. Joe is pretty much the human factor, but he's the heroic human factor.

That's the other thing I like about our show; our characters are all somewhat flawed, they are all somewhat human, they all have their own agenda, and they can be wrong. And there's a difference between being wrong and being evil, which is what we have hoped to show a number of times. Our characters can have different opinions on things, and both can be right. After all, how many Immortals of the week can you develop? Most good shows are about character. And it is inconceivable that someone who has lived that long would not be subject to his own foibles, his own morality, and who he was when he was born.

Another interesting thing is that although our characters grow throughout time, basically their early childhood development stays with them. How you were as a kid directly impacts who you are the rest of your life. Look at Carl Robin-son as played by Bruce Young, who is a wonder-ful actor. Carl was a slave. Throughout his life, no matter where he goes, that part of him—though other things get laid over it—that part of him remains there. Dun-can MacLeod was born and bred to be a clan leader, to take responsi-

bility for people and to make decisions for other people. Some might ask, "Who am I to judge?" And MacLeod would say, "Who else can judge?" He was born to be and is a leader. Amanda stole to live. She was a thief because she needed to survive. And in some part of her soul, there is probably the great fear that if I don't take it, now, there will come a time that there won't be enough. So that in some ways, even though Amanda is joking and great fun, there is that part of her. There's that little bit of insecurity, which makes all the people interesting.

How about Richie?

The truth is that you can't keep a character a street punk for years. The character has to grow and grow on his own. This show is not called *The Highlander and Richie*. For Richie's growth, he really could no longer be the spear-carrier. The show was not inherently about him. And this is not because of the actor. But, for example, the character of Methos leads you into more interesting storytelling. And the character of Amanda gives you things that the young sidekick doesn't, and there are only a certain number of stories that you can play.

Look at the stories that Joe opened up because of the character of Joe and the conflicts that Joe faces. And coming to terms with being somewhat of a hypocrite, which is, "We observe; we don't act." And then you see Joe act. Which happens because he is human and because it's a classic case of "Do what I say, not what I do." And that's the way life is and that's the way people are. And I think that Joe believes that there is something singular and special about Duncan MacLeod, that there may be a destiny MacLeod has to fulfill, which is even greater than the Watchers'. So, those things are always very difficult, and those are the things that he plays with. In **"Indiscretions,"** it is Joe and Methos, and the issue of interference comes to the fore.

Why does Joe think Duncan is special?

Why in our universe does Joe think Duncan is special? Because he has seen signs, **"Avatar," "Armageddon," "Something Wicked," "Deliverance," "Prophecy,"** that separate MacLeod from everyone else, that there is a prophecy that MacLeod is the anointed one. We hint at it, and obviously Joe feels this, plus he feels a tremendous admiration for MacLeod. He loves Duncan MacLeod. This is as deep as one man can feel for another. And I think it's returned.

Peter Wingfield thinks that Methos would take Duncan's head if he had to, to survive. Would Duncan take Methos' head?

I think both of them to survive would kill the other, when you came down to it. I think that you would have to create a scenario where the stakes would have to be enormously high. There would have to be no out, where the winner at the end of the fight could not walk away because the jeopardy to untold millions or to whomever would be so great that he would do this. And I think it would be done tearfully. I mean, look at **"The Valkyrie."** MacLeod made a choice, a choice that not everybody would make, but he made it and he lives with it. I think you are who you are. And if pushed to a certain position, you will act in a certain way. Duncan MacLeod is and always will be Duncan MacLeod of the Clan MacLeod. And Methos will survive.

There are a couple of actors I didn't mention that I would like to mention—Roger Daltrey, who plays Fitz, and Elizabeth Gracen, who plays

Amanda. They bring magic to the piece. Any time that they are in an episode I know that the episode is going to be fun and I know that it is going to be well acted. And I know that they are going to bring something beyond the page to the film. They have been wonderful.

And Alexandra Vandernoot, who plays Tessa, was the goddess. And when I saw her and Adrian standing together, I thought that if I died, and there was a Mount Olympus, that the two of them would be standing together with thunderbolts around them. They were godlike. They were so beautiful and had such presence. She was great. The last two episodes of *Highlander* will be remarkable.

I want to say one other thing; people have heaped a lot of praise on me, and truly, I mean this really truly, a lot of that praise should be deflected to James Thorpe, Donna Lettow, Gillian Horvath, Laura Brennan, Amy Zoll, and David Tynan. They are remarkable. And their job, when they come in, is to never make me seem like an idiot; and most of the time they are very successful. David Tynan was, in many ways, part of the backbone of the show; I could always depend on him delivering. And that's a remarkable thing because sometimes the pressure to deliver on a deadline, continually, becomes enormous. David consistently did wonderful work.

Also, Bill Panzer's impact on the show is enormous. And Don Paonessa; many shows are saved or helped dramatically in postproduction. Bill really runs the editing with Don. And the other thing that Bill does is that Bill knows how good I can be. And most of the time he will not accept anything but as good as I can be. Sometimes we all slip, especially when we do all these episodes. But he makes me a better writer. We fight a lot. We get cranky with each other. We're like an old married couple, he and

I. We go off in the corner and mumble about each other, but we always come back. And the show works.

Any regrets?

Sometimes I think that my failure has been that I haven't been able to make the show so that the casual viewer would like it. You have to pay attention to *Highlander*. Everything plays into everything else. And you have to have some knowledge of what our world is and what Watchers are and Duncan's history. For our hard-core audience and the people who watch it and who know these things, it works very well. For someone who comes in and just watches for the first time, it's "What's holy ground? What's this? What's that?" And I wasn't talented enough to overcome that. But we still stayed on the air for six years.

David Tynan, Executive Script Consultant

Over a lunch of dim sum and tea, I meet Methos' "Dad." —M.R.

Tell me about Highlander.

The thing with *Highlander* is that I think we've always thought we had to do something different. It's wonderful dramatic tension. You would live forever. Well, maybe, unless you meet someone better with a sword. That was good. I have no idea where Bill Panzer and Peter Davis found the original notion, but it is a wonderful one and it has served everyone marvelously well for this action-adventure series.

Every show changes after the first year. The first year is a shakedown year. It's very hard; people are finding out what the show is about, what the tone is, where it's going. *Highlander* had quite a large change of show writers the first year. When David Abramowitz arrived, I think the interest to do stories that were deeply moral in some way came to the fore. David Abramowitz is a deeply moral man. It's one of the reasons I like him a great deal and love him dearly. He would always look for the moral core to the story.

I understand most of the stories come from the staff writers.

With very few exceptions, virtually all of the stories are done in-house. *Highlander* most of the time is a very difficult show to write for, to tell stories for. It's hard for any outsider to write any show, but for them to know a show where the main character is four hundred years old and has a history that confuses even me and kept everybody hopping, well . . . Our time line runs for four hundred years. It's simply too hard to keep track of, so most of the people who would come in and pitch, we would say, "Your stories don't quite work. Why don't we do the story, and we will give it to you and you write the script." A few writers did have great ideas, but most of it was done in-house, which is unusual. A hundred nineteen shows are a lot of stories, and a large number of them are generated from David Abramowitz. David is an extremely generous soul and generous writer. Someone could cough in a room, and David would take that and run with it, and come up with a story area and then tell them they'd done great work; it was a brilliant story. I've seen him literally do something like that. He forgets that often he's done the work. Of course, he often forgets who did actually write a show, as well, because it's hard to keep track of that. And we always had a great team.

Did you enjoy the flashbacks, or were they a special challenge?

The period stuff and the flashbacks were great. I suppose there are challenges to it. But I liked it. Quite simply, I find it intriguing. It was tempting to write in period dialogue, which didn't work. It came across as stilted. You had to not dummy it down, but give it a flavor of whatever period you were supposed to be in. Of course, all of it's smoke and mirrors. The fact that the people in France would have been speaking French anyway sort of obviated the whole question. I think probably more than anything else except the core story, the moral core of the show, the period stuff was the most fun to write. Sometimes you would find yourself itching to get through

the present-day stuff, so you could get to the past. And other times the story in the past was there to give you some reflection on the present-day situation in the story and you could have done the story without going into the flashback. But because it's *Highlander*, you need the flashback, and besides, it's more fun.

Tell me about the actors.

I think if any other actor but Adrian had played Duncan, the show would have been harder to do. He put up with enormous stresses. He, of course, had his own stunt coordinator and sword master, but in many cases, he coordinated the fights himself, simply because it's his neck that's on the line. He is a fabulous athlete and martial artist. He would do his sword fights on weekends, when the rest of us were sitting with our feet up, thinking, "Thank God it's Saturday." He was an incredible workhorse. The sort of work that would have killed, I think, most people. Probably nearly did kill him on a number of occasions. There is a great physicality to the role and to Adrian's presence. The role requires him to act, ride, swim, gallop, sword fight, kung fu, tai chi, use the kendo sticks, and remember the lines and do them well at the same time. It's a tough role, and I think most other actors would have imploded or dropped or simply have walked off, probably after the third year. But Adrian came through every time. He was the broad back on which everybody else leaned, and I think everyone had an immense appreciation for that. Also the girls mostly wanted to date him.

We were shooting a show called **"The Valkyrie"** in which we deal with the attempted assassination of Hitler. Therefore, our production area and studio was full of Nazis in full regalia walking around, practicing lines. We had colonels. We had major generals. We had Hitler, who for some reason, everyone seemed to want to get their pictures taken with. But it was rather unnerving to walk through this lot and see them. They were well chosen. They were usually tall, strapping, Aryan-looking people. I was in my office working when Adrian popped in and wanted to talk about line changes on the next script. At one point, I think I wanted to argue with him, but sitting across from me was a six-foot-plus Nazi in knee-length boots with the Iron Cross around his neck, which meant he'd been valorous in combat. And here was I, just a writer on the other side of the desk. Who was I to argue with him? Not only was he the star of the show and had a point to make, he had a point to make in a Nazi uniform. So I certainly agreed to whatever he asked for.

Seriously, Duncan is not only the show's hero, but an Immortal hero. It's a tough thing. In many ways all that does is concentrate whatever feelings you and I might have. That is, if you knew you were going to die tomorrow, what would you do, now? Would you be working at this, or would you be seeing your best friends or doing something really uplifting, something spiritually rewarding? When you know you're going to live forever, it's simply an inverse of that. There is no point to working to make money or get rich, because you have all the time in the world. It's like having no time at all.

If one moves away from Adrian and Duncan, I like writing for Jim Byrnes. Joe Dawson is an interesting character because he's human. While MacLeod is human in many ways, he's Immortal. Joe is a human like I am or like you are or anyone else is. So he's very accessible.

And there have been a couple of shows where Jim, the actor, has had to deal with Joe, the character, facing the loss of his legs. One was set in the Vietnam War, **"Brothers in Arms."** The character of Joe had been injured. The script was written by Morrie Ruvinsky, a very good, creative writer. In the scene where Joe wakes up in bed to find his legs gone, I had

to ask Jim what it was like. Jim said, "Well, the fact is you don't wake up and scream in terror, you wake up and go 'Whoa,' and fall back to sleep, because you're so shot up with morphine, you have no idea what they're telling you." So we adjusted the script accordingly. And certainly we were very concerned how Jim would feel, as we would be concerned about how any actor would feel about something that approached his personal life in such a way. And Jim was OK with it. I think that's a tribute to him as an actor and as a person, that he's not afraid to explore those areas. Or they are areas that he has in some part explored and he's not afraid to put on the screen.

The temptation scene in **"Armageddon"** was a very unusual scene. It's hard to watch in some way, probably hard to do. That story was done in-house, and Tony DiFranco added his own unique brand of talents to putting it all in script form. And Jim was amazing in that scene.

I liked writing for Amanda very much. I liked any of the episodes that had her because she was great fun and you could write light, you could write quick patter. Elizabeth has a great comic sense, and she and Adrian work very well.

Daltrey was fun in anything. The trouble was that we had killed off Fitz-cairn. But on *Highlander* this is not the problem that it is with other shows, because one can always go into the past, when the person was alive.

Other characters we've killed off, but they weren't dead. Horton would not die. Of course, his brother-in-law, Joe Dawson, was the shaki-est gun in the West. He seemed to not be able to hit the guy in any part of the body that would actually kill him. Horton kept surviving. But when he finally got his, Peter Hudson stumbled over a monument in the grave-yard scene and fell and cracked his ribs. Duncan really killed a double.

Richie, for instance, started off as the wisecracking sidekick. Once he had become Immortal, he had to change and become more serious. For the character, he was going through a learning process and an evolution in terms of his spirit, his soul, and his relationship with MacLeod. He became in many ways less fun to write, I think, because he simply wasn't the smart-ass, wisecracking young street kid. He couldn't be, and that's the direction the character had to go in. There was really no other option.

How was it writing the two-part finale?

In the sense that it's saying good-bye to the series? Very hard. I found I had an approach avoidance mentality when I went into it. I didn't want to be the one who wrote "The End" at the end. In other ways, I was won-dering if I really could put myself into that frame of mind and dredge up the emotions. But the show was not intended to be completely dark; I tried to inject some humorous moments. Having Fitzcairn was inspired. I was surprised that we could get him. But when his name popped up, it was, "Good God, of course, that's the obvious choice; Fitz!" Fitz is an angel in **"To Be"** and **"Not To Be."** And Roger Daltrey, the lead singer of The Who, as this impish character that he's become on *Highlander*, is a lot of fun. But writing the episode was like pulling teeth for me. I almost felt like putting "To Be Continued" instead of "The End," because I hate to say good-bye to it.

And I have to talk about Ken Gord. He is wonderful. He's extremely calm, unflappable, although I'm sure he's been flapped at times. People have tried. The fact that the show gets done on time and on budget, which is exceptional, is largely due to Ken's work. He's been sort of the guardian angel of the show. He's extremely quiet, quite modest and unassuming. No ego to batter around that I know of. He doesn't get in the way of the writing. He points out, and has pointed out, when we're killing people, when we're going over budget. When some things are literally impossible, he certainly makes that clear. And when they can't do something the script calls for, it's Ken's job and the director's to come up with something that works and gets the story told. Ken's good at story. I think the show has run smoothly since he came on because of his expertise and his sense that it could be done, that it's doable. That is immensely reassuring. I think only a couple of times did he come in and say, "This is not going to work; no matter what you do, it ain't going to happen." On occasion, we would find out that the costume department had just blown out their brains or were ready to because they could not keep up a certain pace that we had set. So Ken served as someone who could bring us back to reality and say,

"OK, folks, you've got sixty or seventy people out here, including probably the catering service, working their brains out to get the job done."

Gillian Horvath, Associate Creative Consultant

Over a dinner of stroganoff and matzo ball soup, Gillian and I talk about
Highlander. —M.R.

How did you come to Highlander?

I started in year two, when the new writers' office was opened in our
own bungalow, with our little offices all in a row and our conference room
right there. That's where the writing family is. I started as David
Abramowitz's assistant and the script coordinator. My title changed from
year to year; it was Associate Creative Consultant when I left at the end of
season five.

Tell me about the cast.

We have the best cast on earth. There is something that happens
when you know that your actors can deliver not only what's on the page,
but also more than what is on the page. These guys have gone above and
beyond anything that ever was asked of them.

I'm sure that everyone has talked about Jim Byrnes in **"Armageddon."**
David called him up to ask if they could go there in that story line. And
not only was Jim willing, he was eager. He said, "Let's do it." It's big stuff
for him. It's issues from his own life, but it's not about him; it's about Joe,
but they obviously share some certain traits. That he's willing to bare his
own life, his own feelings, in order to give Joe something that strong. That
he cares enough about the character to say, "Yeah, let's give him this big
scene and in order to do it I will use myself, part of me will be offered up."

Adrian Paul and the fear. People noticed this and we noticed it ourselves, watching the episodes. That he was willing to play being afraid on-
screen. That Duncan didn't have to be superman, Mr. Perfect, nothing ever
scared him. In **"Band of Brothers,"** he's afraid of Grayson. He says so, but
he doesn't just say it with words, he says it with his body language, with
the look in his eyes. During the fight, you see fear. You see him not know
if he's going to live. And that's incredible. That is hard to do. And when
you're the hero, not every actor would be willing to do it. You would get

many actors who would say, "But I'm Duncan MacLeod; what do I have to be afraid of?" For the viewer to feel him as a vulnerable man and not as a superhero, the emotion is so much stronger. And we were able to build it into later scripts. In **"Prodigal Son"** he has a moment when it looks like Hyde is going to win. That was not scripted by us; we set Hyde up as a formidable foe he had faced in his youth, but it was their choice, on the set, in the big final fight for him to almost lose and have that "I'm a dead man" look on his face.

Richie?

I love Richie. Here is this new kid on the block, just learning the ropes, and having the best mentor in the world. This person who you feel can make anything right, and you're proud to be their sidekick. If you look at **"Avatar,"** the inscription on the headstone reads "Friend." There used to be a line in **"Archangel,"** but it was too on the nose, where Richie basically said something along the lines of "I'm your friend; I'm proud to be

that." But the idea is that there are worse things to be, there are worse things to be remembered as, than Duncan MacLeod's best friend. Richie was never the hero of his own show, but he was the support of the hero.

The first season Richie was the same guy for twenty-two weeks. And then certain landmarks start defining your characters and start creating arcs. Richie's going in and out in the second season, I think, helped define his character. I know it was frustrating for Stan—he liked being in every show—but I think it helped define the character because it meant you kept seeing landmark events in his life that kept changing him. He becomes Immortal, gets trained, then when he goes away, he comes back in **"Prodigal Son."** In **"Counterfeit,"** interacting with Duncan on this peer level and in that episode, Richie's right and Duncan is wrong.

If he had been around every week, he would have just had the "What's up, Mac?" scene. The fact that he's in fewer episodes means that when he is in an episode, he has something to do. **"Line of Fire,"** that baby, is about Richie. **"Courage,"** he has those great interactions with Cullen. He's in **"The Lamb"**; he's got his stuff with Kenny. In **"Shadows,"** he's got a great part. Plus it's also the one where he's got the story with Cory. I love that subplot. **"They Also Serve"**: in some early versions of **"They Also Serve,"** and in my preferred version of the story, he raced to the rescue of MacLeod at the end. Not that he came and took the head of Michael Christian, but Mac was in trouble until Richie got there and threw him his sword. And Mac wins because he's got his sword. It's a moment when, if Richie hadn't been there, Mac could have died. The way they filmed it was Mac was already winning when Richie gets there and he doesn't need Richie at all. And I was a little disappointed in that. You will see an echo of this in **"The Messenger,"** and it was conscious on our parts; when Mac rushes to the rescue and throws Richie his sword, this is an echo of this scene that never happened on-screen, but in my mind it did.

Methos?

To me, the things that make Methos so much who he is, are: one, he's the world's oldest Immortal; two, he's hiding in the Watchers. That is such a defining thing about him. The chameleon thing, the wily and devious thing, the scholar thing, is all built into that. And his third key personality point is that he is played by Peter Wingfield.

First of all, it was Bill who decided he was going to be young and hip. He's not going to be a bearded wise-man type. He's going to go against type. Brilliant, brilliant idea. And Bill went casting color-blind, looking at everyone, only knowing he needed to be European because he was going to be playing in Paris at the time. They were looking far and wide. And it was Bill and Ken who picked Peter, and when they told us his name, we thought, "Well, it's a British name, so he won't have a French accent." And that's all we knew until the first days of dailies came in. And when we saw them, we thought Peter was swell. David was the first to decide he was swell. I thought he looked like a drowned rat. Sorry, Peter! He is soaking wet, it's all in silhouette, and he looked like what Adam Pierson should look like. He looked like a geeky Oxford student. It was the exact right look, but . . . And we weren't looking for sexy, but we were looking for presence. And soaking wet, I didn't think he played much presence. But here's what happened; I stopped looking at the screen and listened to his voice. And that's when I said, "This guy is great. This guy is wonderful." We must have watched those dailies twenty times.

Darius?

Darius was an amazing character. When he joined the show it was the first time that someone started talking about peace. The first time that someone actually examined the premise of whether going out and kicking butt is a heroic thing to do or whether it's a mistake. Werner Stocker brought a lot to that role.

Fitz?

Everybody loves Fitz. It was great to have everyone in the finale who was important to *Highlander* over the years. And having Fitz, and Roger Daltrey, being part of that . . . you look at the episode and say, this is the payoff of a whole lot of setup.

Donna Lettow, Associate Creative Consultant

I'm Donna Lettow, and this year, season six, my title is Associate Creative Consultant, which are three words meaning, "She's American and we can't tell you what she really does." The closest equivalent on an American network show would probably be story editor. Only French and Canadian writers can have their names on the scripts, to be what we call the "writers of note." But we have a few Americans who help develop the story ideas and write the outlines, which are then given to the French and Canadian writers on assignment.

From third season to fifth season I was the script coordinator, which is part of what I call the miracle of *Highlander*, or how *Highlander* is different. *Highlander* has probably two-thirds the crew of a regular show, so everybody chips in. Everybody's job description is "other duties as assigned." A lot of times we call it Camp *Highlander* or the *Highlander* Commune. Nobody hides behind their job description. You can't, or things just don't get done. A lot of network shows have three or four people doing the job that one script coordinator does here. But because of that, we've now graduated two script coordinators straight into story editing because everyone's a part of the process; everyone has their fingers on the pulse of the show.

Can you walk me through the process of writing an episode?

We start with an idea, which can either come from a freelance writer, and that's known as a pitch, or it comes from the in-house writers. The past few years we have been using fewer and fewer pitches from outside writers, because they don't understand the arcs and they don't understand the limitations that we have on the show. Before the season even starts, we have to sit down and make a chart of who is going to be in what episode. Not knowing anything about what the story arcs are going to be, but we have to contract with the actors long before the stories are even made. And an outside writer coming in doesn't know that. More and more the stories come up from the inside writers.

So we start with a pitch, and David [Abramowitz] will usually pass the pitch along to Bill Panzer. Bill is the final arbiter of everything on the show. Bill is the Highlander. So it goes to Bill, and if Bill thinks it's a story he wants to tell, then he gives it back to David. David meets what we call "in the room" with the available writers. At the beginning of this year, it was David Abramowitz, Dave Tynan, James Thorpe, and myself for six weeks continuously in the room. Once a pitch is approved we try to what is called "beat out the story" or "break the story." Both are very violent metaphors, and that feels like what is happening—that you are taking the story and shaking it until it confesses. And you figure out the beginning, the middle, and the end. And if it looks like a story that is actually going to work, then you break it down further into an outline.

An outline for *Highlander* is roughly twelve to fifteen pages of prose. Each scene that we envision for the show is detailed in the outline. Here's what's going to happen; here are the emotional beats we want to reach; here's some dialogue that might be in there. For example, in **"Methos,"** "Live, grow stronger, fight another day" came up very early in the process and was in the outline all the way through. The outline goes to Bill; Bill reads it over, makes his minor changes, makes his major changes, sometimes throws it in the trash; and then it comes back to the room and we beat up on it some more until it looks more like what Bill wants. Then it goes to Bill, and it goes through that process until Bill is happy and it's the story that he wants.

Once the outline is approved, we assign it either to a freelance writer or Dave Tynan or James Thorpe, who are the staff writers who are Canadian and can therefore write the scripts. A writer is given two weeks to write and turn in the script. A script is roughly fifty-two to fifty-four pages long. And trade secret: we always save the really good bits for the foreign version, just to piss off the Americans. That was a joke, but there are myths that this is where all the nudity is. There are conspiracy theories that all of Methos' good scenes are kept for the Europeans. No, it's not true. Sometimes you get four extra minutes of square dancing. Sometimes the Europeans aren't that lucky. When you come up short, you do what you can.

Once the script is turned in, we do revisions. We all sit down and go over the script line by line and decide what the changes are. Sometimes the freelance writer will get a second shot at it. Sometimes it gets assigned to one of the staff writers, instead. So we do a second draft. And then David Abramowitz polishes that draft. And finally that goes to Bill Panzer, who, once again, has his minor changes, his major changes, or throws it in the trash, and we start all over again. We usually have about one of those a year, and I won't tell you which ones they are. The really annoying thing about Bill is that he's right. He will give his notes, and behind his back we will bitch and moan and scream and yell and then say, "Damn it, he was right" when we finally make the change. Television is not an easy medium, especially for someone with an ego. If you're in love with your own words, this is not the business to be in. It is such a cumulative adventure. And when it works, it's magic. And when it doesn't work, it's one of the most painful processes in the world, probably, short of childbirth. And in a way, you're trying to do the same thing. You're trying, desperately, to give something life. The beauty of *Highlander* is that it works more than it doesn't work. And the stories don't just change with Bill, because once we have a script that Bill is satisfied with, then we send it to the set for prep.

And it amazes me that the crew and the designer and the cast only see the script probably seven days before they start filming it. And the fact that you can build India in seven days is amazing. The stuff they did with Peru and **"Little Tin God"** takes my breath away. And they had seven days to do it. But because of that, there are times that things in the script cannot be done. So just because we've sent the script up for prep doesn't mean that we are finished with it. As soon as we send it up, the phones start ringing.

I remember for **"The Cross of St. Antoine,"** we had just built Joe's a couple of episodes before, and a memo had gone out, saying, "Use Joe's; we love it, it's beautiful, and we spent a lot of money on it." So we used Joe's a lot in **"The Cross of St. Antoine,"** and we got a phone call saying,

"You used Joe's too much." What? Well, there are some definite practicalities in filming television. You can only film about eight pages of script a day. We try to keep eight pages on a single location, or four pages on one location and four pages across the street, because it costs so much money

and it takes so much time to pick up a crew of a hundred people and all their equipment and schlep them across town. And we had used eleven pages in Joe's. One of the scenes had to change. So sometimes the location is a problem. Sometimes once they finally sit down and figure out the budget for an episode, there are just things you cannot do. I remember, again, **"The Cross of St. Antoine,"** that the budget was so tight, we had to decide between a breakaway window for Joe Dawson to try to rescue his girlfriend or having the priest ride in on a horse. And the funny thing is, for the people who have seen the blooper reel, there are shots in there of Joe, poor Jim Byrnes, trying to break this window with his cane. So when I tell this story people say, "Well, you obviously didn't buy the window." Well, yes, we did. Unfortunately, the window broke on the way to the set. So they broke our horse. And Jim is trying to break a tempered glass window with his cane. And the way they finally broke it? One of the grips had an inspiration, ran to his truck, and got a crowbar and painted it to match Jim's cane.

Besides production constraints, we also get story points from the directors and the actors. There's an episode, **"Indiscretions,"** where we find out that Joe has a daughter, Amy Brennan. And in the version that we sent to the set, she never knows. It's an affair Joe had back in his Watcher Academy days, and he and the girl's mother decided it was best, as Joe says, "To ruin one life instead of four." And Dennis Berry called after the script went up and said, "Don't you think a fiery scene between Joe and Amy about it and then Amy gets kidnapped? Now Joe has unfinished business. They've had a fight; he really has to get her back. Wouldn't that be dramatically better?" And indeed, in that case, it was, and we went ahead and made the changes. **"Indiscretions"** is all about things that Joe and Methos did in their past that have come back to haunt them. Both times when neither of them could keep it in their pants, basically. Methos has a longer track record, of course. But at the heart, I think they're very similar.

Do you have any favorite episodes?

"Legacy" is a big favorite of mine. I love the expansion of the Amanda story and I think Nadia Cameron as Rebecca is one of the most wonderful and magical characters that has ever been on *Highlander*. The problem with *Highlander* is that we get these actors, and then, when we try to bring them back, they're too busy for us. We had Nadia in **"Legacy"** and we managed to get her, again, for **"Methuselah's Gift,"** but she was also supposed to be in **"Till Death"** and in the sixth season finale, and both times she was busy on other projects. We love Rebecca. Rebecca is one of those characters where you think she's a recurring character because everybody thinks about her so much, even on the show, talks about her so much. But she's only been in two episodes.

One of my favorite evil Immortals is Kalas. He was so suave. And David Robb is a wonderful actor. The whole Kalas arc I love. And we were

working on the Kalas arc and we had figured out **"Star-Crossed."** **"Star-Crossed"** came about because Kalas needed to do something really despicable. I don't remember—part of the beauty of *Highlander* is that people's memories are really poor when it comes to taking credit or assessing blame—whose idea it was, who said, "And we should kill Fitz." But it was brilliant. It is possible that if we had not brought Fitz back to kill him, we never would have brought him back at all, because at the time, we didn't know that Roger Daltrey liked the show. And when they were filming **"Star-Crossed"** the phone kept ringing; "Does Fitz really have to die?" And at that time, David said, "Well, yes, for the purposes of the arc, Fitz really has to die, but we could bring him back." And indeed, we did.

"**Take Back the Night**" will always be very special for me, because I am a Celtic reenactor and Celtic and Roman are among my historical specialties. So Ceirdwyn came out of David Abramowitz's saying, "I don't know about doing a woman. Is there a culture where the women fought with the men and were equal to men?" I wasn't in that meeting, and Gillian comes out into my office and drags me back in there, saying, "David, Donna, you two need to talk." So Ceirdwyn will always hold a very special place in my heart.

I remember the birth of **"Methuselah's Gift,"** which is probably my other favorite from that year. Methos wasn't even in it. We knew we had Elizabeth Gracen. It was one of those where we had set up our contracts at the beginning of the year, except for Peter Wingfield. Because at that point, Peter was what we call a day player, meaning that he comes in and he works a day or a couple of days and you didn't have to contract him in advance. Which I think worked to his advantage that year because there were so many stories where we said, "This seems a little light; we need a B story or we need some other action going through." And we'd say, "Put in Methos." So he ended up in probably half of the Paris episodes that year. He didn't star in most of them, but because he was nearby and because he was fabulous, we used him a lot. **"Methuselah's Gift"** started out as a caper. Amanda steals an artifact that holds some significance; we never got down to figuring out the specifics. I think from then it went to, "Well, what if she were vying with someone else?" And we said, "Methos!" And then it became the crystals, and as soon as it became the crystals, David asked, "But why would he want them?" And Gillian said, "Alexa, of course." I think when **"Timeless"** was written there wasn't an Alexa arc. We just knew that Methos would go away and eventually he would come back and Alexa would have passed on. But the moment we thought, "Look, here is something that could make you live forever, what would you do with it? How about your dying girlfriend?" It gave the episode so much heart. And that scene in the train yard with Elizabeth and Peter breaks my heart every time. There haven't been a lot of dailies that make us cry because, pretty much, we know what to expect. We know what the lines are going to be, we know what the story is, but the train yard in **"Methuselah's Gift"** broke our hearts every take.

Similarly, Horton offering Joe Dawson his legs in **"Armageddon"**—not a dry eye in the room. And we watched those over and over and just marveled at Jim Byrnes' ability. And sat here saying, "Oh my God, what have we done to him?"

And then there's a scene in **"Not To Be"** between Duncan and Tessa, where Adrian started crying during the filming and just took us with him. Now it didn't make us cry, but it held us riveted, we weren't breathing, in the scene in **"Comes a Horseman"** where Duncan confronts Methos in

front of the car. Amy Zoll talks about receiving the dailies. We had all gone up to Vancouver for wrap, so we hadn't seen the dailies. Amy is here alone in the office and she puts in the dailies and she said that the first time Peter became that evil guy by the Jimmie, she was so startled she fell back over her chair and ended up on the floor. Because even when you write it, sometimes actors take it to places that you never imagined.

"Dramatic License" is one of the few episodes written for an actor. We had done it once before, with "Chivalry." Ann Turkel was a *Highlander* fan and had asked us to use her, so David wrote "Chivalry" specifically with her in mind. And we were contacted in the fifth season and told that Sandra Bernhard really wanted to do the show, although we figure she probably wanted to be Immortal. Because when people say they want to do *Highlander*, they really want to get out there and wave around the sword. But we liked this for her. I think of the comedies, "Dramatic License" is probably my favorite.

"Money No Object" is probably the crew's favorite. At the wrap party at the close of the fifth season, that is the episode they chose to air. Now I am sure that part of it is due to Adrian Paul's stunning impersonation of director Dennis Berry. Everyone there has worked with Dennis and recognized the character right off the script. And Adrian's portrayal of him was spot on.

"Horseman" and "Revelation" I am sure everyone has talked about, but I will say two things: Valentine Pelka plays Kronos to the hilt. Probably next to the casting of Methos, the casting of Kronos is one of the home runs of the past couple of years. And on the *Highlander* Cruise someone asked whether Methos comes from Peter Wingfield or whether he comes from the writers. And the answer is, "He's an amalgamation of both." We wrote Methos, Peter came in and he gave it a spin we weren't expecting. We picked up on that, we spun a different way, and Peter took that and ran with it. And every time we pushed the envelope a little more and a little more. So if any other actor had been playing Methos, "Horseman" and "Revelation" would never have happened. We never would have pushed that far. But as far back as "Chivalry," Peter started putting in an agenda, a dark agenda. And we didn't know what it was. And, actually, later we talked to Peter about it, and he didn't know. He did not have a story in his head about what had happened with Kristin, but he had enough of an edge in there that we started wondering. What's with this guy? What's his past? We knew early in season five that we wanted to do a story where someone Duncan knew and trusted knew Methos from when he was bad. But at the time, Methos' being evil was like he was the Sheriff of Nottingham, not that he was Satan in a blue mask. But things kept building and building from there. **"Horseman"** and **"Revelation,"** I think, are the pinnacle of *Highlander*. Everyone worked so hard on those. I know that the final day of shooting in Vancouver, they shot for twenty-one hours. It was incredible. Nobody left. Everybody gave it a hundred percent because they knew that they were making magic.

Some days David says he believes he is channeling *Highlander*; he doesn't know where it's coming from. It is amazing how some of this stuff shows up without anybody actually intending it. We are tapping into some universal myths. I am sure Joseph Campbell or Carl Jung would have a field day with *Highlander*. **"Horseman,"** **"Revelation,"** the Ahriman arc, **"Archangel,"** **"Avatar,"** and **"Armageddon"** were all that way. We didn't start with the idea of making Kronos, Methos, Silas, and Caspian the biblical Four Horsemen. It just fell into place. Methos was Death, Kronos was

Pestilence, Silas was War, and Caspian was Famine. It was the same with the Ahriman arc. We had some initial ideas about Mac fighting the devil. But as we were doing research, we found the Zoroastrian myth where every thousand years an Immortal is chosen to fight Ahriman. We did not make that up. Then, as we started looking further into other mythologies, the patterns kept reappearing over and over again. So all we were doing was bringing our mythology in line with the ones that were already out there. Scary.

And what I love about the whole Ahriman arc is that it made some people look into their own beliefs, look into whatever faith they had or didn't have or even just look into mythologies. I know some fans had problems with it, but it resonated with the people who could see the patterns. Technically, they may not be the best episodes we have done. If you want to break it down into technical and artistic interpretation, technical merit may not be as high as **"Horseman"** and **"Revelation,"** but for the themes and meanings there, I think the Ahriman arc is one of the best things that we have done.

Let's talk about killing Richie. It's hard to tell who really made the decision to kill Richie. But David had decided that he wanted someone to go. It was time to make MacLeod face some things. And when it was decided it was Richie, then the next step was to decide that Duncan does it. David wanted something that would really rock Duncan's world. So we had Ahriman trick Duncan into killing Richie.

The finale, **"To Be"** and **"Not To Be."** David knew at the very beginning, before we knew what any of the stories were, that he wanted all of our regulars in the last two episodes. The idea for the finales, the *It's a Wonderful Life* story, the world without Duncan MacLeod, is actually mine. I pitched it for an earlier episode, and David really liked it and passed it on to Bill. And Bill loved it. Bill Panzer is the one who said, "No, this is the finale, we expand it into two parts, and it is the finale."

And then once we decided on the world without Duncan MacLeod concept, the first thing that happened was that I wrote up a chronology of what would have happened to the characters without Duncan and the reasons why. Very early on we knew we wanted Tessa and Richie. We didn't think we'd get Stan Kirsch, so we had a Richie story that we were going to do without Stan because Richie was already going to be dead. At the last minute, I believe after the shooting script went out, Stan finally agreed to be in the episode, which required a major rewrite of the second part. But it was definitely worth it, because unlike some of the rewrites we have had to do, we were very excited about this one, to find a way to let Stan play, too. It was very important to us that everybody be there. We didn't think we'd have Roger Daltrey. In fact, when I pitched it, the "angel" character, the Clarence of the piece, was Sean Burns. And we started writing the outlines with Sean. Meanwhile, Ken was checking on whether Michael J. Jackson would be available the dates we needed him for the episodes, and it turned out we couldn't get him. What are we going to do? Rebecca, we're going to make it Rebecca. We figured she was a good spiritual guide for

Duncan. We can get a lot of good stuff from her. And we love Nadia and we'd like to use her, again. Yeah, well, she's getting married that week. Rebecca's out. And we were at our wits' end. We were afraid we wouldn't be able to do the episode. And in the back of all our minds was Roger Daltrey, but Roger is a major star. But, finally, David decided to contact Roger and see if he would do it. And as you know, he was thrilled and overjoyed to do it. And now it is impossible to imagine it without him. They would not be anywhere near the episodes, if he were not involved. There is something about Fitz that brings out not only the silly side of MacLeod, but also the vulnerable side. Duncan really lets his guard down with Fitz. That works so well in these episodes.

We tried to bring back as many people as we could in addition to Richie and Tessa. There are Valentine Pelka as Kronos and Peter Hudson as Horton. Everyone was playing the "what if" game. There are even two Watchers in the episode who had no lines; they just jump out of a truck with guns blazing. Well, one of them died in **"Methuselah's Gift"** and one of them died in **"Judgment Day."** Ken Gord brought them back deliberately because, you know, they'd still be alive in a world without Duncan MacLeod. Even the extras are playing. It's fabulous. But I really think that this is a fitting end to the television adventures of Duncan MacLeod, to show how important he's been. This is our gift to the people who have been with us every episode. We're hoping that it's a legacy for the show.

Laura Brennan, Script Coordinator

I am Laura Brennan, and I am script coordinator and assistant to David Abramowitz. The script coordinator is given the pencil revisions that the writers frantically write in the margins. And I put all the revisions in the computer, so that the next draft that comes out is fixed and perfect and wonderful. And then they can start the process all over by tearing that one apart. However, on *Highlander*, it is the most open, generous group of people in the universe. I'm welcomed into, invited into, the process of coming up with stories or helping solve problems with the writers. David Abramowitz is the most wonderful human being on the face of the earth. He welcomes my input. Occasionally we even disagree on things. And he respects that. He respects people's opinions. So I feel like I have a voice and I love that. I love being part of *Highlander*.

Amy Zoll, Production Assistant and House Archaeologist

I am Amy Zoll and I am production assistant for the writers' office. I do odd jobs around the office. Mostly I provide support for the writers in any capacity necessary. Often I am doing research for them on extremely bizarre subjects like ancient Persian demonology. The weird thing about working here is that I now know more about television than any archaeologist ever should. It has allowed me to apply my skills as a researcher to wildly diverse subjects. But I think my favorite part of the job is answering the viewer mail.

Can you tell me about some of the more interesting mail?
We got some Richie letters, but one of them, that we read out loud, was completely vitriolic and just mean. And it started out, "Dear Murdering Bastards."

I was there to see it happen and I was glad to see the thought processes that led up to it. It was never ever "Who can we kill?" It was that this demon had to do something so heinous that it would have to put MacLeod in a different place. What's the worst thing that we can do to him? They all looked at each other at the same time and said, "Richie's gotta die." They're storytellers. They're here to tell a powerful story, and that's where the narrative led. *Highlander* is one of the few shows that I think would have the balls to follow through with the story. By the time they got to it, they knew that they were going to alienate a lot of people with it, but they were true to their integrity as writers, and I truly respect them for that. We were very sad to see Richie go. No one wanted to kill him, but it had to be done. So instead of taking these "Dear Murdering Bastards" letters to heart, we said, "Yeah, we knew those were going to come, but we are standing by our choice."

CHAPTER THREE

Production/The Shoot

"There was a mad Englishwoman at the gate."

*V*igny, France, September 1997. A forty-five-minute drive from Paris, and I have arrived at what can only be described as a small picturesque town in the countryside. As I wind my way down the narrow streets, I spot the spires that surely indicate the Château de Vigny, the location for the week's shooting of episode number 113, **"Unusual Suspects."** I park in the town's central parking lot, near the church, and walk to the private driveway that leads to the Château.

There is a guard. He politely tells me that they are shooting; this is a private residence, and no visitors are allowed. In my university French (I should have taken that crash course from Berlitz), I attempt to explain that I am a writer and that I am expected. Either my French is worse than I thought, or I am simply not convincing. I go back to the car and pull out my files. I show him a series of faxes from Gaumont and *Highlander* and try again. He finally decides that I am beyond his purview and tells me he will go get someone "important." I wait. He soon returns with Jeremy Swales, who is, as it turns out, the architect working on the restoration of the Château. Jeremy checks out all the paperwork and realizes that I am, indeed, who I claim to be and that my arrival is anticipated. As we walk down the driveway, Jeremy explains to me, "I didn't know what to expect. He told me there was a mad Englishwoman at the gate."

Well, at least I made an impression.

So, however, does the Château; at the end of the driveway, I get my first real glimpse of the house. It is an imposing sight . . . dating from the sixteenth century, with spires, seven floors high, and a moat! (As I am to later discover, stocked with what Jeremy calls "mutant carp.")

There are trucks parked all along the circular driveway in front of the Château. We walk around to the back of the house and discover a hub of activity. They are shooting on the main floor. Scaffolding frames the side of the house, and lights shine through the windows, lighting the interior. We cross the bridge over the moat, walk down the gravel parkway, and enter through the back door into what was likely the kitchen area in earlier centuries. One small room to the side is set up with a computer, printer, fax, phone, and so on. It is the on-set office. In the main room, there is a large table set up. It is filled with baguettes, coffee, a basket full of fruit, including bananas, and a large pan of quiche. As I will learn during my time on the set, Catering always makes sure that there is food and beverage nearby for the hardworking cast and crew.

Jeremy introduces me to the assistant director, William Pruss, who greets me and offers to take me up to the shoot. We walk down a long, narrow hallway and enter a large, impressive main entry hall. Tapestries hang on two of the walls. There is a huge main stairwell, as well as a small circular stairway that leads to the family's private quarters. We walk up the stairway to the right. We have found the shoot.

The cast and crew are in a large, formal room. It is dressed ornately in an astonishingly bright shade of red. Adrian Paul and Roger Daltrey are shooting a scene. Duncan is talking to Fitz about—what shall we say—the highly exaggerated reports of his death. One, two, three takes. They're done. Move on to the next scene.

As they block the next scene, director Dennis Berry holds up his hands as if they were a lens through which he can look. Clearly, he is visualizing the scene for the camera. The actors read their lines, checking for timing, any difficulties they might have or changes they need to make. Wardrobe, hair, and makeup are checked. The prop man enters with a fairly large, seemingly dead, rat. We learn that the prop rat is named Mort. Adrian enters the room. He nears the table, and, clearly to Adrian's surprise, the prop man, hiding under the table, offers up the rat on a large, fancy dinner platter. Not precisely what the script called for, but Adrian breaks up with laughter, as does everyone else on the set.

A certain number of pages must be shot each day, yet there are definitely many moments of laughter and camaraderie on the set. One day, I hear the sound of what I think is a ladder or perhaps some of the metal scaffolding being dragged down the narrow, circular stone stairwell. However, rather than the anticipated grip carrying a ladder, what emerges is a clanking suit of armor, with Roger Daltrey inside. He is greeted with thunderous applause when he makes his entrance.

They say an army travels on its stomach. The same can be said of a film crew. Lunch and dinner breaks, though brief, always seem to be a time of boisterous good fun. Yet Adrian often seems to have as much fun in the after-dinner time, enjoying a few moments practicing his golf game on the vast green expanses surrounding the Château. Best part: he doesn't need to go out and collect the balls for another round. The castle dogs make great sport of retrieving the balls and returning them to Adrian.

Actors, clearly, need to have a keen sense of perception about their characters. Throughout the first days of the shoot, the hair department makes sure that Fitz's hair is a perfection of pomade and finger waves. When I commented on those perfect curls, Daltrey replies, "Well, I have to have perfect hair. I've just been buried." —M.R.

Ken Gord, Producer

It's a beautiful afternoon in the French countryside. Ken and I sit down over a cup of coffee. —M.R.

First question: What do you do?

There are lots of different producers. What I do is take the paper and turn it into plastic. I could elaborate. Paper says anything; it says, "The Huns invade Europe." So my job would be to physicalize that. But I don't actually do anything myself. I just make sure that it gets done. Everyone is a professional, and they all know their jobs. They're really great. It's kind of like a train, and it starts up, and it's up to me to make sure that it stays on the track. But everyone is really good at what they do.

But there are certain areas in which I get more involved, like casting is me. And I make sure that the locations are right. And make sure the extras look good and check the main props and the set dressing. And make sure that everything conforms to budget because if we really can't afford "the Huns invade Europe," we can maybe afford a group of Huns and an

Immortal. It's all done within a framework, and the budget is a framework and the schedule is a framework, because there's only so much you can physicalize in one day. And it comes down to pages per day. And so many pages of talking heads are different from so many pages of fighting. It's putting together a jigsaw puzzle.

Once you put those pieces together, are there any that you have especially liked?

Yeah, I do have a few favorites. In no particular order? **"Courage."** I liked **"Courage"** because I thought it was a really well-done show, really brutal. I think **"Courage"** pushed it to the outer limits. It pushed us to the limits of action. I don't want to use the word "violence," but it was pretty rough stuff. I don't think we'd go any further than that because we pull back a lot, but that showed just how far we could go. I don't want to open a whole can of worms here about violence.

But I guess *Highlander* is violent by some people's definition, but to me it's action that comes out of character. Maybe we're just splitting hairs, right? But we don't exactly show spewing guts and heads being cut off. We show the aftermath. Also because we're a mythology, they're not real people. It's like vampires. The vampire sucks some blood and you stick him through the heart with a stake and nobody takes that seriously. These are Immortals.

Having said that, we have had MacLeod murder regular people. I'm thinking about **"Warmonger."** That one was pretty great. I was excited to read that.

I liked **"Color of Authority."** I thought that was a great show. I liked it because I thought the show was kind of like baseball. It's really cliché to use baseball as an analogy because how hokey can you get; but really, there are so many things that have to go together, acting and the script and a tone and pacing. And sometimes you get one or the other. But sometimes it all works. And I think in that show it all worked. The A story worked, the B story worked, and there were great flashbacks. I thought it was really compelling.

I liked **"The Valkyrie,"** the one Richard Martin did. Ingrid was likable. That was a tough choice. I loved that. That was a good show. I liked the two-parter where Mac goes bad, **"Something Wicked"** and **"Deliverance."** That was a terrific two-parter. I thought we did more in those two parts than a lot of features. And having your hero go bad is a great concept. Adrian's bad was scary. Little things like looking in the mirror and licking his lips. It was creepy. It was great. I loved that; it was different.

I liked some of the comedies like **"The Stone of Scone"** and **"Till Death."** A different kind of thing; they're funny. I could name more and more, but those are ones that come to mind.

Now that you've named your favorites, were there any episodes that were really difficult to do?

I'd say most of them. This is a tough show. Oh yeah, if you just do a regular talking-head show and you do it in seven or eight days, in North America, it's difficult. And if you do an action show in seven days it's more difficult. And if you do a show with action and special effects it's more difficult. How about action, special effects, and flashbacks? Where you have to follow through on everything, wardrobe and sets. You know the show, so you've seen what we've turned into what, and that all comes with a lot of hard work. And we prep these things in seven days. And sometimes in Vancouver, we're doing them in six days, so it's all put together, everything you see is physicalized, in six days.

And we're prepping and shooting and doing postproduction at the same time. For example, on Monday, I'll sign off on the mix for show three, but we're also editing show four, and we're doing pickup shots and ADR [automated dialogue replacement] for show five.

And in less than seven days you have to have the cast because Costume and Hair needs them. So you get the script seven days before and you're really casting the whole show in three or four days to get the actors in time. So it's tough because you have to put all the pieces together. The show can be a nightmare, but it is a challenging and creatively stimulating nightmare.

And you don't always get the people you want just from casting. Because a lot of times you can sit through a casting session and you don't see somebody that you envisioned, so I've pulled people off the street. Literally. In the show that Richard Martin just shot, **"Black Tower,"** there are five bad guys. Two of them are supposed to be Spanish. Those are actual twins from London. One of them, the computer guy, he was from London. One of them is supposed to be an American Southern guy; he's from London. Then there's the French guy, Benoit, and this is a guy that I just found. I was walking by Notre-Dame, and he was roller-skating with music and he looked like he was dressed from *Road Warrior.* He was doing ballet with a hockey stick. And it was a pretty bizarre act, but you could see that he was really graceful and athletic and strong. And I said to him, "You look very Immortal; you have to be on this show." And he was very happy to do it. He gave me his card and it didn't have a name, it just said, "Skating for the adoration of God." You'll see him on the show; his name is Alain Creff. Literally pulled off the street because he looked great.

The whole show looks great.

The art directors are wonderful. They are brilliant. Geaghan was brilliant. Rex [Raglan] did a fantastic job, seamless. And Chantal [Giuliani] is exquisite. She has the best taste. And what's good about it for me is that

I can just trust them. Otherwise, I'd be ragged, because you have to pace yourself.

There are different philosophies about producing. There are people who produce from fear and power. I believe the opposite. Yeah, a little bit of tension can be good and I'm not averse to providing tension if it needs it, as directors will tell you, but at the same time, let creativity have some space. Because these people are really talented, and I don't know more about dressing a location or what's going to make a good thirteenth-century castle than Chantal, so trust the experts. The producer doesn't necessarily know more about things; he's just there to make sure that it stays between the lines.

And everyone makes mistakes. We don't kill people for making mistakes. A lot of shows, if you do make a mistake, they kill you. And so people get petrified, and then creativity gets totally stifled. And some shows there are so many producers that one guy says, "Paint the set red," and another guy comes along a half an hour later and says, "Paint this blue." And you know what happens? Nothing. And then ten minutes before you're supposed to shoot, the producers all fight it out, and then they have to bring in fifty guys and $50,000 to do it fast. The fish stinks from the head down. So I love Bill Panzer and Marla Ginsburg because they trust me. I'm the creative producer, and they've given me my wings. I pass that along. And it really works well.

The barking of the Château Labradors reminds us of our location. —M.R.

How does Highlander *find these amazing locations?*

You read the script. It's broken down as far in advance as possible, seven or eight days. We have a creative meeting. We talk about possibilities. And then there's a scout. There's one scout here in France, Sophie [Musset], who's great. Because it's not just finding places, it's finding places that really work, and not just work, but are magical. Anybody can find a location, but to find a location that brings a script alive is a talent. So we have boxes and boxes of files. And people have ideas, because people know places. And I've even come up with suggestions. Most of the ideas I come up with, people generally fall down because I say, "Let's shoot at the Eiffel Tower." And everybody says, "No, no, no." But we did. It took eight months to put together. But you see? It was too obvious. They were horrified.

How did you get the Eiffel Tower?

I asked for it at the end of one year, and they said, "No way." And when I came back the next year, I started working on it. So at the end of the third season, Mac and Kalas fought that big sword fight. It was good. But it took that long for the paperwork, because the Eiffel Tower is something special.

Let's pause a moment and set the scene. Ken and I have been talking while sitting at a large, shaded table at the back of the Château, near the moat. The view for acres and acres is verdant fields and forest. It is quiet and serene, the silence occasionally broken by the splashing of the moat's fish population. Suddenly, a booming voice is heard. Director Dennis Berry exits the main floor of the Château, proclaiming: "Friends, I have delivered, with brilliance and exquisite precision, an extraordinary scene on schedule. And I can guarantee you a hundred percent efficiency as to the laughing humor of this show. I am going to sit down, now, and have my tea because it is tea break time. A little shot of vodka would be appreciated quickly."

Dennis joins us. —M.R.

KEN: "You've obviously met D.B., the one and only."

I HAVE.: "He's been our good host."

DENNIS: "This show is coming along good. It's funny. There is a natural elegance to the costumes and the castle."

KEN EXPLAINS: "I was just telling Maureen how we decided to shoot on the Eiffel Tower and how petrified you were because you were going to have to deliver a sword fight and a Quickening on the Eiffel Tower. And what incredible pressure it was for a French director to have to shoot on the Eiffel Tower. Remember that I told you that, Maureen? That he was absolutely petrified about it? He was so worried, so nervous."

FRENCHMAN DENNIS, SON OF FAMED AMERICAN DIRECTOR JOHN BERRY, TONGUE BARELY IN CHEEK: "I'm an American director and basically, I am used to working in the studio, where you can order the Eiffel Tower. The Tower is easy; you just build it. I was shocked to find out that's not how they work over here in France. I realized there were budget constraints when I signed on, but I was told it was a big, huge show. That it played in ninety-nine countries. And then I find they can't even afford to build the Eiffel Tower, and you have to go schlep with the tourists."

KEN, ALWAYS THE VOICE OF CALM AND SANITY ON THE SET: "Luckily Dennis rises to the challenge, and we came through with flying colors."

DENNIS: "Really, we had a great time up there."

The assistant director calls for Dennis. Tea break is over. Later, when we hear the shout of "Moteur!" (the French version of "Camera!"), we know that Dennis and everyone else are back hard at work. —M.R.

Where were we? Was the Eiffel Tower the most unique location you've gotten?

Maybe that was the most obvious, but bizarre at the same time, because it's so difficult. But I would say the most bizarre was the underground submarine base in Bordeaux. It was used during the war, and it was a base where they used to bring in the submarines and refit them. It

was bombed by the Allies. You could see the bomb craters. And the amazing thing was that Adrian and I were scouting and they were showing us something else because the script said Kronos lives in a château. And we thought, "He's not really a château kind of guy." But we weren't sure what we were looking for. And someone was showing us a bridge, I think. And we looked over at this building, and Adrian and I just looked at each other and said, "That looks like the dark empire, doesn't it?" We just twigged on it. And you know that set inside? There was an artist in there who had done all that metalwork. It was just sitting there waiting for Kronos and the Four Horsemen to come and take it over. It was great. I think maybe it was too dark, but the double Quickening looked good.

Is the Quickening strange to shoot?

The Quickening? No, actually, it's four hours of waiting and ten minutes of *boom-boom*. It's really all setup. Hurry up and wait.

Have you ever had any special difficulties with the Quickening?

The weirdest one was the one with Michael Siberry, the English actor who played Hyde in **"Prodigal Son."** We brought in this special effects guy from England because we had this huge castle in Chantilly. We had the whole thing lit for night. He set maybe a thousand charges. We were going to see all the way across the moat. It was like a huge, huge feature shot. And as soon as the Quickening started, about five seconds into it, it caused some kind of power surge and all the lights went out. We were horrified. It literally took two days to set that up, and then the lights went out. So what you see is basically the light of the explosion.

There is one other weird Quickening. It was the first Quickening with a new special effects company. **"Star-Crossed"** with David Robb playing Kalas, standing underneath the Bastille tunnel. If you watch the film, watch the Quickening carefully, you will see a little piece of debris come and hit him in the face. That was definitely not intended to happen. I died. No one is ever supposed to get hurt on this show. It's all magic. With all credit to David Robb, he felt this thing, which was supposed to blow out that way, blow in one inch from his eye and he kept in character. He went crazy afterward, after it was cut. And he was absolutely right. I was horrified. That isn't supposed to happen. But David was OK and he kept going. Is that amazing? A real actor. I love our cast. They're all really good.

Dennis Berry, Director

I have been watching you all week; your energy is amazing. What do you think you bring to Highlander?

I try to add a dimension of madness to the surreal *Highlander* dream because *Highlander* is like a dream. Have you heard of the imaginary museum? It's how people used to learn about other civilizations. Well, the *Highlander* concept created a kind of way for the modern man to travel through time and learn about other cultures and civilizations.

I think *Highlander* is a fiction that corresponds to the consciousness of today. We are aware of more civilizations than ever before because communication and travel happen so fast. But at the same time that the world is becoming like a village, we're also feeling more and more confined. And inventing a fiction where the audience can travel through time gives you an enormous impression of freedom and dimension. You're not claustrophobically closed in, and we're not bogged down by standard episodic "naturalistic" television.

Highlander's surreal dimension has a dreamlike quality, and I love that. That's what has kept me going so long on *Highlander*. When I go and do other shows, I always miss it. I also miss *Highlander* if I'm not here because it's an affectionate family. It's not run like your usual television show. The director gets almost as much freedom as if he were doing his own little feature of forty-six minutes.

And what is nice is that when you talk to David Abramowitz and Bill Panzer and the creative end in L.A., often they're open about ideas and changes, so that you can design with what you find under your eyes and the elements you have. For example, in **"Archangel,"** they wanted to kill Richie because it would be a great way for Duncan to be victimized and traumatized by the devil. And what happens is that you look for a way to justify his cutting off Richie's head. So I invented the idea that all of the evil characters that he had met in the last two years would appear in front of him, as if the devil is playing with many, many spirits. And that they all circle around Duncan and even double themselves, so that when he cuts off Richie's head, it's in a moment of total confusion. I found what we would call a choreographic concept to sell the fact that Duncan's sword is cutting off Richie's head. And that's what a director does on *Highlander*. Whereas, when you do something else, it's very specifically written.

And I get along great with Adrian. He is a real creative force; his commitment and dedication have made it possible. He spent all his time trying to give the most possible creatively, so that *Highlander* could become the best. He's creative choreographically. Scriptwise, he knows his character. He developed it. He has conviction as an actor. He brings credibility to what he does. If you team up with him, there's a complementarity [sic] that works great.

And the thing is that we're very different. He's a very logistical kind of person, he's very methodical, very it-all-has-to-make-sense. I have a vision. I don't care if it makes sense. And he tries to make sense of my crazy vision. And what he does is, he translates it for me and to a certain extent makes it better. He helps me make it work for the best and to be the most acceptable to an audience. So it's interesting, our relationship. I am a little bit on the visionary mad side. I try to treat it like a dream. And he wants to make sure that it also makes sense as an actor, and between the two of us, there is a great chemistry.

Though, I would say that when he takes off as a director and has a mad vision of his own . . . You have to have a mad vision to do these shows. You can't be too down-to-earth. You have to let go of the boundaries of your daily reality. You have to cross the bridge where the ghosts show up.

So what else can I tell you? It's tough. It's very tough, because there is never enough money. I am reminded of those RKO B directors from the forties and fifties who would make masterpieces in nine days. Or John Ford or Howard Hawks or Fritz Lang, all those guys used to make movies in very little time. You find that the confinements sometimes make you very inventive. You have to create a period and you have two horses and four villagers and suddenly you put in fog and you find frames and it becomes another world and you're in another century. That's really a pleasure. You go elsewhere, you really go to another world, to a *Highlander* world, not anyone else's. We've invented a whole new world, and I think it grows on you. A lot of directors have delivered some great and interesting shows.

Adrian Paul, Director

Directing I love. The reason I began to direct was because I wanted to see what it was like on the other side of the camera. What the problems were. What the advantages would be as an actor to see what it was like for a director. Then I realized I enjoyed it.

I really wanted to be technically knowledgeable about directing. I think directing has many facets. You must be able to talk with actors. What I've learned is that everybody has different techniques and different ways that they work, so if I can connect to how they work, I can direct them.

You must have a good eye for re-creating a story in a visual sense. Richard Martin has a fabulous eye. He's incredible. And all directors can learn from dailies. I've watched every single daily since the show began. And what I learned there is how different techniques work at different moments. You must understand the different techniques that you use to produce a moment or produce a story. Then you also have to know how

to pace a script, how you want it to be slower in some parts, faster in other parts. Whether certain moments need more close-up, more time. So those things gradually, gradually, I began to learn and I began to like exploring them.

I think my technically best episode is **"The Modern Prometheus."** I specifically shot things in a certain way to give them a certain edge. **"Modern Prometheus,"** originally, was supposed to be my easy show after the hundredth episode. But, in fact, we had a carriage race, two huge stunts off a roof, two sword fights, and two Quickenings. So it was an enormous show and we got through it and we were very lucky.

Don Paonessa, creative consultant, postproduction, said "The Modern Prometheus" was one of his favorites. To quote him:

> I rather like **"The Modern Prometheus,"** which Adrian directed. I thought that was a pretty cool show. First of all, I thought the cast was quite good. And the story was trippy, the idea of a famous poet being a rock star and an Immortal. Then, when Adrian and I talked about the execution of the show, we came up with a solution where the past would be soft and impressionist and romantic and the present would be edgy. I had suggested the idea of a documentary approach, like *Don't Look Back*, the Bob Dylan film. They shot a lot of the present day in hand-held to give it a documentary, you-are-there, vérité look. And then, in post, we gave the present a kind of washed-out, contrasty look that gave it an edge, which contrasted with the soft and frilly side of the past. That was fun. I thought that show was pretty well executed.

Don said that? That's nice, because Don's seen them all. I really spent time in constructing how I wanted the flashbacks and the past to look. If you look at the way they're shot, the flashbacks are shot entirely differently than the present day. And that's what we wanted, a romantic feel in the flashback and an edgy, hard, rock-and-roll feel in the present. We used a hand-held camera in the present and a lot of dolly and Steadicam in the past.

I wanted it to be a poetic show. I read Byron's biography before I did it so that I would know who he was, what he did. It was my belief that the Byron in our universe had had enough of life. I think he almost expected death. He'd tried everything else: drugs, women, rock and roll, whatever;

nothing was giving him any satisfaction. The only thing that did was the words; that's why he stole them from other people. For me it was a very complex, really interesting script, although I think some of the others had a real heart to them. **"Homeland"** had a real big heart to it.

"Revelation 6:8" was very special because it was the hundredth episode and because it was the largest Quickening that we had ever done. We chose some amazing locations, and I was able to work with the actors. Peter Wingfield and Valentine Pelka were so good, so strong. It was just big in all respects.

And when I direct a show like the hundredth episode or **"Homeland,"** there's a mourning period afterwards. You put yourself a hundred ten percent into it. I eat, drink, and sleep it. As I'm going through the day, I'm thinking about a scene that is going to be shot later on. How should it be played? How should it be filmed? Is there anything I am missing? When that is over, you think, "Well, what should I do, now?"

Do you find it difficult to return to "just" acting; is it hard to let go?

It is. You were totally emotionally involved in something, and suddenly you have to take yourself out of that. And it's a new and different episode. The people are different and the space is different. It's almost as if somebody has died. I think the biggest mourning period for me was with "**Homeland**." Because I spent so long with it and because it was so emotional for Duncan, it took me the entire following episode to recover.

Gerard Hameline, Director

I meet with director Gerard Hameline and storyboardist Marc Goldstein in West Hollywood. We enjoy a lunch of Chinese chicken salad and white burgundy while discussing *Highlander*. —M.R.

What vision did you bring to Highlander?

That's a big question. I think what I brought to *Highlander* was something a little bit less mechanical. I thought in terms of the emotional relationships of the characters. I tried to get the actors confident with me. And I think I did. I think I created a good relationship between the actors and myself. We were able to discuss details, emotional beats that they could change or switch a little bit.

Of the episodes that you directed, do you have favorites?

I like "**Comes a Horseman**." I was lucky to get those actors. The acting was really good. I could create with Valentine Pelka. We were always talking together. I could ask him the way he would like to do a scene before we shot. I was able to spend some time. It was wonderful. And Peter Wingfield was so fantastic, just so fantastic. I wish on every television show there were actors of this caliber.

And I did like **"Judgment Day,"** maybe because it was my first one. There was a very interesting atmosphere in **"Judgment Day."** It was very dark. We shot in a place that was confined and small and tense. I was looking to create a dark atmosphere and I pushed it in postproduction to make it very grainy.

"Richie Redstone" was not so easy, but I took very good care of Stan. He's a wonderful guy.

How did you come to ask for storyboards?

It is the way I work. This comes from my background in advertising. Everything has to be well prepared. I like, also, to have a board so that I can show it to each department and I can communicate with them. With the boards, in one second everything was clear, there was an image in the head of each one of us.

And they help me to prepare. When I work, I have a vision, but when I work with Marc Goldstein, he has a different vision. He brings something in, and when I am on location and am confronted with the reality, I am prepared enough to change.

Marc Goldstein, Storyboardist

You have little time to improvise on a shoot, everything is so fast. So to have the luxury of being prepared allows you to do better work.

Highlander *usually does not use storyboards; how did you get hired?*

Gerard Hameline asked me. The first one I worked on was **"Glory Days,"** then **"The End of Innocence,"** then the big one, **"Comes a Horseman,"** and finally **"The Ransom of Richard Redstone."**

How many storyboards do you draw for a script?

You do the most important scenes, those that require special effects or those that you think that you can pull off a very evocative, epic visual for. In TV there is never time; the pace is insane. But you do your best. The boards served as an inspiration for the director to shoot from. Eventually, if they shot five percent of what was drawn it was an achievement. But storyboards are the first visual step from the script to the shoot, so the director has something to work from.

How do you begin?

In the best of all possible worlds, you read the script first and when you have the time and a comfortable budget, you sit down with the director, the director of photography, the art director, the production designer, the producer, and everything works out. With *Highlander*, I read the script, shot the whole thing in my head, and presented it to Gerard.

I understand that you were a fan of **Highlander**.

When the first *Highlander* film came out, I was about eighteen years old and part of the gothic crowd in Paris. That film struck a very special chord in all of us. So ten years later, to participate in something that had been my own personal inspiration for all these years, was a love story of sorts. And another great satisfaction for me was that a friend of mine from that time, Marcus Destory, became Silas, one of the Four Horsemen.

When I read the script, I said to Gerard, "You know what? I have your headhunter horseman. He's got a mohawk, he's got a tattoo on the side of his head, and he's perfect." Eventually Marcus went on to compose three or four tracks of original music for **"The Modern Prometheus."** It was full circle from being fans to being part of *Highlander*. It was a thrill.

Charles Lyall, Production Manager, Vancouver

Can you tell me what you do?

Technically, I am the one who looks after people and equipment working directly for the producer. The production manager really is in charge of hiring crew, maintaining them, keeping them happy, and finding out where the problems are, making a change if necessary. And at the start-up, it's amassing the equipment that is necessary, all the rentals and perhaps purchases, and then maintaining it.

A big part of the job is paperwork, so you work closely with the accounting department. The producer is responsible for the budget, but I manage it. So if we're building a temple and it's going to cost $300,000, I have to speak up

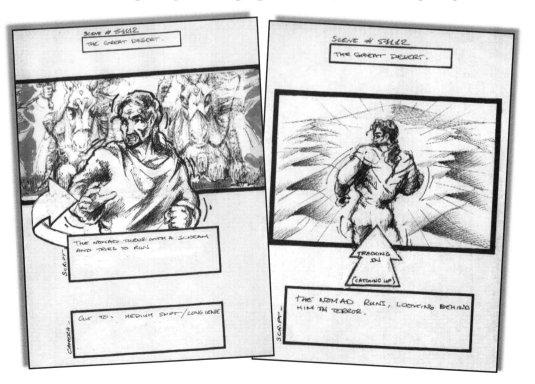

and say, "Let's find something else to do or scale it down." In **"The Valkyrie,"** in front of Hitler's bunker, well, they could have had seven or eight Nazi staff cars. We managed to make do with one. With very creative camera work, and tighter angles and stacking the shot, it looked really good and you're not left wanting.

In the film business in Vancouver nearly everything is rented. Capital cost is so high and maintenance is so great, the technological change is so great, that it's better to rent and build it into the budget—camera, lights, grip stands, any form of hardware, trucks, cars, anything with the possible exception of some set material, set decorating, and construction items we might buy because the cost of renting would outlay the cost of buying. Certainly in any series, the smart thing to do is to rent studio space that encompasses a few standing sets. It's worth paying for and building those, so you own them. Duncan's loft and dojo area and Joe's Bar were all sets we owned and went back to.

Where was the studio space?

Our studio space was in an old warehouse in Vancouver. We chose a large, hundred-thousand-square-foot ex–equipment warehouse and used thirty-five thousand square feet for our sets. We pretty much created our own soundstage. You have to make sure they're reasonably resistant to the outside ambient noise, and there you go.

How many people work on the production?

There are probably 125 or 130 people who work in a week, construction people, Accounting, Post, all those areas that aren't on the set, plus the shooting crew. And a crew usually lasts one season because it's a freelance business. The job of making films is similar when you're up to a certain standard. The great part is that it's art you can mold on the day. You seize the moment.

I think part of the way that Bill Panzer, Ken Gord, and the producers like to run things is in a trusting environment. I agree. So you give a lot to the department heads. They do their best. I had people coming in and being proud of the fact that they'd come in and had saved money. And they had done the job and done it well.

CHAPTER FOUR

Sets, Costumes, Swords
"How about a yurt?"

Chantal Giuliani, Production Designer, France

I'll try to answer your questions the best I can, but it is difficult to summarize a six-year experience. I am Chantal Giuliani and I am production designer. I've been working on *Highlander* since the beginning, six years ago. And the pleasure has remained the same, from the beginning to the end. Of course, I often complain because I get the scripts at the last minute (but that, I think, is part of the game) and my budget gets cut from one year to the next. I have a wonderful crew, which helps me build and decorate the sets, and I take this opportunity to give them the credit they deserve.

I must add that in France we are particularly lucky because we have an extremely rich cultural heritage. The Île de France (Paris and its neighboring regions) is stock full of châteaux, which greatly contributed to the quality of the decors.

One of my favorite episodes is number 100, **"Revelation 6:8,"** directed by Adrian Paul and which we shot in Bordeaux. For this episode, we built a barbarian village and a nomadic village on the Cap Ferret dune, and other complicated sets. This brings back wonderful memories.

Steve Geaghan, Production Designer, Vancouver

Over souvlaki and a bottle of Cava Boutari, Steve and I discuss his tenure on *Highlander*. —M.R.

I'm Steve Geaghan. I was the production designer on *Highlander* for four years. I was the originating designer on the show and was given several caveats by Bill Panzer and Marla Ginsburg when I came on about the look of the show. When they took the show to Paris, the designer there, Chantal Giuliani, was given the same set of orders and was shown all the shows that we had done prior to that. And I think by and large, over the four years that Chantal and I were involved, the show had a very consistent look.

What is the Highlander look?

What I remember Bill telling me was that in the *Highlander* world you could turn a corner and run into something completely different. The look of the show was gritty and dark and very stylish. This is what we tried to do in the first four years. And there were some interesting things about *Highlander* that made it unique. The art department consisted of me and my art director, Richard Cook. That was it. Two people. Any other show of comparable size would have at least four people in the art department. And somehow between the two of us, we managed to keep the show looking fresh every week, and unique in terms of the period stuff.

The period pieces must have been a special challenge and joy for you.

There are some interesting things that evolved over the first couple of years with the period stuff. Originally, the flashbacks were only small segments, tiny little moments. And feedback began to come back to the producers that the audience wanted to see more. So we started insinuating longer and longer segments and larger and larger sets until the vast majority of the shows took place at least half in present day and half in period. And that's the way the show evolved. Unfortunately, the budget did not evolve to assist that. So we had to be increasingly ingenious every season as the requirements got bigger and bigger and bigger. And we did find ways to do it.

In the last three years that I was there, the set decorator was Andrea French, a very talented German set decorator. That European flair helped in keeping the look of the show consistent between the Vancouver and Paris parts of the season.

What's a European look?

Quite decidedly in year one, we wanted to have a very Philippe Stark look for Tessa's apartment. It was extremely European. We were dealing with a French woman and a Scotsman. She was an artist. He was an Immortal with many years of education and experience behind him. He ran an antique store. The look in the antique store that year was very reconstructivist. I used metal bridges running across diagonally, insinuated into deteriorated brick walls with frescoes painted on them. The whole feel of the place was decidedly Old World in a New World environment. Basically, we kept it very rich and extremely textured. And the textural quality of the show, the grittiness, remained throughout all four years that I did it.

When we started the show, Bill Panzer had certain requirements. Having fathered the original films, he didn't want a look in the series that was decidedly different. And I think that by show three or four of the first season, we had the look of the  show in hand and we knew where we were going. Throughout the four years, the show never got easy, because, as I said, the requirements continued to increase as the show metamorphosed, we did more and more period stuff.

The period stuff is, one would guess, where you got to be your most creative. I remember you did China, Mongolia . . .

This is interesting that you bring up China and Mongolia. **"They Also Serve,"** the show that starts off with Mac in Mongolia, the original script indicated that he was in China. And I realized that we could not do China of that period. It was impossible. Imperial China was beyond us in opulence and access. So I decided we wanted to do something different. I asked, "Why don't we do yurts?" And everybody said, "What are yurts?" I said, "They're these neat things that the Mongols live in. They're like round traveling house tents and they can break them down and put them back up." And we all agreed and then thought, "Where do you create the steppes of Central Asia in British Columbia?" Well, we did find a place, a very flat tidal plane. And when the tide was out, you didn't see the water in the distance because it was obscured by slight, green

hummocks in the distance. Then you saw the mountains of Vancouver Island and it looked like the steppes of Central Asia. And you got a couple of local Chinese guys riding ponies in Mongol dress and MacLeod striding across the steppes of Central Asia into this yurt village, and, for all intents and purposes, we had solved the problem.

Except when the tide came in and the crew had to get under the yurts and lift them up. They looked like Kurds walking across the plains. And the tide kept coming in and they'd have to carry the yurts a little longer and get them a little higher. That was kind of a funny moment.

Clearly, location is important to the look of the show.

Vital. Having to shoot both period scenes and present-day scenes in the same day, we ended up having to find locations that allowed us to do untrammeled wilderness along with highly refined present-day environments. Much of my job was spent with the locations department. And I can't stress entirely too much that putting together these shows is very much a collaborative effort between the production department, the locations department, and the art department.

In year one we had to build a Scottish Black Hut for Duncan. These are little stone huts, and they have a very distinctive look. We built one up here in the local mountains, fairly high up on Cypress Mountain. And we got the thing dressed and did an interior/exterior. The scene is where Duncan is reviled by his father, after he awakens from death. We had just completed dressing it and around the corner comes this Scottish family. And this old Scot looks and says, "What's a Black Hut doing here?" I said, "It's for *Highlander: The Series*." He asked, "Can we look?" I said, "Sure." He goes in, looks around, and then tells me that he works for a Scottish museum. He said, "This is a better example of a Scottish Black Hut of the period, in its furnishings and dressings, than we have in our own museum. This is good." We knew we were on the right track.

And each week for four years, we had to come up with something new, regardless of the period. We researched out everything, constantly. And when scripts came in, they were not engraved in stone. In season four I said, "You know, we should do MacLeod in India and the palace of the Rajah of Guipur." And we did **"The Wrath of Kali."** We have a local theater, the Orpheum Theater, and aspects of it were done in classic Indian Victorian style. We shot in there, and it worked beautifully. We created a classic Indian harem bedroom using some of the existing architecture and supplemented it with murals, insets, and other walls. That was the major interior for that show. Then we had exteriors. We built a temple of Kali and put that up in a forest. When Sue Mathews, the Indian actress who played Vashti, saw it, she said, "This is amazing. It looks just like the river delta south of Delhi in the summer." So we managed to put together these shows with bits and pieces, baling wire, and a little ingenuity. And we got the looks that we needed.

I have been told that I should ask you about the statue of Kali.

We built a five-foot statue of Kali. It was designed by Richard Cook and sculpted by Susan Parker. We thought we had a full seven or eight days to sculpt the statue, pull a negative cast, and make a positive when we realized, much to our horror, that it had to be seen on day one. We all somehow neglected to read in the script that we had to see the statue in MacLeod's apartment. So we constructed a shipping crate, tarted up some clay to look like bronze, and managed to get it in there in time to shoot the scene. MacLeod looks at it and we see the head and part of the arm, which is all, literally, held together by baling wire. He closes the crate, and that's the end of the scene. But we also had to make the actual cast statue for the location. It ended up weighing four hundred pounds, just out of the casting material. And when it came out of the negative mold, it broke. Shattered. There was a crew in all night, gluing, drilling, and putting in pins to keep it together. I walked in at six o'clock the next morning, and there was the crew still hard at work. I felt a bit like the captain in *Das Boot*. We were on the bottom, and there were only a couple of people who could get us off. I had better just keep my mouth shut and let them do their job. And if we got off, great, and if not, well, we were going to die there. Fortunately, I had an extraordinarily good paint crew and carpentry crew, and they pulled these bits and pieces together. We then put it in a truck, got it out there, and carried this four-hundred-pound statue the half a mile into the temple location. They shot the scene. And I'll be damned if you never saw the statue, because it wasn't lit. Designer nightmare.

What happens sometimes is that you run into a hell prop. This is something that will kill you. For example, we were always breaking swords. We started off using steel blades, but they were deemed much too dangerous by our sword master. We ended up learning how to manufacture jewel aluminum blades. But the problem was that by the time you fit them through the subo, which is that chunk before the hilt, you had to narrow down the blade to a point where the aluminum began to lose its strength. So sometimes we would go through two or three katanas every sword fight. I think there must have been hundreds of them made in the four years that I was there.

So you designed the katana?

The design of the hilt of Duncan's dragonhead katana was a joint effort between Richard Cook and myself in year one.

What else would you like people to know about your job?

The production designer, in the capacity that I was at *Highlander*, was instrumental in making the scripts visually interesting and shootable within the confines of the limited budget of episodic television. I think the production designer makes sure that the artistic integrity of the script is not compromised by the necessities of production.

Could you give me examples?

"The Samurai." We hauled a sixteen-foot by ten-foot-high wall section with a gate in it up to a fairly remote beach location in coastal British Columbia. Once we shot the exterior of the wall and the gate, we took that gate and used it again in the house in the set that we shot on the stage. What it says to the audience is that we are here at the exterior, now, and as we turn the camera around, we are here at the interior. And I would have a bit of the matching foliage outside to insinuate the fact that the interior was looking out onto an exterior. And if it's lit properly, and that's up to the director of photography, the transition will be flawless. And I think, by and large, between the two directors of photography we had while I was there, Phil Lindsey and Rick Wincenty, the show maintained its look very well.

"Song of the Executioner." That monastery played as a scriptorium, a chapel, a communal dining hall, a monk's bedroom, a hallway, and an entry hall to the monastery. It was designed in such a way as to accom-

modate insert pieces, insert sets, and walls that would give the illusion of its being a much larger space. I think we shot in there for three out of seven days. We turned it around in lunch hours from a hallway to a scriptorium. Another day we stripped out the scriptorium and turned it into a chapel. This is a good example of taking one set and making it play many different functions as a unit set. That's a theatrical term, where one set will turn into many different sets. In *Highlander* we had to be as ingenious as possible. We had to be extremely creative with the materials that we could afford to produce and the materials we had in stock.

And we rescued everything. For example, the antique store from year one was used as different things well into year three. The last time we used it was in **"The Zone,"** the worst episode I think we ever did, as the medical center or hospital. After that I had it destroyed, dismantled, and dismembered, because we'd seen enough of it.

"Shadows," the episode where MacLeod's Immortal friend is burned at the stake. We had to create an English village. And there's a place called Fantasy Gardens, south of Vancouver. It's a funny little period Dutch town, built by a former premier of British Columbia. I've always had it in the back of my mind. The streets are small and narrow and there are all these cute little buildings. They're badly done, but some aspects of it work for period England. So I suggested that we shoot **"Shadows"** down at this little fantasy village. And the place was sufficiently small scale that we could handle it on our budget. I changed boards on the fronts of buildings, I changed windows, I largely left brick and stucco alone. We covered the place in hay and bark mulch to get rid of the cute stones on the street. We put up period signage. We put on period raggedy old wood doors, took down the nice white gutters, and put up bent Styrofoam painted to look like old guttering. We put in period lampposts and basically dressed down the entire place. The only thing that was disappointing was that normally it rains in British Columbia all the time in the winter. But on the day they shot it, it was a beautiful sparkling clear day for a witch-burning. But the night scenes of MacLeod walking through the town with the old ladies and

the smoke and the whole period feel of seventeenth-century England worked exquisitely well. We were very pleased with that. And it was one of those things where you have to look beyond the obvious as a designer, especially when you don't have a huge budget. And in the four years that I did *Highlander*, I think we tackled just about every possible location that the writers could think of and a few that we suggested.

How long would it take you to dress a set?

No dress for *Highlander* ever took more than a day and a half. When we were doing the Scottish village for **"Homeland"** we took a couple of interiors that we had and turned them into exteriors. Then we built facades of other buildings. The roofing was very straightforward; it is straw that is stapled down. We have a scenic way of doing a reasonable thatching look without having to hire a thatcher from England. I think the construction on that village, which was four or five buildings and a couple of facades, took a day and a bit. Halfway through day two of construction, the set decorators, the set dressers came in and started flushing out the interiors and the exteriors with bits of clothing and whatever else the decorator deemed necessary. That was a heavy dress. And on that particular show we didn't start shooting on that set until the middle of the following day, so they had the morning to tweak it. That's when all the animals came in.

The animals?

The budget would allow for one Highland cow and a few sheep because in the fight they have to go through the fence and into the sheep pens. I think it was four mouton sheep, plus the inevitable chickens that always run loose, and we shot it.

The budget would allow only one cow?

Well, the cow itself is probably the least expensive item. But when you say "Can we afford the cow?" what you have to do is look at the wrangler who has to get the cow on his truck. You have to support the pay for the wrangler, the use of the truck, the wrangler's time, and the pen for the cow. Then there's the shooting day. The cow has to be wrapped at an appropriate time. That's a big chunk of money, and this happens with the use of every animal. The sheep are the same deal. And it gets more expensive with cougars and bears and tigers. In **"The Wrath of Kali"** we had tigers, but we knew they were coming, so we budgeted. And they were very well-behaved tigers. No crew members as snacks.

But I still haven't told you any of the funny stuff. There were some funny moments. We'd done an episode called **"Epitaph for Tommy"** where Adrian had to climb up a roller coaster. In one of the sword fights, the other actor smashed the subo on Adrian's sword, and it sent it into the web between his forefinger and thumb, cutting it very deeply. Then Adrian had to leap over a fence to chase someone, whereupon he crotched out on the fence, doing some damage to the family jewels. So the following day, after all this has happened, we're out on set for day one of **"The Fighter,"** and Adrian is standing there and I said, "Adrian, what's this?" I lift my right leg to the knee, hold my hand putting my thumb inside it, showing only four fingers, and it looked like a pretty gimpy human being. He said, "What's that?" I said, "Adrian Paul after season five." And he started to laugh and shook his head.

And one of the more infamous stories . . . One day we were on set and we'd had a tough day, and one of the crew walked up to Dennis Berry. Dennis would get into his job and didn't want to be disturbed. He was the auteur of the show. Some grip walked up and was standing there eating a banana. Dennis looked up and said, "I've had it with you people; no more eating bananas on my set." So, needless to say, about a week later, a T-shirt appears. It's got a great big banana on it with a red circle with a slash through it. No bananas on the set. And the entire crew was wearing them.

But, seriously, I must say, the people who produce this show are some of the most creative minds I've worked with, ever. Any show. Any company. To separate any of us made the show a little less. We were a team. It's why the show was so effective.

Christina McQuarrie, Costume Designer, Vancouver

I am Christina McQuarrie, and I was costume designer. I put together the look of the show for the individual characters in conjunction with the producers, directors, writers, and the actor, of course. The costume designer helps to put together the look of the show in terms of clothing. Jewelry and accessories are a big part, and there's a bit of a dividing line between other departments, but you orchestrate it to a great extent.

Sometimes I think the best way to describe a costume designer is that it's like the conductor of an orchestra. You have all the members of your orchestra together and you give them direction, and if you have good people they go off and they do wonderful things. You give them the direction you want it to go in, and usually it works out beautifully. But I think the important thing is to have a really strong and creative team around you who also understand your vision and are willing to work with you to achieve that vision.

And that vision comes from the producers. And it comes from the interaction with everybody else. Then you're all creating. And it's very

strongly directed by the production designer. For the years that I was there, it was Steve Geaghan. He and I worked very closely. I have a great deal of respect for him, and we had worked together in the past. That has a lot to do with where you go; you're not an island. Any show like *Highlander*, which is what you might call an art show, as compared to, dare I say, a jeans and T-shirt show, is a very collaborative effort. If you've got a good team together, it's the best thing in the entire world. It's wonderful. But if you don't have a good team, it's a nightmare. But we did; it was an incredible team. It's everybody together painting a picture.

The other thing, and this is one of those secrets of filmmaking, if you're only doing a small area, like a corner of a room, you can make it look very, very lush; you don't have to see the other seventy-five percent of the room that's not on camera. That's the magic of filmmaking. If you think about the way that television is shot, a lot of it is from the neck up. So the roses at the hem of the skirt never get shown. That's where you spend your money, from the neck up, on the accessories, the jewelry and all the embellishments. You don't worry too much about the shoes, unless the director says we're going to have a foot shot going down the stairs, then, of course, you have to worry about shoes. But, otherwise, they could be wearing mukluks under there and nobody is going to know. And sometimes they do wear mukluks on a cold day. You have no idea what the actors sometimes look like in front of the camera. But that's where the emphasis is, and it allows you to concentrate your budget in a small area. You concentrate your good extras right behind the principals because it's those six people that you're going to see and not the other thirty who think they're on camera and they're not.

You must have a great knowledge of historical costumes. . . .

A fair amount; a lot of it was learning by doing. I worked in theater for a long time. I think that's where I became so fascinated that I learned a lot of costume history. And certainly there are historical sources to go to once you're presented with a problem.

For example, if the script reads, "Duncan, Japan, 1778,"
what would you do?

Go to the library. You get a lot of your inspiration from art sources, from the painters of the time. Sometimes it's interpretive, a nineteenth-century view of eighteenth-century Japan, but there are all sorts of ways of going about it. I have to say, you may know more about it than some people, but a lot of people don't know the finer details. And while you might not see it on television, the finer detail is very important and what gives it the feel.

Finer detail?

Accessories, headgear, jewelry, embellishing the costume as much as possible. We probably didn't make too many hats, but we used a wonderful costume house. Should I give away the secret? I would say it's one of the finest costume houses in the Western world, Angels and Bermans in London. Of course, a lot of their stuff is made for features.

As I'm sure you know, the costumes used in "Chivalry" were
from Restoration, *which won an Oscar for Costume Design.*

When I got those, when I unpacked those, the detail was amazing. We were almost in tears because they were so beautiful. The materials, the lace, the trims, you can't get stuff like that on the West Coast of North America; you can get it in New York, London, and Paris. I will never forget those costumes. They were exquisite.

Most people will want to know about dressing Adrian Paul as
Duncan MacLeod.

He looked good in a gunnysack. He's interesting, because he's not your classic period body size. He's very big. Generally speaking, for a lot of the period clothes, there's a period shape to the body. Adrian is a very modern body shape, so it did present problems on occasion. He's tall, extremely broad-shouldered, wide chest, narrow waist; it's a 1990s body. Also, a secret, he has very long arms, so he was always pulling his sleeves. We did manage reasonably well, but sometimes it was a bit of a squeaker because tailoring takes a long time.

Adrian has a very strong sense of style, which I liked. He loves clothes and he wears them really well, if he likes them. If you found clothing that he liked, then it was wonderful and you could go shopping. We built up a stock and created a look for him. Silks and natural fibers or rayon silks, anything with a real weight and a beautiful drape. The clothes

flowed over the body and gave him a nice look. And he wore jeans quite a lot. He wore them more than the dress-type pant because he looked good in them.

Coats were a big part of Duncan's look.

Of course, we always had to hide the sword. There was this convention, theoretically, that there was always this long duster coat, of which we made many. Making those was a matter of finding a fabric that had a certain weight and drape to it. That's all very well, and it hid the sword, but sometimes we had to have shorter leather jackets, and then this convention became "Where does the sword come from?" Well, it's magic. So where is he wearing it? Is he wearing it under the coat, strapped to his side? No, it's magic. This was sort of an ongoing debate. Was it like a gun on his belt or was it magic? And it just appeared out of nowhere. We did a bit of both, and sometimes they'd pick them up behind couches or chairs. The expandable sword. The magic pocket. But that's what was so neat about *Highlander*; it's a bit of fantasy.

And as far as I was concerned the duster coat was signature to the show,

so I had to keep the pattern secret. Well, I tried to. Even in the industry, people wanted to borrow it. And I'd say no. The duster was with the *Highlander*, so I was not going to let anybody use it. You can make your own, but I don't want you to use that one. And the coat evolved. In the very first season, it was a purchased coat. Then we came up with this pattern, which worked really, really well. Then we just kept the pattern and remade the coat in different weights. And they'd get slashed or destroyed in the sulfur pits, so we had to keep remaking them. The duster coat was a big item.

That and Duncan's hair ornaments.

The hair ornaments were found bits and buttons on elastic and all sorts of weird things. The original ones were just bits and pieces. We didn't think they were anything special, but everyone asked about them. Later, they became made.

How would you define Duncan's look?

Immortal sophisticate? Except in his very early days, when he was a rough-and-ready Scots boy, he had a casual elegance throughout the ages. Even if you put shirts with jeans, they were silk shirts.

What about dressing the other characters?

I loved dressing Amanda. She was the cat woman. Amanda was wonderful. Elizabeth Gracen wore clothes well and she was a delight. We did make some things for her. We made these wonderful Western gowns for **"Double Eagle."** Her gowns, which unfortunately we didn't see very well on-screen, were fun, and she looked like a million. I loved those. We made those because I knew I couldn't find them. I think they worked out really well. Her gowns were beautiful, and they fitted her with this wonderful hourglass shape. It was great.

It was funny; the character that was the hardest to find a look for, because he kept evolving, was Richie. He started out as this street kid, and then he became Immortal. I'm not sure why exactly, but nobody could

ever really nail down who he was. His look kind of waffled through the years. He was a tricky one, in the end it was jeans and T-shirts because what else? Then he became a mini-Duncan, and that wasn't right.

Joe Dawson was fun. He was your blues singer. He's wonderful. And Jim Byrnes is an incredibly handsome man. Joe was stylish casual. There wasn't anything too wacky.

How many costumes might you be responsible for in an episode?

Say fifty. We didn't have huge numbers of extras. One of the other things that was interesting on *Highlander* is that we didn't prefit extras. So I have to tell you, those mornings when we had our extra scenes and we would be flying around trying to dress people were a nightmare. But I've learned from that. I don't do it anymore. It was terrifying. But I am always amazed when I look at the show, now, and I think, wow, we dressed them in an hour and there are thirty-five extras there and it doesn't look that bad. It was fun, and it was amazing considering how fast we worked.

The action and the sword fights must have presented special challenges for you.

With Adrian, we would always go for three. Obviously in a show with a larger budget or more time, they might want ten, so they can keep doing it and doing it, but we're assuming that with television within three tries they had it. This was one of the tricky things with Adrian's wardrobe, because he's a large guy, sometimes trying to find triples was hard. You'd go to the store and they'd only carry one extra-large and they couldn't get another one, so then you somehow have to fake one or two. With his stuff, we never bought anything unless we could buy it in threes or manufacture it or multiply it, because he was always fighting. The period stuff, no. Sometimes we made the shirts so that they could deliberately "slice and dice," as we used to call it. But there are some things that we couldn't. And I know it restricted what they could do, but we couldn't afford the cost of replacing some of those period clothes. I would always have to say, "There's only one; no you can't."

Everyone wants to know about Duncan's plaid.

What does he wear under his kilt? Ahhh . . . trade secret. That MacLeod tartan was made for the original *Highlander* movie, so it was created. There were a couple of episodes that we did when we went right back to when the Highlander was a boy. At that particular point in history, it would have really been a woven cloth. They would not have been wearing the tartan plaid, as we know it. I remember there was a bit of a controversy. The dress that we used for that particular episode had been used in the original movie, so it was correct in a way. It was the modified MacLeod tartan. I dressed the young ones in a rough blue, just to try and indicate.

Geaghan talked about "hell props"; did you ever have a "hell costume"?

If you want to hear one little anecdote: There was a show where I was trying to get some armor and chain mail from this wonderful company in London. We ordered it, and they shipped it out. Somehow the shipment had come through customs, gone to the States, and back to London. I told Ken Gord, "This is what's happened, I can send them out in their long johns, I don't know what else to do." There were twelve guys; it was a fairly large scene and we couldn't manufacture armor. The company reshipped it. The next day we got to the set, which was way outside the city, and we discovered that it had arrived at the airport and that our driver was waiting to pick it up. When it got to the set, I literally unpacked it and threw it on the extras. They walked onto the scene, fully dressed, and to the people who didn't know, nothing was ever wrong. I think poor Ken nearly had a heart attack. I remember him wearing sunglasses because he couldn't bear it. That was one of the more horrendous experiences. Because of the time constraints, it was frightening. We didn't know how we were going to pull the rabbit out of the hat. It was just so funny because it arrived, we dressed them, and ta-da!

Rex Raglan, Production Designer, Vancouver

I am Rex Raglan, production designer. I work from the script, designing the visual aspect of the film or, as we sometimes joke, all the fuzzy out-of-focus space around the actors' heads, at least on television. But that was one of the joys of *Highlander*; it wasn't always fuzzy and out of focus. In fact, it played a large part in the show because of the flashback element. You had to see these places and times to know that it was different than contemporary times. It was a very rewarding experience for a designer. But it's a rigorous schedule. There's no time to catch up or relax or take a breath; you just plunge and keep on plunging.

We had three standing sets: the bar, the loft, and the dojo. Those were sets that Steve Geaghan did. The immediate department was Richard Cook and myself. We did the design, the supervision, the scouting, the breakdowns, the notes, and disseminating the information to the rest of them. There was the set decorating department, the props department, the construction department, the paint department, and sometimes Wardrobe. Basically, the designer's job is to keep everybody on the same page, so there's coherence to the look of the show.

Do you have any favorite episodes?
    One of them was **"Little Tin God."** The script was written with the budget in mind, and it was written very modestly. And I read it and thought, "This does not deserve to be a hut; this deserves to be in a

temple." Everyone said, "We know that, but how do we do it?" My idea was to find a controllable space and then by matte painting build in the top of the temple. And we found a spot that worked really well. We built the bottom of the temple to look like it was spilling out from the overgrowth, like the jungle had long since reclaimed it. Post matted in the temple top. We built a village at the base of the temple. The village was two two-sided huts. We'd take them and turn the good side to the camera when we were looking from the outside in and we'd do the opposite when we were looking from the inside out. We also took a number of stills, so in Post they multiplied these two huts into a crowded little village. The Moche Indians predated the Incas and were fascinating. We worked from one museum catalog that David A. sent up, and a *National Geographic*. Within the temple we had the Decapitator's throne. His attributes were the hatchet and the lightning bolts. We had open fires and braziers, which gave it a more "primitive" quality.

Ken Gord is one of the most laid-back producers in the business and rarely goes to set unless there's a problem. But for whatever reason, he went out to the Moche temple in the evening. All the little campfires are lit, the torches are going, the lava pit is steaming, everyone was out there in full costume, the llamas were milling about, and Ken was knocked out. It was magic.

The fantasy bedroom for **"Dramatic License"** was fun. It was a two-walled set, ten feet by twelve feet, but it was made to look like it was in an elaborate gilded villa. The bed was about eight feet high. Gold and candlelight really do wonders.

I think one of my other favorites was **"The Valkyrie."** I had been hoping to do a show where we could try and do something based on the scale of Albert Speer's designs for the Third Reich. Just to work in that scale and create that illusion of being there. In Hitler's bunker, the scale of the fireplace was huge. The top of the fireplace was at his shoulders. And the Effects guy kept turning the fire down so it wouldn't get too hot, and I said, "I made this huge fireplace because I wanted a huge fire. Behind Hitler we have to have the flames of hell burning; turn it up!" So he did. And the table was made to look like it was a four-inch-thick slab of oak with a swastika inlaid in it, in ivory surrounded by ebony. And the beauty of television? That ebony and ivory was paint and the oak was mahogany plywood.

That's the same thing as everything else: paint, the cheapest mahogany plywood, and sometimes there's Styrofoam. But the beauty of it is that you can't tell until you touch it. That's the art. That's the fun. Creating the illusion that it's something other than what it is. Every week we create a different world.

From whence do you draw inspiration?

Once you have the concept nailed down, it's historical research. We get a script seven days before we shoot. It sets the scene; then we go to work. Everything that we didn't know accurately, and the more accurate the better, we would research: photographs, drawings, paintings. Then you notice the details and think about how to integrate them. The details can help the story.

The look of the show was always beautiful.

It was amazing. One of the things that made it possible was the vast warehouse of stuff that we recycled. The Moche temple became Hitler's bunker. And it's interesting to note that once you get back before the Industrial Revolution, a lot of the basic things are the same anywhere in the world. Pots and pans or open fires and kettles, barrels, baskets, wheelbarrows or carts, with a little bit of tweaking or a bit of decoration or dressing; it could be South America, it could be Western Europe, it could be Scotland, India, anywhere.

Richard Cook, Art Director, Vancouver

I am Richard Cook, and I have been art director on *Highlander* since day one. Everyone else changed. Seasons one to four, production designer Steve Geaghan and I did all the artwork on the show. Looking back on it, that was an absolutely astonishing feat because we were a two-man band. Steve did all the conceptual stuff, went to the meetings and dealt with the producers, and I did everything else. For a series as ambitious as *Highlander* with so much historical content, and a show where the art department is required to make an important contribution, it's amazing that we could do it with two people. It was one of those things where Steve and I clicked. We understood each other's visual vocabulary, so we could shortcut things. He would give me an outline, and I would take it and expand it, enhance some of the work in terms of adding detail and color. Looking back on it, it is one of the most creative experiences of my career.

The show had such a rich look; how did you maintain it?

Highlander was an incredible burst of energy. Year to year the show grew, and it developed a definite look. By season four, *Highlander* achieved texture, patina, and a wonderful rich saturated look. That was something that seemed to just grow and develop. Steve and I started in theater, which has always been a great help. We would pull all these theater tricks out of the hat. Instead of using the real thing, which most people do in television because they don't know how to do an alternative, we would cheat it to the camera because ultimately your image is reduced so much.

Can you give me an example?

For instance, we were often required to provide tapestries as set decoration. We couldn't afford to go out and buy them or even rent them because they cost hundreds of thousands of dollars. So we would paint them. And we had a wonderful scenic art department, and they would paint these wonderful tapestries, and to the camera, my goodness, you would never know. They just looked so wonderfully rich.

One year we did an ancient Chinese temple, and Steve said to me, "We need some really amazing wall paintings here." So I went off to the library to do research. Steve and I went through the books that I brought back and grabbed a bit of this and a bit of that and talked about it. And we developed these amazing backdrops. They looked like crumbling wall textures, but they were painted on cotton. Once we had the appropriate

lighting, added some incense burners, the right furniture, and some good set dressing, there we had ancient China. Those were theater backdrops that worked for us. And a lot of the stuff was carved out of Styrofoam.

I've heard Styrofoam was a show staple.

One episode, "**Shadows**," scripted a character who was an artist who sculpted gargoyles. We had to quickly find a good sculptor. Fortunately, there's a really good talent pool in Vancouver. I did some quick research and came up with drawings and the sculptor carved these gargoyles all out of Styrofoam. They were big and very imposing. Once they were painted and we added a gritty overall stone texture to the outside, you would never know. They looked so massive and solid.

And we would do that all the time, find ways to make it work. We had to be really inventive. And we had an amazing paint department and all the great construction guys. Our technical staff was absolutely wonderful and grew, year by year, into a family.

How many people were in the technical staff?

We had a permanent staff of four to six construction guys and three to four paint people. And if we were doing a really ambitious episode, where we were doing a big build, it would go up to fifteen construction guys for a short period. We had a core of people who were really, really talented that we cultivated and valued. Without them, we were sunk. The thing about the medium is that it is essentially a collaboration. Steve was very aware of that, and really valued his people. He valued me tremendously. I have learned so much from him, and I think he learned from me in some sense. Working together, there was no question of who was calling the shots. It was just working together. It was a good experience.

Were the flashbacks a special joy and challenge for you?

It gave us a huge opportunity to be far more creative than almost any other episodic television series you could think of, especially given our budget. *Highlander* was an art department dream. And it was very, very hard work. There was no mistaking. I can think of all the many, many Celtic villages we set up on Mount Seymour in North Vancouver. That involved dragging scenery up there, plus all the animals and the stock pens and the sheep and the goats and the highland cows. And sometimes it would be summer and there would be clouds of mosquitoes. And, again, we were dependent on our crew. By the end, the guys in Construction were so good at doing sheep pens and lean-tos. We did lean-tos for everything from Mexico to Celtic village to Chinese market because it's a cheap way to provide a good look and it's construction that happens on-site. The guys would literally cut branches and lash them together. Then we would put tarps or skins or fabric over the top, depending on what period and what look we were after. And you bring in the set dressing, the animals, the smoke, the carts, the wagons, and then the costumes, and there it is. You have a village. Incredible.

Do you have any favorite episodes?

Each and every episode held some kind of challenge, but I enjoyed them all. Some really pushed the limits. We did a great Mexico for **"The Revolutionary."** The Location guys found just the right location. It was late summer in a sandy beach dune environment. We put in lean-tos, of course. We did rush matting over the top and got these wonderful patterns of light. We built a cantina facade. We did this big broken and ruined archway. There was a well in the center. We were in Mexico.

We did a Vietnamese village, which we shot just outside of Vancouver.

We only built one three-dimensional building that was actually used in the action. Steve and I decided we were going to try matte painting. I painted in all these little additional huts, and we set up one very wide establishing shot and locked off the camera, and then I worked from still and overlaid that with acetate.

Exactly how they do matte painting in the big movies. To the camera, it looked like we had twenty little houses. Also, this is the Pacific Northwest; the natural vegetation is mainly evergreen. There are no palm trees. So I painted in palm trees, as well. We got up to all kinds of things. Just the cheek of it was amazing. People would say, "You're doing matte painting on episodic with two people in the Art Department? Are you crazy?"

There was another episode, **"Homeland,"** where the heroine was supposedly standing on the edge of a precipice. The location didn't quite work because although it was a fair drop, it was more of a sandy bank than the edge of a cliff. Steve said, "Let's try matte painting." So we took the shot and put a clear cell acetate over that, and I painted a sheer rock face at her feet.

I'm beginning to understand what you mean by "cheating the camera."

We did it a lot. For instance, we made all these icons. And they were just color Xeroxes that were pasted on, aged, and then we added gold leaf. We cheated all the time, but it was so creative. There is absolutely no creativity in going out, spending a million bucks, and coming back with a real icon. The creativity is to spend twenty bucks and come up with something that works just as well to the eye and to the camera. That's what's creative. And that was always the challenge.

F. Braun McAsh, Sword Master

Highlander's resident sword master is at the Château de Vigny to get in some practice time with Adrian and the guest star of the week. During a break in rehearsals, Braun stops for a chat. —M.R.

My title, if you can call it that, was something that I inherited when I came onto the show. Bob Anderson created the name Sword Master.

What does it mean?

It means that I choreograph all of the action involving bladed weapons, not just swords, but knives, bayonets on rifles, anything that involves something that cuts or pokes, slices or stabs. And I also do a little of the unarmed combat and advisory on firearms because I have a very wide violence background. I'm a violence professional, if you will.

How did you become a violence professional?

When I was in drama school, the curriculum still included stage combat and stage fencing. At the same time that I was in theater school, I was also a competitive fencer. And I'd always been very interested in history, and, of course, when you're younger, history is knights on horseback and arms and armor. I've been doing martial arts for twenty-four years. And I was in the army and the Canadian army reserve. I started as a paratrooper and ended up as an intelligence officer.

How did you become a fight choreographer?

When I first started as an actor, I spent five years at the Stratford Shakespeare Festival [Ontario, Canada]. They have a resident sword master and I apprenticed myself to him. My last year at Stratford, they asked me to choreograph several major shows. That's where I really started hard-time professional choreography. I've been doing almost nothing else but *Highlander* for the last four years.

Can you walk me through the preparation for a fight?

I get the script, I page through the script; then, when I regain consciousness, I ask, "How many fights do we have?" The main thing is, the fights have to tell a story. The fights are not there gratuitously; they are there to further the plot, they are there to tell things about the characters, just like the lines. So you have to figure out what does the fight mean, why is it there, what dramatic purpose does it serve, and how can the choreography help tell that story?

The next thing is, how much information do I have on the actor? Is he right-handed or left-handed? Till I get that information, I can't even begin to choreograph. Well, I could, but it would be a waste of time, because I'd have to choreograph two fights. One for a left-hander and one for a right-hander.

The next thing is, what weapon am I going to use? How do I choose the weapon? Should the weapon say something about the character? How old is the character? When would he or she have decided, "OK, this is the sword that I'm going to use"? Methos is five thousand years old, and

the sword he uses is a late-thirteenth-century medieval sword. Why would a person five thousand years old choose that? Well, it's his style of fighting.

Has the actor had any training? Can I use a one-handed sword or a two-handed sword? You can control a two-handed sword more readily than a single-handed sword. Have they had any training or experience? Ninety percent of them have never touched a sword in their life, so then you have to assess their abilities. I had a fight this season with a relatively young man, in his late twenties, early thirties.

He had two artificial hip joints, so the fight has to then take into consideration how he moves from the waist down, as opposed to how he moves from the waist up. Can't have him going really quickly backwards, because if he trips, be-doom, that's it. So there are all those physical considerations.

Then, what's the set going to be like? How much room do we have on the set? How is the designer going to dress the set? Are we building the set? What can I use? Can we dress in stuff that I can use in the fight? Like rolling over a table, knocking him through a glass door, picking up a lamp and throwing it, breaking furniture with the sword. Most of the time, it's not in the budget.

When I'm choreographing a fight, I also have to take into consideration how much rehearsal time the actor has. How many days do I get the actor? How many hours a day can I have the actor? There's no point in choreographing something that you don't have the time to rehearse. So I have to scale the fights to how much rehearsal time is available and what the actor's skill level is. I'd rather have a short fight that is well rehearsed and looks great than a long fight that is underrehearsed and is just a long series of tentative blows, then, "OK, cut. OK, cut. OK, cut." You just eat up time that the director often doesn't have.

What's the costume? How does the person move? Especially in period pieces, a lot of men's clothing was designed specifically with fighting in mind. So if you're going into certain time periods, you have to realize that the clothing puts restrictions on the weapon because it presupposes a certain weapon and a certain fighting style. Sometimes that has bearing.

Footgear; what surface are we working on? I was doing a fight as Hans Kerschner in an episode last year where we were on cobblestones. Well, that was no big deal. But then we shot at night and it was French winter and the cobblestones froze so that we had this glaze of ice. Then, of course, we had the blinding lights right in our eyes, so every time you turned you were staring into a 20K spotlight and you could not see at all. We were slipping and sliding all over the bloody place. When I was killed as the character, I lay down and when I got up, I had like two pounds of gravel frozen to the front of my costume. That's how cold it was.

Above all, the fight has got to be safe. You learn that in rehearsal. You can't be above changing something. I might spend hours and hours and hours choreographing a fight and if I then find that the actor can't do it comfortably or safely or is tentative or afraid of a move, then that move has got to be changed.

And, of course, Adrian, being six years on this show, has evolved a style of sword fighting that is very different from when he first started the series. His style is a mélange of many, many things. And, right now, Adrian is more than skillful enough so that he feels comfortable making decisions about parries and the like. You've got to be able to adapt the fight to Adrian's character because, after all, he knows Duncan MacLeod better than I do. I haven't played him for six years.

Are the battle scenes choreographed differently?

Every pair has to be choreographed individually in the battle scene duels. I just don't let these nuts go at it. In a battle scene with forty guys, one guy will kill another, then seek out another, and so on. One guy might have two or three fights. So between forty people, there are probably thirty to thirty-five individually choreographed fights. And they have to be choreographed, they have to be taught, they have to be rehearsed. It's just that they're done with stunt men, so you say, "Come here, do this, this, and this, you got that, OK, go away. You two, now. You two, now." Well, the French stunt men.

With nearly three hundred fights, are there any that stand out for you?

Many. What comes to mind immediately are all of the rapier-dagger fights in **"Duende"** with Tony De Longis. Not only is Tony an actor, he's a very fine swordsman himself, a fight director in his own right. These fights were a little bit different for Adrian because he hasn't used an off-hand short-bladed weapon for quite a while. And most of the fights we were doing on the Magic Circle, where extending the arm allows you to hit the person. There are no lunges, so you're working perilously close. We were using forty-two-inch steel blades because the aluminum blades would bend too fast. The daggers were steel, too. So, there we are; we're basically using real weapons, but without edge. And during the last fight scene, it was absolutely pouring rain. So, they're out there fighting a very, very complex, extremely precise fight in the pouring rain, on a slick piece of painted material, because they didn't mix sand in with the paint. They were slipping and sliding.

I have a lot of sword fights that when I saw the final cut, I thought, yeah, that really cooks. Again, Tony De Longis, in year three, in **"Blackmail,"** the fight through the mansion and into the pool. Again, very complicated. That took two days to shoot. That was the only sword fight that took two days to shoot because it was six phrases and two stunts and a lot of furniture being broken, a television being sliced in half.

The fight in **"Rite of Passage"** with Rob Stewart off the boat, going up the ramp, all the way around the dock, and falling into the water, all in one shot. That was a continuous shot using four cameras. No cuts. Very, very fast, too.

"Homeland" had some very good sword fights. That's the first time I've actually been able to use not just the Viking axe, but also the shield the way the Vikings used it when they used the axe, which was strapped to their back. You turned around and took parries on your back or used the sword and the axe simultaneously.

The saber and katana fight with Wolfgang Bodison, who played Cord in **"Brothers in Arms,"** was a very well-executed fight. We introduced hand blocking, pummel striking, and close-in fighting. And the knife fight between Cord and Stu Akins' character, Charlie De Salvo, on the roof was an extremely good knife fight. Interestingly, Wolfgang is a man who had never touched a sword in his life, before, but he's a very, very physical actor, a very coordinated actor.

Dara Tomanovich as Alex Raven in **"Sins of the Father"** had a very interesting fight. She had a short version of a Russian sword, and she takes on MacLeod who is just using a Philippine fighting stick, so it's sword against stick. Again, very, very close. Hand blocks, pummel strikes, elbow strikes, and quite fast, too.

I'm quite proud of **"The Revolutionary"** with the bayonet fight in the Mexican Revolution, where MacLeod takes on four soldiers and basically strews them around. Bayonet is quite different because you're using a weapon that is a weapon at both ends. The bayonet is on the butt.

There are so many good fights. I designed all the weapons for **"Horseman"** and **"Revelation,"** the ones that Kronos, Caspian, and Silas used. Those weapons never existed in history. And even though there weren't any fights in **"Horseman,"** we did have to choreograph that bit where they come streaming down the hill, mowing people down. You try riding a horse down the side of a sand dune on a thirty-degree rake through a village with about thirty people, hacking and hewing with weapons, with a mask on. It was interesting.

CHAPTER FIVE

The Actors and Their Characters

"I'm the leprechaun of *Highlander*."

Adrian Paul as Duncan MacLeod

*T*hey are filming at La Cité this week. The university is *Highlander*'s home away from home in Paris. Much of the day is spent shooting an encounter on a rooftop. When Duncan is shot with an arrow, the always busy Adrian has some downtime. We sit at a small table near the dormitory. Adrian's assistant, James, brings us coffee. —M.R.

Can you tell me how you became Duncan MacLeod of the Clan MacLeod?

March, six years ago, I walked into a meeting with Bill Panzer, Marla Ginsburg, the other producers, and the writers in a hotel room at The Four Seasons in California. I was the first person they saw for the job, but not the last. Four months later, I did an audition and then a screen test. Then I waited three weeks and got the job. So that's how.

What did you think when you saw that first script?

I knew the premise, I'd seen the films, I liked the films, I liked the idea of the films; I thought it was a good idea.

Duncan has evolved since that first show.

I think he takes more things in his stride, now. I think he lets things happen a little more. This year is the first year that you actually see him changing the present; usually you see him changing the past. You know there are certain moments in his life, in the past, that make him go a different direction in his life. This time, because of the death of Richie, he looks at things with a different eye. He doesn't jump in as much as he did in the first five years. Now he says, "OK, well this is how it is and you make your own decision." And if it's going to hurt somebody then he'll probably try and stop them, but he's not as aggressive, I think.

So the changes are linked to Duncan killing Richie?

I think now he self-doubts what he does. I think it's a question of having killed his best friend; is everything that he does worth it, when it comes down to it, in the end? He questions himself. He went away for a year and tried to cleanse himself of everything that he knew before because he was up against something he wasn't familiar with. It wasn't an Immortal, it was a demon.

People have said Highlander is like a morality play, dealing with the big issues of right and wrong. Do you agree?

A morality play? Let's put it like this: David Abramowitz came on the seventh show of season one, and the scripts started getting better. *Highlander* has such an interesting premise: Immortals dealing with human problems and human morals. But I don't think MacLeod is "moralistic." He is a person who still makes mistakes. He may have his way of thinking about things and he has a certain moral code, but I don't think he should impose it on anybody else. He will tell people what he believes are the rights and wrongs of a certain situation, but that's only from his point of view.

As an actor, do you have a favorite episode of Highlander?

I've had fun on a lot of them. I enjoyed **"Something Wicked."** Being the bad MacLeod was fun. I enjoyed that. Gosh, there are so many scripts, so many shows that we've done. I could say that I've had a fabulous time. I like the comedies.

Roger Daltrey said he liked the comedies.

I love working with Roger Daltrey. He and I want to do a film together at some point, a totally different thing, because the comedy we have is just there; it's natural. He's a very good friend, like a brother. And it was strange, because when I was growing up The Who were huge. And it's Roger Daltrey playing Fitz. Yet we get on like a house on fire. We have a lot of fun.

Has the action part of the show provided any special challenges for you?

I've always been very physical. I played rugby at the county level. I played semipro soccer. I was on the school cricket team. I was on the school running team. I played basketball when I was a kid. I've played volleyball, tennis, and done jet skiing. I've always liked sports. And martial arts I've been doing now for about nine years. With that background, picking up sword work was another level of what I was physically able to do. What I've learned on the sword is immense in the past six years.

F. Braun McAsh said you were good enough to choreograph your own fights.

He's very kind. And I have done it. I choreographed the fight that is in **"Armageddon"** at the very end. I choreographed all the hand techniques and put sword techniques within that because F. couldn't choreograph it with me. I was the only one who knew the Qidong moves, so we had to do it that way. We needed the spiritual side of a noncombative fight, if that made sense. What's interesting is that it's basically a set of movements.

F. said you have your own style.

F. will choreograph something and I will always go in and change it slightly because his body to my body movement is very different. That's something I've learned. You have to have your own type of style with the piece. It goes hand in hand with the acting. A lot of actors F. will fight with; then when we start rehearsing, they forget it totally because my movements are so different than his, it puts them off. It's bad in a way, because we have to have rehearsal time, and if they forget something, the consequences are I go to hospital with a few stitches. Once, twice, three times that I can remember, and that's not including a lot of other bloody moments.

Are there any sword fights that you especially liked or found especially difficult?

Oh my gosh, I've done something like three hundred fights. The fight in **"Timeless"** was very good. Ron Halder was very good. It was fun to do. Different type of thing.

The other fight that was interesting was fighting myself in **"Something Wicked."** You do some with a stunt double, but I had to do both sides, so I had to learn both sides of the fight. Stan and I also have a good fight in that episode. It was fast.

Anything with Anthony De Longis was great. He is a fabulous fighter. He's very talented as a swordsman and when you have somebody like that you are both able to pull things if anything goes wrong, so you have speed. I did a good fight with Anthony in year three in **"Blackmail."** And in year five we did **"Duende."** **"Duende"** was beautiful. **"Duende"** was a great show. The opening of **"Duende"** was a beautiful shot. That's why I was talking about Richard Martin having an amazing eye. It's a very good episode. The scene with Duncan and Theresa by the fountain was one of the most romantic-looking flashbacks we've ever had. It was a beautiful, beautiful flashback.

Peter Wingfield said he liked the fact that on Highlander all the actors listened to each other.

Peter's a strong actor. He works hard. I would like to work with him again as a director because he's so good. As actors, we've had good scenes together. Methos and MacLeod are friends, but they don't necessarily agree a lot of the time because their ideologies come from such different times and places, but that's one of the things that makes them so interesting.

It's the same as Joe and MacLeod. Joe and MacLeod are friends, but they can't quite be buddies because MacLeod is an Immortal and Joe is a Watcher. Joe and MacLeod have an uneasy friendship.

Highlander *has a large following; have your experiences with the fans been primarily positive?*

Yes. It's been really nice to have people appreciate the work that we've done. OK, their main comment is often that they like Duncan MacLeod, which is nice, but it's very definitely been a collective effort. And I think that if you treat people with kindness and respect, most of the time they will return kindness and respect to you.

Stan Kirsch as Richie Ryan

How did you get the job?

It was really just another in a slew of auditions that an aspiring young actor would go on. I think I went back four times. I did a screen test. The audition scenes that I read were out of the **"Free Fall"** script with Joan Jett. And then one day I got the call and was told I had to be in Vancouver in five days and would be working for the next nine months. It was exciting and daunting and nerve-racking and thrilling all at once.

Richie is probably the character who has evolved the most over the course of the series.

In some ways the evolution of the character slightly mirrored my life as an actor at the time, because I was growing and learning a lot. It was the first time I had the opportunity to work on something for such an extended period of time. In some ways the development in my life and my life as an actor specifically mirrored the development of this guy trying to find his way in this world, in this new territory.

And then Richie became Immortal.

I was excited to become Immortal because it's a show about Immortals, so you might as well be one and play the Game. And in a lot of ways I was left to my own devices, episode to episode, to discover the reality of that particular situation. So I looked at each episode slightly independently and used some to craft a more comedic approach and some to take a more dramatic approach.

I understand you pressed for a leaner, meaner Richie Ryan.

I wanted to explore the darker sides of the character. I thought, what if somebody really became Immortal in today's world? They would realize they couldn't die, they'd probably take some chances. They'd do some things that they normally wouldn't do, put themselves in precarious, dangerous situations. I did want to explore that, but I also think I was saying anything I could along the way to fight for the character, for the independence of the character, the evolution of the character. The independence being the big thing, to be not just the sidekick to Duncan, but to be an independent character on the show.

Do you have favorite episodes?

I think **"The End of Innocence"** was a good episode. I hadn't done the previous year's Paris shows, and that was my decision. So I had had a bit of a distance from the show and from the character of Richie. I had very much become my own person. I had spent a bit of time in the gym, so I felt a little bit stronger and little bit more independent from the series as a person and as an actor. It was nice to come back, but I think from that point on, there was a marked change in the relationship between Richie and Duncan.

And I know this episode wasn't well received, but **"The Ransom of Richard Redstone"** was a lot of fun for me because I enjoy comedy. It was a chance to be funny, to get out of my brown leather outfit, put on a tuxedo, and really play as an actor. Constantly pretending to be pretending to be pretending to be something. For instance, in the scene where they drugged Richie, that's the kind of stuff that I enjoy as an actor. You are in a circumstance that is not about looking cool and being tough. It's a playground and you are like a kid. You don't know what's going on and you've been given a horse tranquilizer. Go for it. So although I don't think that show was one of the better *Highlander* episodes, I had a lot of fun. We got to shoot in Bordeaux, in a town called Bergerac, and in Paris. I thought it was exciting to take one episode to three different cities. And I got to take my own story and do something with it. And I enjoyed working with Sonia Codhant.

I always enjoyed working with the guest stars. On a series you see so much of the same people, and you have done so many scenes with the same people that there's a familiarity, which you can use. But to then work with somebody new and somebody fresh is exciting. And I always enjoy working with a woman.

Too bad the readers can't hear that wicked laugh. Richie did seem to lack a love life for much of the show.

In the beginning, because Duncan had Tessa, the random love interests were delegated to me. Which was great. But once Tessa was gone and Duncan was sort of out and about, Richie's love life was severely cut off. So to speak. Richie got a woman a season. So I would look forward to and enjoy those few moments.

Speaking of relationships, Richie and Joe—in terms of the show, perhaps not one you would expect.

Yes, but no. Jim Byrnes and I are actually very close as people. We had an initial click. I always found that being around Jim, as a person, was inspiring and somewhat of a reality check. And, on top of that, he's a really

funny guy and we got each other. We got each other's sense of humor. The only thing that I wish is that we could have been more ourselves on camera. Because we never stopped laughing, and Richie and Joe didn't get to do much of that. On location, Jim and I have spent a tremendous amount of time together, especially when we were in Paris. Adrian would be working for the most part, and Jim and I would be staying at the same hotel, on a very similar schedule, and hanging out a lot together. And I think because we connected as people, we could get in there on camera and do a scene. I think the relationship we had as people just sold. I love Jim. I think he's a great guy. He's terribly funny and I admire him so much for what he has accomplished in his life.

Everyone will want to know how you felt about "Archangel."

I knew it was coming when they asked me to do that show. I could have said no, I could have not done the episode. At the time I was not contractually obligated to do the show. But I elected to do it, knowing that Richie was going to get killed. I wasn't out to keep Richie alive. I'm an actor and that's what I do. I will go wherever and whenever to act and to play interesting stories.

How was it returning for "To Be" and "Not To Be"?

I saw it as Richie from the antique store in the beginning. This Richie is a little bit lost; he's still got that streety New York thing in him. He's very familiar with talking his way into and out of a situation. He's familiar with small-time thievery. He is not familiar with death. He's not familiar with killing. He's not a murderer, just like Joe says. So I tried to focus on the vulnerability of the character, not knowing about Immortals, not having been properly trained and taught as Connor was, as Duncan was, as everybody else was. He's in over his head, and he's really a good guy at heart. He's not merciless. To steal money is one thing; to kill a person is another. I tried to focus on the vulnerability and the desperateness of this young thief who probably doesn't want to be Immortal, who doesn't know what's going on and is thrust into this situation and forced to believe and trust Methos and Kronos because he has nobody else to turn to. And they end up turning on him. I think it's a sad story, when I step out of it. Richie has nobody to turn to, and he desperately wants to be accepted by the people around him because he has no family. In the moment when Methos and Kronos say, "We want him dead," nobody has ever asked Richie to kill. That must read there. And then Richie masking it, "No, I can do it." And then the scene with Jim was very desperate. Can't do it. But looking for any way to do it.

Jim Byrnes as Joe Dawson

I watch Jim doing ADR (automated dialogue replacement) at Post Modern Sound in Vancouver. When he is done, we sit down in the studio and talk over a cup of coffee. —M.R.

I am Jim Byrnes and I play Joe Dawson. The character was originally called Ian Dawson and he was either North American or English, somewhere between forty and sixty. That was that. Immediately, I said, "No, I'm not an Ian." So we changed the name to Joe. And, originally, I knew I was doing this one episode where we were going to introduce the character and then we were going to take it from there. And they promised me *x* number more episodes just to kind of sweeten the pot to get me to do the show on short notice, and then I had a good rapport with the crew, with Adrian, with the writers, the producers, etcetera. Obviously, I didn't get in the way, and what I did didn't hurt anybody. And people seemed to enjoy the character, so it's continued. This is the fifth year I've been with the show.

Tell us about the first show.

My first show was the first show of the second season. The last show of the first season they had shown to me because it had Horton, who was Joe's brother-in-law, and these bad Watchers. They introduced the whole concept of the Watchers with that episode. I think that's part of the reason that the character caught on. We are all Watchers, everybody that's a fan of the show. We are all members of the same organization, so I think that puts me, an ordinary guy, in extraordinary circumstances, and that gives everybody something to hang on to.

I think that's why the character has worked. We all get older and have our aches and pains and we look different every day, you know, a couple extra miles, so it gives that sense of continuity. I just put everybody, all the viewers, I think, a little bit closer to the picture. Because they see me, and some days I don't look so hot and some days I look all right. It's the human element. Joe's just an ordinary person witnessing extraordinary events.

And we've seen Joe move from Shakespeare and Co. to Joe's, where both you and Joe can play.

In the first episode, the line that I loved was, "I have a weakness for beautiful things." It's probably the most human thing Joe said in that episode. And we've seen over the while, he does. Music is a thing of beauty, and it was like he said, "I got tired of hanging around museums and dusty bookstores." And I wanted to get into a milieu that I enjoyed and that Joe enjoyed, just as the character. And it happened because everybody had discovered that it doesn't just say on my résumé that I'm a professional singer and guitarist. I actually am. Everybody came out to hear the band play and then thought, "How can we incorporate this into the show?" And we found a way and it's been great. It really helps you as an actor because it broadens Joe's scope immediately. It gives him a wider palette.

In the first episode of this last season, **"Avatar,"** there's a scene I like. There are some flashbacks, and I'm sitting there playing guitar and remembering. And it had not been written that way. I had my guitar with me, and I said, "Music is Joe's form of meditation, where he would go; it's Joe's martial art." So we filmed this and thought we'd see what we got, and they ended up using it.

Are there any other episodes where they have showcased your music?

The last episode of season five, **"Archangel,"** they had a montage of Richie's exploits and they wanted to use a piece of music. They said, "Do you think that you could come up with something?" And oddly enough, I had written these words just verbatim. In Paris the year before, I was sitting at a café on the last day of shooting. You're counting through your money, checking all this stuff because you're leaving the next day. And my own personal angst was going on at the time. I sat at this café, I had this little journal that I write in, and I wrote those twelve questions just in a row. I looked at them and I talked to one of my musical collaborators and we sat down and in about a half hour, out of these words, we had this song, which I though fit great at the end of the episode. I didn't know exactly what it was about, but it certainly seemed to work, because it expressed mentor/brother love between men. I thought it turned out OK.

Did you enjoy "Avatar" and "Armageddon"?

It was great to really dig in. Because so many times, it's the nature of the game, I end up saying, "Well, you know, in 1865 they found this guy" and just do exposition. You got to tell the story some way. You're like the narrator because of the nature of the show; it's not about me. But **"Armageddon"** and **"Avatar"** really got into Joe and Mac's relationship and the humanity and the temptation. It was great. I really had a good time.

The writers said they spoke with you first.

"Yeah, I do think about it." That's what I said when they asked: "I deal with this every day, so sure, I can handle it." You don't think about it, really, because it's obviously not going to happen, but you do. Man, to run down a beach and put my toes in the sand would be . . . couldn't ask for that; it would be like going to heaven. It's impossible. Something that would never happen, but, as I say, it gave me a chance to dig in. I was more than glad to do it because it was something that I could really get into. I didn't have to make up anything.

It wasn't too close?

Yeah, but at the same time, that's why I wanted to do it. Also because I generally try to avoid mention of disability. I go through my life and do what I do and let people see it that way, as a positive thing for others, whatever their disability might be. I've got this life and I deal with it. I think the episode dealt with it without really hitting you over the head, but at the same time, it really made you think, "What would you give?"

This is another thing; people always come up to me in airports and say, "We love your show, and I let my kids watch it with me." You know, at one time, we had this thing that we were the most violent show on TV because we had these constant beheadings. OK, ostensibly, on one level, you can see that. But there's no blood, and it's symbolic in a way. And we always deal with every consequence. The show is about consequences. And the show is about nobody gets away with anything. It always comes back to you. You always have to deal with the consequences of an act of violence, of a lie, of telling the truth. It's about moral issues.

Do you have any episodes of which you are most proud?

I like "**Brothers in Arms**"; it's good. I like many of them. The opportunity to work on "**Avatar**" and "**Armageddon**" was great for me. Whether they come across or not, I don't know. And it's hard because I don't particularly like to watch myself. I do it now and then and if something's good I enjoy it, but I don't really learn much from it. Little things really bug me. Just details, little stuff. I hate the way I walk. I do. Let me be frank.

But at a convention I heard a woman say that Joe is the sexiest guy on the show. . . .

I can dig that.

I have also heard people ask you about Joe and his girlfriends or lack thereof.

Joe is very attracted to the opposite sex.

But no domestic bliss?

No, Joe's been through the wringer. When you really think about the consequences of what this would do to somebody seeing this shit happen, it's like, whoa . . . devastating. It would be hard for people to be around him too much, I think. He's kind of a loner, because at some point he's got to have some serious demons. These people have witnessed this crazy stuff; how do you deal with it? It's hard to be ordinary. Joe is extra ordinary, he's really ordinary; I mean that in a good way.

Has your experience with fans been positive?

It's been amazing. Generally, people get to know you and they find out that you're just a person. I like to show them just who I am. I don't try to make anything out of it. It kind of mystifies me to some extent that people could be so wrapped up in a personality that is made up. But at the same time, it's very gratifying. But I don't believe my own PR, and I can't, because I've been around the block. Maybe if I was nineteen years old, but I've had a whole life, great stuff and miserable stuff. I know there are ups and downs, so I appreciate it for what it is. You can't help it. Particularly when, that swooning nonsense aside, people say that with a performance or with a song, you said something to them or, on an emotional level, you touched them. That's what you're trying to do as an artist. You're trying to make people think and feel. So in that way, it's great. But at the same time, I know the reality of me, and I know that I'm not on this pedestal.

How do you feel now that Highlander is drawing to a close?

End of a job. It will be good. It will be bad. You'll have your pals around you and say what you want to say. We're all going to miss doing the show, but we're not going to miss it, too. It's work and it will be nice to get a different perspective and put Joe to rest. And, who knows, he might show up every now and then on the new show. And there's talk of the *Highlander* movie, and Joe might play a part in that, if all things work out. But that can change. I know we're going to shoot the final episodes of this particular version and this particular mind-set of *Highlander*. And then we'll take it wherever else we'd like to go.

Elizabeth Gracen as Amanda

How did you find your way to Highlander the first time?

I was recommended by someone, and *Highlander* called me up and asked me if I wanted to go to Paris for ten days and get paid. Let me think about it for a nanosecond. Yes. So it sort of came into my lap.

And when they asked you to come back?

I said yes. I had so much fun doing it. It was great fun. And I guess the fan response was pretty strong, so they had me back.

The fans like Amanda, the writers like Amanda. . . .

She's fun to write for, I think. She gets all the funny lines and gets to be the wisecracker, and it's fun to do that. David Abramowitz, Dave Tynan, the writers all wrote some good words for her.

How would you describe Amanda?

I think that at the base of Amanda she is a real survivor. She was a street urchin at the beginning of her existence, and that's her undercurrent. I think she makes a lot of bad choices and is pretty wily, all coming from a basic place of fear. Fear of lack. Fear that it will all fall in around her. I think being a thief and her getting up to all the things that she does, it comes from that place. But she has a great sense of humor, and it has served her well to have lived that long and come up against the things that she has.

Was Rebecca a big influence on her?

Definitely, I think without—when you talk about fantasy, it starts to get weird—I think Rebecca balances out Amanda and makes her think twice. Rebecca is like MacLeod as well. They are more logical, reasoning creatures than Amanda. Rebecca called out the innocence and the best in Amanda.

In "The Lady and the Tiger," your first show, Amanda and Duncan clicked.

Adrian and I had chemistry. You can't create that. It either happens or it doesn't. And for some reason we had a bit of comedic chemistry together. I don't think it was a sexual chemistry, but more of a comedic timing thing with each other. It was very weird. We looked like we had been old friends.

In the finale, do you see Amanda turning into a black widow without MacLeod's influence?

I thought it was kind of predictable, but whatever. It's a logical stereotype for a pretty woman. I guess it's as logical as anything else that I suppose could have happened to her. But she could have also turned into a hotshot ruthless lawyer. Who knows what she could have done? But it's more glamorous to put her in a black dress like that and have her poisoning her husbands.

Speaking of dresses . . . Christina McQuarrie said she always thought of Amanda as the cat woman.

My wardrobe went through many permutations. Some of it was very cat-woman-like. Amanda has been alive for twelve hundred years. You

know, sometimes the writers and producers would sort of freak out because I would come in with my hair different or wearing a nose ring or whatever, and I would say, "You know this character has been alive for fifteen hundred years, she would have tried everything." She gets bored very easily, I am sure.

Did you prefer the comedies or the dramas?

I like doing drama; that is usually what I do as an actor. So I enjoy doing the comedy because I never really get cast doing comedic stuff, ever, just because of the way I look. I don't look wacky, or I don't have that look. So that was a nice surprise that it developed into more comedic and downright slapstick at some point. So I had a great time. The episode we did with Roger Daltrey, **"The Stone of Scone,"** was so much fun. We were just completely over the top, and laughed. I love Roger Daltrey. And he and Adrian and I all get on so well. It was so much fun. And **"Dramatic License,"** with Sandra Bernhard, those were great episodes to do. Lots of fun.

Has your experience with the fans and going to the Cons been positive?

The fans are very loyal. I have never been a real fan of anything. Maybe when I was eight or nine, I was a member of the David Cassidy Fan Club. But it's odd to me. The fans are very strong-willed and romantic, and they're an interesting group of people, but I am not very comfortable at the Conventions because there are so many people. I was Miss America, and my brain just clicks back to that time and I get exhausted almost immediately. It's not a bad thing; it's just strange to me. Peter has done very well with his fan club and is very comfortable with it. I thought about a fan club, people asked me, but in the end, I just didn't do it. But the fans are comfortable with Amanda. A part of everyone wants to be Amanda.

Peter Wingfield as Methos

Here we are at the Teriyaki House of downtown Vancouver.

Thanks, Peter. Can you tell us how you ended up on Highlander?

I got the job from an audition back in 1994. I got a phone call from my agent, who asked if I was interested in a show that was filming in Paris. It was going to be four days' filming in Paris. That was it. No follow-up. Come in, get paid, that's it. And there was a possibility that they might bring the character back at the end of that season, which was season three, for the **"Finale."** They were going to bring him back to get his head chopped off. But that was not guaranteed at all; that was a suggestion.

Were you familiar with Highlander?

I knew nothing about it at all. I was aware of the original *Highlander* film with Christophe [Lambert] and Sean Connery. I suppose I vaguely

knew about immortality and chopping heads off, but the idea that in the end there can be only one, but at the moment there were lots of them, I didn't know any of that stuff.

What did you think when you saw the first script?

The first thing I saw was the scene where Methos offers his head to MacLeod. I thought it was very, very strong. I liked it a lot. For the audition I had that piece and I think I may have had the pages for—oops, here comes the beer—Methos and MacLeod walking beside the canal and Methos saying how long it is since he took anyone's head. I liked it a lot. I thought it had a depth to it, which kind of resonated and touched something in me. So I did this audition, and the casting director videotaped it and, I presume, videotaped a whole bunch of other people. The videos went off to Paris, and they then called back and asked me to do a recall about a week later, again, by video. I went in about five o'clock in the evening on the Wednesday; the tape was then going to be biked to the airport, flown to Paris; they were going to watch it and make a decision on Thursday. They offered me the job on Thursday, and I was filming on Friday. The first time I ever met anyone was Friday evening under a bridge in Paris, and the smoke machines were going. I dread to think if they'd decided after the recall, no he's not right. Because it was only me that went back in, and they wanted me to do the same scenes but with a slightly different feel to them. If they had decided it wasn't going to work, they would have been in big trouble, because there was no time to see anybody else.

As an actor, how did you view Methos when you started? In that very first script, he offers his head to MacLeod. Assuming he meant it, that says a lot about the character.

Oh, I think he absolutely meant it. It's a hell of a game to play, a hell of a risk to take, if you don't mean it. It's funny, I have spent so much time with him, now, that it's hard to remember what it was like when we first met. You know what I mean?

There have been changes . . . have you ever looked at a script and thought, I had no idea that Methos came from that place or would do that?

Yes, certainly—"**Horseman**" and "**Revelation**," the two-parter. That was extraordinary. The first I knew of that was the Props guy, the crew in Vancouver saying, "Have you read the next episode? Man, you are the baddest of all bad guys."

Do you know that you inspired the writers to write that?

Really? My God.

They said that in the previous season you were adding mystery and dark subtext, and they took the ball and ran with it.

I think that is the great strength of this show and many long-running shows. When it really works, the writers put an idea down on paper, which sparks something in you as an actor. And what you give back sparks something in them as writers and it spirals in this positive feedback tornado. When it really works, it is very exciting. I am very pleased with that. I like that because in season four I did consciously try to give him a bit more of an edge. I was very wary of him becoming MacLeod's sidekick. I think that

is a difficult position in any TV show where there is one character that holds the show and everyone else is a supporting role. It is very difficult for those characters to retain an independence, a life, of their own, so I tried to make sure that he wasn't just MacLeod's sidekick.

And it's really a position he could not take. Methos is the oldest living Immortal.

Absolutely. That position wouldn't do me any favors, and it wouldn't do Adrian any favors. Adrian is at his best when he has something to play with, someone to spark off. The more you push him, the more he has to offer back.

*So what did you think of "**Comes a Horseman**" and "**Revelation 6:8**"?*

I loved them. They are such a gift, to get that kind of script through the post. Normally, as an actor, you would get that kind of stuff and go and audition for it, knowing that they were going to give it to some Hollywood name who . . . I almost said a terrible thing. But you see it over and over and over, again, you see roles played by people and it is not their territory and they are playing it because their name will open the film. So I am very used to the experience of seeing a script, reading for a script, knowing that I am not going to get it because I don't have that status. That can be heartbreaking. So to get "**Horseman**" and read it and think, no, I am going to be playing this. I don't have to audition. There is no question about them giving it to someone else. I am going to play this. Absolute joy from start to finish. There is such breadth in the character, if you forgot every other thing that Methos has ever done, just those two episodes, the range of emotions and the range of challenges in terms of playing it. It is wonderful. Thank God.

You clearly relished discovering that Methos was, possibly, the ultimate evil.

Yeah, because it expands his character. This show is interesting because you keep going backwards. Every time you define something about a character, you fix it. You fix them. You narrow them. But what they seem to have achieved with Methos is that by going backwards, they actually made him bigger rather than smaller. They didn't close off avenues by saying something about where he'd come from. They made it bigger. That was a superb idea on the writers' part. The concept of him having been so completely different from what you would expect means that anything else is also possible. He's been around a very long time; if you went back a couple of thousand years and he was still basically the same as he is now, then there you go. But for him to be that different, it means that you could go back to any period in the past and he could be completely someone else. And that, in the end, is why he has survived this long. The thing that he is good at is changing and adapting. He is good at disappearing, blending in, and becoming someone else. So there is nothing specific to him that you can hang on to. He is like the wind. He is like the ether.

What do you think appeals to people about Methos?

I think he has a great strength about him, which is to do with acceptance. Because he's seen it all before. He's seen everything over and over again. And he knows that there are some questions that don't have answers and that there is a part of him that is at peace with that. That however long he lives, he still will not be able to answer particular big questions. That there will be personal dilemmas that remain personal dilemmas irrespective of how wise or how old you are. Because of that, there is a tremendous strength at his center. That contrasts with the fact that he is

very human. I think he is very vulnerable. I loved **"Methuselah's Gift"** and **"Timeless."** The arc of that story was just . . . I found it heartbreaking, the desire that Methos has to find love. It is just so beautifully human. I think he's deep.

It's very tough to play a good guy. This is true right through, because you are immediately limited in what you can do without offending people. One of the great strengths of Methos is that it would still bear reading that every single thing he has ever done has been a manipulation to get Duncan into a position where he can kill him. I don't personally believe that is true, but I am aware of that reading. If a script turned up that said that, there are no clashes, it would fit. And that, I think, is an enormous strength. It is that the possibility is there. And that is Methos' strength as a character. He is full of possibilities. He is not nailed down. The good guy is trapped by what we accept as good behavior. That is all that he can do, and if he does anything else it has to be because he has had a bad Quickening, he's on a bad trip, he's sick, he's not normal. Methos is a great character. I don't know how many episodes I've done, now, all told, something like twenty or so, and every one of those has broadened him, not limited him.

I think it is a compliment to you and the writers that a certain world-weariness is avoided with Methos.

Absolutely. There is still a youthfulness about him. My feeling about the point at which we join Methos is that he's been in hiding or undercover or generally avoiding the Game for a very long time. There was a weariness to him. And I think that's why he offered MacLeod his head, because it had become just too much. But he's getting back into the Game. He's becoming more and more involved again. And he's touched an excitement in him that he's been suppressing for a long time. And I think he likes it more and more. It's like a drug that he's been trying to abstain from for a long time. He's just had a little taste, and now he's hooked again.

Do you find special demands or joys from being in Paris 1997 and then being in the Bronze Age, Thursday?

No, I don't find that a problem at all. I just finished a show where it is set all in 1997. It is absolutely contemporary. And we shot four episodes concurrently. That is a nightmare. Changing periods, no. A piece of cake. The great joy of filming *Highlander* is the freedom on the set. That absolutely comes from Adrian. It is also because of the producers, the directors, and the writers. People being open to it and not immediately calling for their lawyer when you change a line. But that is the great joy of this show. If somebody changes a line, then you respond to what they've said to you. And I didn't realize how much I'd taken that for granted until I was back in England filming this summer. Where if you asked somebody, "What time is it?" when the script says you were supposed to ask what day it is, they will either stop and say "Sorry, you asked me the wrong question" or they'll answer the question they were expecting, because they don't actually listen to what you are saying. And it's incredibly revealing when an actor you're working with answers a question that you didn't ask.

And it just made me suddenly aware of how used to that I am. If somebody changes a line, then the scene goes off in a completely different direction. And sometimes that's useful and gets used. And sometimes it's a complete dead end and we have to shoot it again. But we play. Jim and Elizabeth and Adrian, all of us, we play with each other at that moment. We talk with each other, so if someone asks a question, they answer it. We trust each other.

I have only become aware of what a great deal I have on the show by going off and working on a different show. Jim does a lot of work outside *Highlander*, and so I am sure he is more acutely conscious of that than maybe others are. You have to have something taken away from you for you to realize how much you took it for granted. It's fun filming on *Highlander*.

Everyone has talked about the creativity and freedom and trust and "If we really crash and burn, that's OK."

Yeah, let's do it again. It's only a few little bits of celluloid; chuck it in the bin. Let's put some more on. I think always, this atmosphere comes from the top. It comes from the people who actually have the power to say "Don't behave that way." Because there are plenty of people around who exercise that power.

Moving back to character . . . did you play Adam differently than you play Methos?

Yes, I did. I made a conscious decision that Methos was playing Adam. Adam was a disguise, was an identity for Methos. Therefore there had to be a sense that Methos was the person and Adam was a character. That's very delicate territory. There's nothing that I hate more than seeing somebody put on their pretend role. You just look and think, "OK, well, you are clearly now acting being someone else, why can't the people around you see that person isn't real?" So Adam has to be as convincing, but his psychology has to be that of what Methos is looking to do. Adam has no motivation of his own. But I tried to make Adam softer and more unobtrusive and psychically smaller. I tried to make my body shape slightly different, less confident, as Adam. That was what I was looking for, that Methos would try to become slightly less visible. Because that's what Adam is about. The idea that people would say, "Oh yeah, there's that kid who works in the library, but I can't remember what his name is, Alan or something." That he would not draw attention to himself in any way at all.

Was that a strain on Methos?

No, I don't think so. Methos likes dressing up, dressing up in someone else's body and their mannerisms, the feel of them. I think he likes

that. That's what's kept him going all these years, because he's not a big one for picking up a sword and fighting. When he does fight, he tends to fight dirty. It's quick. It's a trick to make someone vulnerable and finish him. He's not one for big, long drawn-out battles.

Did you enjoy "Chivalry"?

I loved it. I loved it. I always describe that episode as the one where I whack that bitch. At the end of it, the following day, there's the scene with me in MacLeod's kitchen and I'm just going to get some beers and put them in the fridge. And I have a line, which I really like, I can't remember exactly what it is, but it's very close to Hamlet's line in act 5: "They are not near my conscience." When he's killed Rosencrantz and Guildenstern or sent them to their deaths in England. It's something like "She had it coming," but it's classier.

Would Methos have a notion of chivalry?

Absolutely. We have to be nice to girls. If they're nice girls, fine. Every man, woman, and child for themselves when I grew up.

But that has shaped him. Methos is five thousand years old. He could pick and choose his philosophy.

I think there is a strong element of truth in what you are getting at there. Philosophies, a lot of them, are fashion. They come and go. There are deep fundamental truths that he believes in, but there's a lot of superficial stuff. Sorry, man, I remember the guy that made this up and it became trendy for a while and then disappeared. And there are a whole bunch of other philosophies that you don't even know about that have come and gone. This is just another one of those. There are good people and there are bad people.

I liked your analogy of him being childlike.

For anyone to survive that long, they'd have to have a special quality of some kind, or a special balance of qualities. They'd have to have some strategy that is going to allow them to survive that long. But they would also have to have the desire to stay alive. That first meeting with MacLeod, where he says, "Listen, man, finish it; I just can't take it anymore." I think that was a real cry from deep inside him. At the end of **"Revelation,"** MacLeod saying, "Why didn't you go up against Kronos?" I said, "Because I wanted to survive and I still do." I think that is deep, very, very deep in him. He likes being alive. And he keeps finding new things.

If there can be only one, what would Methos do if it came down to Methos and Duncan?

He would kill him. What are you, nuts? When it comes down to it, Methos wants his own show. We all know that. I am aware of it. I'm not sure I want to do the show, but Methos does. I am aware of how strong his desire for his own show is.

How did you feel about Methos getting his first on-screen Quickening?

I thought that the homoerotic overtones of that scene were undeniable. I laughed hysterically for several hours. When they were staging it, setting up all this stuff, and we were talking it through and they were talking to the effects staff, saying

things like, "Into Duncan's eye and out and in through Methos' mouth" or something, I thought, "Man, what are you, crazy? What are we doing?"

I wondered if you noticed. . . .

Did I notice? Why do you think I'm on all fours at the end? Yes. I was fully aware of it. I was a consenting adult. You'd have to ask Adrian if it was good for him. I had muscular spasms in my arms for days after that, holding that heavy weapon for such a long period.

Do you have any favorite episodes?

I have several. I am very proud of **"Horseman"** and **"Revelation."** I am also very proud of **"Methuselah's Gift"** and **"Timeless."** I didn't do a huge amount in **"Timeless,"** but I think the B story of that episode with me and Ocean Hellman is very strong. She was wonderful. She was so good. Man, I can't bear how positive I am being about the show. The director of that episode, Duane Clark, was just fantastic. He trusted Ocean and me. We never rehearsed scenes. But what we would do is we would run it once for shape, so they could get the cameras positioned and get it lit and everything, then he would whisper something to Ocean and he would whisper something to me and we'd film it. And then he'd whisper something to her, again, and whisper something to me, and we'd film another version. What it meant was that every time we filmed it, I knew something about what she did was going to be different, but I had no idea what it was. And it just made the two of us very focused on each other, that we were looking for what was different and responding to that. That episode was, again, thrilling to be part of and, as an actor, deeply fulfilling. The story was strong, but the experience of putting that on-screen was great.

I feel very privileged to have done this work. In my entire career, there are only a handful of things that I can point at and say, "I think that was good work and I am proud of it. I think that stands up." And probably half or three-quarters of those are from *Highlander*. It has offered me challenges that I have not encountered in other work, and that's why I am in the business. It's what I am here for.

Tell me about the Joe-and-Methos relationship.

Methos and Joe . . . I think there is a common humanity to the two of them. I think that's why they work, why they seem like they are together.

They see the world—I'm making all these assumptions about what Joe is like—I think they seem like they're from the same island. They have a similar kind of acceptance of: there is so much that you can do and after that people have to fight their own battles. You can't make anyone do anything. And they share that heart, but also the same sense of humor and attitude to life, generally. I dunno, they feel good together. And I think Jim is a great man. The character completely aside, there is such bravery. He has such humanity himself. He is a great man.

Jim said you were all friends.

I love them all. It's true. A couple of days ago, I went out to dinner with Bill Panzer; not business, purely social. Don Paonessa . . . I went to a gig with him and his wife, Renee; purely social. Jim, I have many times

been out with socially. Adrian and Elizabeth and Stan, over the New Year, we went out in Italy and did a road trip together. We get on really well. They are my friends. And I have no comparable experience with a show before. And I would expect none in the future. It is a very rare thing. It is, I have no doubt, the reason for the success of the show. The people in it get on, they work together well, because they like each other, they respect each other.

You are saying good-bye to Highlander.

I am very tempted to say these were the best days of my life. I am no longer clear whether Methos became like me or I became like Methos. But I feel that my life has utterly, unutterably changed because of my association with Methos, particularly, and with the show in general. And I like it.

Roger Daltrey as Hugh Fitzcairn

It's my very first day on the set. Daltrey simply walks up to me and asks, "Français or Anglais?" "Well, I speak English, but . . ." He hears the accent. "You're American. You don't speak any version of the Queen's English." And then he laughs. That's enough. It's clear why everyone adores him. A day or two later, we sit down, near the moat, to talk. —M.R.

How did you end up on Highlander?

Just came through as a job, and I'm a jobbing actor and I thought, well . . . I didn't know anything about the show. I hadn't even seen the

films. I didn't know anything about it. And when I got on the show I thought, well, this is absolutely ridiculous. This is the most stupid scenario I've ever been in, in my life. People get killed, but they're not killed and they're coming back to life. I thought, well, this is so silly it deserves to be funny. So Fitz can play the only Immortal who doesn't want to fight anybody. He'd much rather fuck than fight. He knows what life is all about.

And the first episode I did, of course, there was a terrible tragedy in the cast. Werner Stocker died. And the whole episode revolved around Darius. So then MacLeod and I had to literally patch the thing together. That's when I developed a rapport with Adrian, whom I like immensely. He really is my main reason for doing the show. I have such great fun with him. If I ever had brothers, he would be welcome to be one of them. We just had great fun; that's what it's been ever since, it's great fun. And killing me off was the pièce de résistance because I couldn't stand being Fitz in modern day. It just felt so ridiculous.

Too much tweed in the present?

Not enough shagging goes on in the nineties. I'm talking very honestly and candidly about my character. It's one thing having it coated in armor, but rubber isn't quite the same. I'm right, aren't I?

Moving right along . . . So you like the fact that Fitz has been on more dead than alive?

Yes, he's the most alive dead person that I've ever played. This is an extremely silly interview.

Which everyone will love. You know that the writers like writing for you and Fitz.

Well, I must say, I really do have fun playing him. He can get out of any scrape. So to go on a set with that as the character, you've basically got a license to do anything. And believe me, he does. He always has. He's always scraped through somehow by his wits and his wit. Fitz is, I suppose, the leprechaun of the Immortal world. That's exactly what he is, the leprechaun of *Highlander*. And he gives MacLeod all kinds of headaches, which he loves to do, of course. He doesn't even have to decide which ones are deliberate and which ones aren't.

I wish the readers could see that smile of yours.
So, you like the past?

I've always thought with a face like this, I belong in the past. There's no doubt about it. I just got very lucky in the seventies for a few years there. With an old boat like this, it just belongs in the past. I've done an awful lot of period pieces: *The Beggar's Opera* and *The Threepenny Opera* and Shakespeare. This face suits an older period; it's not a nineties or even an eighties face at all.

What has Fitz been in the past?

Anything at any time that he thought he could get away with. Really. And anything that he would have thought he could have had some fun doing. If it wasn't fun, he wouldn't want to do it. It's as simple as that. Fitz is really simple. He wants to have fun, especially with girls. Why be complex when you can have so much fun being very simple? Who wants all these moody types? They're about as exciting as an oyster race.

Have you ever shot in Canada?

No, they can't afford to send me there, and if Adrian gets any more wage rises, we'll be living in wardrobes. None of this is going to appear in this book, is it? [To Bill Panzer] I dare you to put that in, Bill. It's nothing I haven't told Adrian. I've said, "Adrian, for fuck's sake . . ."

I love film, I really do love film. And that's another thing I really like about this show, the production value on this show is tremendous. I've only worked in France. And it's not just a talking-head show, which so much TV is now because of budgets and because of time. TV should be much more. It's a moving picture. It's not just talking heads. But you watch more and more shows because of those limitations, becoming where the directors only have time to get the faces on the screen, and it's boring. This show manages to capture great sets, lots of actions. It's good. I am amazed at what they do for the budget they do it for. I'd be even more amazed if we actually got paid. I wouldn't do this for the money. I couldn't do it for the money. I do not need the money. I love doing this part. Well, I thought when they killed him, I thought that was going to be the end of it, I really did. I was surprised when Fitz came back.

I did have a talk with Bill Panzer at the beginning about the problem you have with a series like this. It's dark, and how many shades of black can there be? And to then reexpress and go through another dark period, you've got to put something in to break it up, and there's nothing like humor. If you make people laugh and then it goes dark, that's the darkest of all. When did I die? Was it the Cordon Bleu thing? **"Star-Crossed."** Bloody ridiculous script; I even put on weight during that week. I've never eaten so well on this show in all my life. Best food I've ever had in my life. We were in the kitchens, and it was all around you. Everything you looked at was something that some young master chef had worked all day on it. A bit of this, a bit of that. I made myself ill, but Fitz died happy. He died extremely happy, under the Bastille.

We know Fitz doesn't enjoy it, but can you use a sword?

I can use a sword all right, but I'm an old chap, now. Fitz would rather use a scam. There's far more ways to get what you want without a sword. I enjoyed **"The Stone of Scone"** last year. My golf spoils my good walk. It was good fun, and Elizabeth is wonderful. I enjoy working with her.

And the two before that were fun, too. I've enjoyed all of them. I was worried when I saw this script, "**Unusual Suspects**." This is a very dangerous script. It could be so wrong, but I've got a feeling. . . . I'm very impressed with Dennis Berry's work on it. He's kept it exactly at the right pitch, and I think it will turn out to be the funniest one of all. But it is a very dangerous line that we're treading here. But you've only got one life, and you live it. Or several. Fitz has screwed himself up his own butt so many times, he doesn't know who he is.

And now we've seen Fitz Senior. . . .

Fitz Senior is something else, a different kettle of fish, altogether. He's a complete buffoon.

Fitz Senior has a different motivation than Fitz?

No, I think they've both got the same motivation. Let's put it in right order: money and pretty women. At the moment, I think Fitz has been fizzled. I think I will go and feed the fish. My pleasure. [To Panzer] Good luck to you, Bill. Thanks for the job.

And Daltrey goes off to feed the fish, tossing bits of baguette to the carp in the moat. —M.R.

Peter Hudson as James Horton

How did you first arrive on Highlander?

The first time I met *Highlander* I was in just a couple of episodes as the bad man interest. And I think it went quite well, and so they wrote me back in for a couple more episodes. And I think when they got short of ideas they thought of me again, over the years. That is slightly frivolous, but I think, partly, it was geography because I spend a lot of time in France, anyway. My wife is French, my family is French, and so I am going back and forth from Paris to London a lot. And I was well placed when they were shooting over here, so although I did four or five episodes in Vancouver I did quite a lot here, too.

How would you describe Horton?

The trouble with Horton was that as a character, it wasn't easy to see how he evolved. Each time he reappeared, I found out more about him. And they weren't necessarily elements that I would have expected. I suddenly found out that he had a daughter and was established in the States and so on. It was fantastic in one sense because it was always a piece of work that kept on coming back over a number of years. But it was frustrating in that we didn't really get to

know what was going to happen to him next, or what had happened to him much in the past. But I think the basis of him was that he had a genuine hatred for the Immortals. I think he was an intelligent man, but he was also a kind of military type. I always tried to play him as someone who had definitely had military training. And he felt that he had a mission, which was to remove the Immortals. And then, of course, that evolved until the final episodes, when he became one of the manifestations of evil.

How did you feel about playing Horton more dead than alive?

I enjoyed it because playing bad guys is interesting, but it can become monotonous if things don't change. But Horton did change, even though it was sometimes more of a brutal change than a real evolution. Suddenly he became someone who could take different physical forms, and he would suddenly appear from nowhere. That is always interesting to do, so I enjoyed that. But he didn't smile much. That was the downside.

What about Horton and his brother-in-law, Joe?

He used Joe whenever it suited him, and there was never any sign of his having any real affection for Joe at all, not any more than he had any real affection for his own daughter, whose fiancé he threw off the terrace without any kind of thought at all. It was a big drop. But he was very sympathetic with her afterwards when she thought that he had committed suicide.

Are there any episodes that you especially liked?

I was lucky in that Horton had interesting dialogue. I enjoyed all of them really, except when I fell over and got injured.

Can you tell me about that?

We were shooting in the cemetery; I tripped over a tombstone, fell on the corner of the marble tomb, and I had the beginning of a collapsed lung. So I had a few days in hospital. What I should have done is stop shooting immediately, but none of us realized. You think you're a hero when you're playing somebody like Horton; you forget that you're not really invincible.

Horton is the man you can't kill.

That's right. That was a nice line, you see. He got good dialogue. But it was fun. I very much enjoyed working with Ken Gord. He was very supportive and one of these guys who is really interested in acting, which is unusual for a producer. And also he liked to be involved even in the detailed choice of costumes and such. He was always there, and that was really nice.

How did you feel about coming back for the series finale?

Well, it was a nice idea. I was very happy to be able to come back and do something right at the end. It was a great *It's a Wonderful Life* scenario, which I liked the idea of doing, and it was such a great film, anyway. And I very much enjoyed working with Adrian throughout and so I was happy to come in, even very briefly at the end. It was a sort of gesture to get the characters who were regular, or almost regular, to come back, which was nice. I was touched by that as I wasn't a regular. At various times during the series, I thought that Horton had probably disappeared, but he did come back, so it was nice that he was there at the end.

Valentine Pelka as Kronos

How did you arrive at Highlander *the first time?*

It was very strange, actually, because I had been at *Highlander* a few times. And I have to say that each previous time the part wasn't Kronos. The impact wasn't so immediately great. The minute I read Kronos, I thought, "A character with no scruples; interesting." So I went for an interview and heard nothing for ten days and just presumed, as one does, that it hadn't worked out. But then they called and I was given some very last-minute instructions. Yes, you've got it—this was Thursday—and you're traveling on Monday. And I went to Vancouver, and everything just clicked. The part felt right. I immediately got on with Adrian really well. I immediately got on with Peter Wingfield very well; we're now sort of best mates. And the whole setup there was just great. So it was, basically, quite the normal start, but it didn't quite finish that way.

So you knew going in that you were playing the baddest of bad guys?

Well, yes, it was written that way. As I was traveling over on the plane, I was reading over the part again. And I was thinking it's unusual to play somebody who has got no second thoughts about what he is doing. Of course, he has a very good excuse for what he's doing; he's one of the Four

Horsemen of the Apocalypse. He's supposed to do this. There were no scruples to have. His function is that. Therefore, you can just go out and enjoy it. And I thought to myself, "That's probably the best tack to take with the part. Just enjoy it."

One of the writers said that you were one of the home runs of casting.

That's very sweet, but I have to say I got a hell of a lot of support from people like David Abramowitz. The whole writing team was great.

And what was good was their feedback. It's all right you thinking, "Oh, this is a good idea," but they have the overview, the big picture. And in the second episode, **"Revelation,"** Kronos was killed, and then David Abramowitz asked, "Would you care to come back?" And I said, "Yes, sure, but how?" He said, "You have five thousand years of flashbacks; we have no problem with that."

How was it going back, after Kronos had been killed, to do "Avatar" and "Armageddon"?

It felt slightly weird because in the first two episodes Kronos is very much in control of his own destiny; he knows exactly what he is doing. But this time he was potentially, one doesn't know, the figment of somebody else's imagination, in which case, it's their imagination which is the puppet master pulling the strings. So that felt quite strange, but it felt great to get the sword back in my hands. Although I have to say, between playing Kronos modern and playing him Bronze Age, I think I prefer modern because there was less time in the makeup chair. What was ironic about doing *Highlander* is that the last two years I've been in a lot of costume work, and a few of my so-called friends have been jokingly calling me Mr. Costume. So when *Highlander* came up, I thought, "Well, yes, there is costume stuff in that but the majority of it is right up-to-date, modern." And they did suggest that I might need to have my head shaved, or crew cut at least; my hair was quite long at the time. And then I thought, "Yeah, I could do with a change," and it worked terrific. It was great fun. But the great thing about the Bronze Age was the horse I got to ride. The horse was fantastic.

Braun mentioned that he liked the choreography of the ride down the hill in the sand.

Well, it did go very well. It was just very, very good. It had a real sense of a feature film, especially the stuff Adrian shot in Bordeaux; he directed very well. And I love riding and fighting anyway, and Adrian is the best fighter that I have ever fought. I really like to go for it, but to be able to go for it you have to trust the other person. I have been in a production before where I wasn't able to trust the guy I was fighting, because he wasn't pulling anything. When Adrian and I first had a crack at it, I missed a parry, and he really goes for it, too, and he stopped the sword two inches from the side of my head. Whoa. And we looked at each other, and I grinned at him and I said, "Thank you very much, Adrian, for not taking my head off. But I completely trust you because I've got eye contact and I know if I make a mistake you're one step ahead." And a couple of times we forgot the choreography. I always pull my blows anyway, but once you know you can trust each other, then you have the safety net, if you like, to be able to really go for it. So we tried to get it as real and as fast as possible. And I just love fighting with Adrian. We did one take, in the second episode, when we are fighting on the bridge and we really, really went for it incredibly fast. And at the end of it, because we got away with it, we were both laughing and giggling so much because it's a real thrill to do that. And that's what makes the job so worthwhile, every time. Even if you get a sword across the knuckles, that's just part of it.

I'm sure both Adrian and Braun were happy to have an actor on set who can really ride and fight.

Funny you should say that. The first time I met Bill Panzer was at Adrian's party in Vancouver. And Gerard Hameline introduced him to me and said, "This is Valentine, and by the way, he really does ride." And Bill stopped and looked at me and said, "An actor who says he can ride; I've heard that one before." That is really what he said. And I said, "Well, you'll see tomorrow, won't you?" I've been riding for a long time, but he's quite right; actors do say they've been riding for a few years, then you find that the horse seems to have more of a mind of his own than they have.

In the series finale, when Kronos enters and says, "Greetings, brother," everyone in the room just looks at each other and cheers, "He's back!"

I understand that's a very popular line. And I felt like that, too. I'm back. It's very strange, it's one of these strange perfect mixtures of the right people, the right project; everybody just jelled together. Peter and I, we acted off each other; he helped me a lot. Peter is such an easy guy to get to know. I was there stuck in the makeup chair and the girl was trying to sort where to put the scar and he just popped his head around the corner and said, "Hi, I'm Peter, and welcome to Vancouver." That really made all the difference, because you do feel a bit like a fish out of water.

I'll give you another example: Ken Gord did everything he could to make me feel welcome the first time I went over. Quality control is really important to him, and he asked, "Do you know the show very well?" And at the time, I didn't. He said, "Look, I'll make sure there's video in your apartment when you get back; take these tapes and look at them." And then you could say that the Kronos look is right down to Ken Gord. He picked it. I said, "I quite like this." Then he said, "Well, yes, but . . ." He had a good idea of what he was looking for. And then, at the end of it, they very sweetly gave me my jacket. That was a nice souvenir. Kronos is now stalking around London.

Do people recognize you?

I went to my hometown of Leeds and some people came over in a restaurant and said, "Even without the mask we recognize you." And I didn't know whether to take that as a compliment or not. A part like Kronos does make an impact. The response has been absolutely fantastic. In fact, it's almost twelve months to the day that I did the first one. And the twelve months since have been probably the richest twelve months I've spent as an actor. The variety of the stuff has been extraordinary, going back to *Highlander*. It's like one thing mounting up on top of the other. It's a pity the series is over, but it's nice I was involved.

Has your experience with the fans been positive?

The fans have set up a fan club, which is a first for me and very sweet. And I've just received a quilt, which is absolutely fantastic. We, as actors, get a hell of a lot out of it. If you work as an actor and get to do all these nice jobs and go to all these nice places, you are there because people want you. There's no point in me kidding myself. I got asked back, very nicely, by *Highlander* because people watched and obviously said, "We quite like the character; can he come back?" That's very important, but I think there comes a time when you have to pay back. You can't just keep taking and taking all the time. You have an expression in America: What goes around, comes around. I am a big believer in that. My great-aunt's expression for that was "Do as you would be done by." I think that's very true.

Anthony De Longis as Lyman Kurlow and Otavio Consone

Anthony De Longis and I meet in Santa Monica, California. Over a lunch of papaya and lobster salad and a glass or two of a fine Sonoma Cabernet, we discuss *Highlander*. —M.R.

I played Kurlow in "**Blackmail**" and Consone in "**Duende**." I like *Highlander* because it demands all of your very best. It takes all the experience that you have; it takes all your creative imagination to work under these extremely difficult situations. No matter what the weather, no matter what the location, you get it done.

Adrian and Braun both talked about your skills as a swordsman.

I admire the mental and physical chess game that swordplay is. I admire the style, the élan, the dexterity, the accomplishment, and the romance. It's the stuff that heroes are made of. The sword is the weapon of choice for the hero. I also cling to a certain romantic notion that people who use swords have to have a little more honor. There is a noblesse oblige.

Tell us about your first episode of Highlander.

My first episode of *Highlander* was "**Blackmail**." It was funny on that one. Normally, they try to schedule the fight at the end of the shoot, but due to the availability of the location it got pushed to the second or third day, so we had no real rehearsal. As a matter of fact, much of the last fight, we essentially evolved on the spot under Braun's eye—of course, with the proviso that it had been predetermined that the TV had to die and the bookcase had to be butchered, as Braun smilingly told me.

*In "**Blackmail**," you used a cape in the first fight. Was that planned?*

You get to the set, and the first thing that they do is troop you off to Wardrobe because they have until the next day, when you're going to appear on camera, to put something together. So they took me for a fitting, and they had given me this sort of Mad Hatter hat and this Restoration-style clothing, but it didn't quite fit, and I had a big heavy coat. And I said, "Is there any chance of me getting a cape?" There was. So that whole opening phrase of the fight would not have existed if I hadn't gotten the cape. We made it part of the story. I think that's how it's supposed to be.

*How did it happen that you returned for "**Duende**"?*

I had been doing research for another project and read Braun's translation of several of the Italian rapier masters. In the treatise he had said that the mysterious circle is overly articulated, deliberately obtuse and abstract. They don't call it a mysterious circle for nothing. I'm paraphrasing, of course. He said, if anybody can figure this out, let me know how it works. So I added my own research and years of experience and came up with a style, which I presented to David Abramowitz. To make a long story short, David and Bill Panzer liked the idea, and I went to Paris. It was really nice working on "**Duende**" with Richard Martin. He was wonderful. I had also worked with his father, Dick Martin.

A number of actors have mentioned Richard.

He kept giving me these entrances. My favorite scene is the one with Anna Hidalgo at the club. We shot it at the end of the second day. I walked in for camera blocking and there, in the club, is this chair sitting in the middle of the floor. Richard indicates that I am going to be in the chair, in the dark, and then the lights are going to come up. Right away that says a great deal about your character, that you would have come in and set it up and given yourself a spotlight. The arrogance is pure Consone.

*Tell me about the fight in "**Duende**." It is a real favorite.*

For the fight in "**Duende**," the rain made it so dark, we had only two hours to shoot. Then we lost the light and had to stop to wait for it to get dark enough for the lights. I think the fight looks best under the lights because that's the first time you see the downpour. It had been raining that hard all day, but it isn't until the lights are behind it that you see it. God was our art director. He did a fine job, too.

It was a tough day. We were standing under a constant deluge. Adrian started singing "Singin' in the Rain," and we were an instant kick line. That was very funny, but our platform was as slippery as an ice rink. You should have seen the dailies. Thud. I'd just disappear from frame, and Adrian is saying to the camera, "See, we told you. See." When I fell, the first thing I wanted to do was dump the swords because I was thinking about Adrian. I thought, "I have got to clear these." And all of this is taking place in that split second when I know my feet aren't there anymore. I am now horizontal. What do we do? And also, you think, "Do we curse here?" No, no, just get up and try not to be too wet. Too late.

And Braun is wonderful. He always does his homework, which is the mark of a true professional. He's used to having to work with people who don't have a lot of experience with the sword. This is tough on him and on Adrian, especially with the fact that there is no time. He had sketched out some of his ideas and he would start a premise and he knew that I would answer with a response, which would provoke a response from him, and together we would evolve the fight. Into that mix comes Adrian with his energy and knowledge. And we all knew that not only was Adrian doing the sword fight, but also he was flamenco dancing, so rehearsal would be minimal. In fact, the night before our final confrontation, Adrian had never even seen the completed fight. So he halted filming for thirty minutes while we rehearsed. Good thing. Because of the rain, that was the only rehearsal we got.

We wanted to do something special, to tell a story. I know that's what Braun tries to do, and I know it's what I try to do. If it's not story-motivated and character-driven, then you may as well stay home and fight in front of the mirror.

CHAPTER SIX

Postproduction

"Ken, can you put more steam on the shower door?"

*T*he writers, the directors, actors, set designers, and so on have all done their job. The show has been written, filmed, and is now "in the can." What comes next? Postproduction. —M.R.

Don Paonessa, Creative Consultant for Postproduction

I meet with Don Paonessa in the Henry Room (Henry V8 is the "king" of effects editing systems) at Gastown Post in Vancouver. Guest Services provides bagels and coffee. —M.R.

My title on the show is Creative Consultant for Postproduction. What I do is oversee and supervise all the creative elements in shaping the show once it has been shot.

Can you walk me through the process?

If you want to take it step by step, we can begin from the production side. We use a number of visual effects in this show, and one of the signatures is the transition. Once I read the script and see how many transitions we have, I go through and earmark each one. Then I work with the director to design a way in which we can make the move from present to past and past to present. So, when the director talks to me about how he's going to shoot a scene, how he's going to block a scene, and what the location is like, I take that information and I try to design something to make this window into another world.

That's number one. If there are other elements in the script that call for a visual/optical effect, we go through that same process. We discuss what the shot is, what's going to happen, how we can design it. Then it's shot, we get the dailies, and, if we're lucky, we get what we asked for. Then we go to the next step, which is cutting the show. The editor will do a cut, and, as far as I'm concerned at that point, I let the editor do what the editor does: cut the show to script and get it in as good a shape as he or she can within the time frame. The director sees that cut and has a day or two to give notes. The editor does another pass on the show, implementing the director's notes. At that point, I come in and work with the editor to make the final cut and get the show working as well as we can.

Because the script is the script and it reads one way and doesn't necessarily produce the same way, sometimes when we get an episode together it doesn't work, so we will restructure the show. We will move scenes around. Sometimes we will split things up. On occasion we'll make a single flashback into two flashbacks. But we continue to push through the show to get it into shape. At the same time, Bill Panzer gets involved, and since he has creative control of the show, we work together to make the domestic version—which is the forty-two-minute version—our primary goal. When I say primary goal, we know that the show is going to have a foreign version that is forty-six minutes long. We work through that one, because when I'm working with the editor we get to a point where we've

got the show in pretty good shape at forty-six minutes. Then we keep pushing through to start eliminating elements that will bring the show down.

For the first five years of the show, Roger Bellon was the composer. For each episode he would get a cut of the show. Then we'd have a telephone conversation, because he's in Los Angeles and I'm in Vancouver, and we would discuss the tone of the show and we would spot it for music. We would go through the show from start to finish and discuss where a cue should come in, where it should go out, and what kind of music it should be. For season six, we brought in a music editor, Hal Beckett, who is also a composer. We all worked to create the music that best suits a particular episode.

Next, we lock the show, which means lock the picture. Then I sit with the colorist and work on color-timing the show. Overall, we're trying to get the best-looking picture that we can with the *Highlander* style to it.

So the show is color-timed; now what?

Back to the sound end of it. I usually sit in on the ADR [automated dialogue replacement] sessions. We do a lot of them for technical reasons. We shoot in practical locations on a low budget. You can't stop traffic. You can't wait for airplanes. So you have flashbacks where you're in 1760 and you can hear the din of Vancouver in the background. Those scenes have to have the dialogue replaced. One of the other advantages of ADR is that sometimes we can enhance a performance a bit or we can massage a scene.

That is, if we want to change the attitude or the way a line is delivered, we have the advantage.

Next, I am in here [in the Henry Room] with the compositors, Steven Pepper and Tom Archer. We do the transitions and Quickenings and other visual effects that are optical,

132 / Maureen Russell

not practical. That's when we play. A lot of the time, the compositors will come up with solutions that take a scene to another place. When you're working creatively, you have an idea, somebody else adds to the idea, and then a third thing happens and, hopefully, it's for the better.

Now we're ready to mix the sound. I sit and work with the mixers. Not to make it a bigger deal than it is, but if it were a feature film, the director would be mixing the show. In television, that's the producer's function, so that's what I do. In a weird way, I work as a postproduction director more than a producer. It's cutting and designing and doing the creative stuff. And I do the same thing for the sound mix. Then we send it off to Ken Gord; he will look at it and he will have a few notes.

We're doing a show that really should be a two-day mix because it's very complex, it's very textured, and it's very ambitious. But we have to do it in a single day, which puts a pretty heavy demand on everybody involved. It can be frustrating, because you don't have the time to nurture it or to tweak it. We get into action scenes with sword fights that we have to mix in an hour. We could be spending five hours. The end result is that you have to broad-stroke. The idea is to use a sleight of hand to create the illusion of a full sound track. Some work really well; some stink. It's just a matter of the amount of time we have.

Do you have any final words?

Everybody who works on this show does a great job. Everybody contributes to it. They work hard, but it always comes down to time and money. So we do the best we can under the circumstances. We try to find creative ways to make things look and sound good. We create an illusion. It's my job: The Illusionist.

There's a book called *Zen Mind, Beginner's Mind*. It starts with an axiom that says: In the mind of the beginner, there are many possibilities, and in the mind of the expert, there are none. My attitude is to be a beginner. Keep it fresh, be inventive, and have an adventurous approach to it. If I am proud of anything, it is the idea that we've kept it fresh. After 119 episodes, they're all interesting. And the people who follow *Highlander* are really strong fans because, I think, they lock into all of the levels on which the show operates. On the surface you look at it and it's about a guy who whacks people's heads off, but it goes much deeper than that. That's what has kept my interest in it.

Tracy Hillman, Postproduction Supervisor

Tracy and I meet at the Pub at Rainmaker Digital Pictures. Over Merlot and chicken fingers we discuss Highlander. *—M.R.*

I am Tracy Hillman, postproduction supervisor. I keep the postproduction end of the show on budget and make sure that the show gets delivered. I work hand in hand with Don Paonessa. Don and I have this symbiotic relationship. If there's a way to figure out how to do it, adjust the budget and make it work, I will. Postproduction, and the result that you see from it, is really a team effort between the two of us. Don handles the creative end, but it's a question of would you be able to do the creative without the support that's around you?

Don's handprint is all over the show. It would not look, smell, feel, touch, and resemble what it is without him. Don has great ideas, and I think one of his most exceptional qualities is that he's great with story. He will see story problems and know how to resolve them in editing. They do their best to make it better.

My job is budget. For instance, we have one-tenth the optical budget of a comparable show, but we make that parlay. It's a bit of negotiating, a bit of creative, a bit of compromise, and a bit of knowing how to get almost the same thing in a way, but cheat the camera. And, I confess, sometimes the effects are bad. But most of the time they're good.

Janet Kendrick, Postproduction Coordinator

I speak with Janet at the *Highlander* offices in Vancouver. —M.R.

I'm Janet Kendrick, and I'm the postproduction coordinator. It's my job to make sure that everything that has to be somewhere in postproduction gets there on time. It's my job to make sure that everybody in the chain, who has to know something, knows it. My job is not terribly glamorous. I answer all the phone questions. I am the one who sends all the dailies to Paris, to L.A., to the producers, to the actors, to the executive producers, to the story department. I am the one who sends the finished shows where they have to go. I send out the master tapes. I am the liaison for the staff between the production office and postproduction office. I talk a lot and I fax a lot to the coordinator in Paris. And I coordinate all the postproduction ADR with the coordinator in Paris. That's a tough job, because the tapes have to get where they need to be and we have to make sure that the actors are available and the studios are available.

When UPS was on strike, that created huge problems for us. Production is in Paris, Postproduction is in Vancouver, and Executive Production is in Los Angeles. Getting something from Vancouver to L.A. during the strike was nearly impossible. One time Bill Panzer had to get a cut because the show had to be locked. But, because of the strike, it didn't get there. I got a call from Bill, saying "I don't have my cut." I tracked it and found that it was sitting on the shelf in the FedEx office. Earlier that day, Bill had made the decision to go to the FedEx office himself. Now here is this highly successful executive producer going to FedEx, standing in line, waiting for his shipment, and then being told they didn't have it. Finally, a courier picked it up. So, the deadlines of this job are tough. It does, absolutely, positively, have to be there overnight.

Stein Myhrstad, Editor

Each season, there are two editors who normally work on *Highlander*. Stein Myhrstad is one. Some of you might know Stein as the voice singing "Macnanza" on the *Blooper II* video. I join Stein at his editing station in the Vancouver office. —M.R.

I am Stein Myhrstad, and I am an editor of *Highlander*. I cut all the footage, all the dailies, together and try to make it seem like one cohesive show. I listen to input from the director who shot it and the producers and come up with a product that everyone is happy with, within the given time of about forty-six minutes. Domestic cut is four minutes shorter. Without editing, no one would watch TV because it would be boring. People making mistakes. Someone closes a door, the set moves, and you can't show that because the door is supposed to be made of stone and stone doesn't move.

How do you begin?

I do a first pass on it, and then we all look at it and talk about what's working and what's not. Sometimes it's a question of if it's overall a good show—then we talk about how to get the best out of it—and other times we are stuck with problems. Our first cut might come out to forty-four minutes, so then we have nothing to cut out and we have to figure out a way to fix that and get back up to the allotted time. *Highlander* has the advantage of being able to go into Mr. MacLeod's memory. Playing clips from past episodes is a nice, inexpensive way to fix a short show. Writing and shooting a new scene is the expensive way.

What can an editor bring to the show?

An editor can determine the mood of a shot. I'm now working on a scene from **"Diplomatic Immunity."** An old Immortal friend of Duncan's is bugging him for money. He's saying, "If you won't lend me money, I am going to move in with my wife on your barge." So Mac fishes out his wallet and digs for money and he says, "Is that enough?" and then looks away. The guy says, "I want more, I want more, I want more," they share a little

look here, and then he grabs the money. That's the way I cut it because I think it's funnier for them to share that little look. That may be different than Adrian would want it because it's not in continuity with how that look came in on the dailies. The way I've cut it, I've had Mac say, "Enough," hand over the money, and then play that look as a buddy-buddy moment that I think strengthens their relationship. But who knows how it is going to end up? And, yes, it can be something that subtle and a lot of time it is. But it can make a big impact. And over the course of the whole show, in every scene, there is something in every scene that determines the mood or the feeling of the scene.

Do you have any special concerns while editing Highlander?

Since this is a sword fighting series, a lot of the problems are with the sword fights themselves. Sometimes we don't have actors who have handled anything larger than a kitchen knife. They write you in a script as an Immortal who has been around a long time and survived a lot of battles, but if you're holding the sword like you would hold a butter knife, it's hard for me to sell that. But I have to sell it. So sometimes that involves maybe adding a ten percent speed change to a shot to make someone seem more agile than they really are.

So your edits really wouldn't show to many of us?

That is the key with editing, to try to make it as seamless as possible, so that you are not aware of the cuts themselves. We can't fix everything in Post. You know there's a joke that all shows are fixed in Post. If we can't do it, here, we can maybe stick in some sound effects or something. But that is not true. Directors have to get the footage.

As the editor, what do you contribute to each show?

I think I contribute the same as the director and the producer, I think we are all working together as a team. And if you're not, you should be fired. I just finished cutting the scene in **"Armageddon"** where Jim Byrnes is playing Joe and the devil, Horton, is offering him his legs back. For Jim it's an emotional scene. So you're trying to pick the best pieces where he is giving it all of his emotion and you're trying to get that whole scene. You're trying to put yourself in his place. It's very creative. That's what I love about this job.

Are there any shows that have been special for you?

I think every show is a challenge. Like in the last show I just finished, which was **"Armageddon,"** they shot a couple of shots where Horton was going to blow up and turn into a skull. His head was going to start shaking and it was going to catch on fire. And they only had two elements for that, a close-up of Horton and the skull that catches on fire. And once you see it in the context of the show, which was the third and final show in a three-story arc . . . Well . . . it was all the director could do given the time he had. When we got it into the editing room we looked at it and said, "Well, this is anticlimactic for a guy MacLeod has been battling for three shows. Shouldn't something else happen?" This thought came at about noon on the day it was supposed to go online. Well, what are we going to do? Don had an idea of doing a series of flash cuts. Good idea. It takes time. I only had a couple of hours to pull all those one-frame, two-frame segments from the other shows. So it ends up being what it ends up being. The directors don't always get the shots they want, and we don't always get the shots we want, and we have to try to work around it. And we do. I think the Horton example turned out good. I would have liked to adjust the pacing a little bit more, but you got one shot at it, you cut it in, you spend fifteen minutes changing it, and somebody pulls you off the machine. Away it goes. Jettison that torpedo.

Because of the fantasy nature of the show, are there special demands on you?

No, not really. A lot of the stuff for this series that is the fantasy stuff happens after it leaves us. They paint on the effects. To the average *Highlander* fan, it would be quite funny to sit here and watch a Quickening. Adrian Paul doing an epileptic shakedown with no lightning bolts or anything, without the big sound. The magic goes out pretty quickly.

Lisa Robison and Lorie Olson, Assistant Editors

My name is Lisa Robison, and I'm one of two assistant editors on *Highlander*. What I do is I organize all of the takes that are in the show. I pull a list out of the computer and Lightworks, which is the editing machine that tells Gastown where to put what shot. I look at the show, which is compiled within the editing machine, and there is a running time code for the edit and it starts at zero-one hours, even, and it usually goes to forty-eight minutes and forty-three seconds. So we have that running time code, and each shot refers to that time code and in that place. And we also output the show, which means we play it out onto a three-quarters tape. That is what I do. I sit in.

It sounds like a very small thing, but it builds up over the show. If there are lots of flashbacks, you have to go back to source dailies, previous episodes. Does it really fit? How does it look? It could be seventy hours for one episode for each of us assistant editors. Lots of paperwork and organizing where stuff goes. And I will catch myself watching the show. "I should be fast-forwarding; sorry, Don." And he will remind me, "Just spin down to the end, Lisa. Take it home if you want to watch it."

I am Lorie Olson, and I'm an assistant editor. It's pretty basic. I pick up the tapes and then I write down briefly what it is, if it's a wide shot and who the character is. Then I put that information on a disk and that goes into the computer and it digitizes from tape onto the hard drive. That's most of my job, getting it from tape to the hard drive. And I also make dubs—a three-quarters tape to VHS tape, so that the people who need to look at dailies and the first cut and the second cut can have copies. And then I organize all the paperwork into a binder for the editor. Lots of notes from the continuity person, script pages that change all the time with revisions, film processing logs, camera reports, sound reports, shooting logs, crew sheet calls, and film-to-tape transfer notes. That's it.

Technically Speaking

The next stop on the postproduction schedule is Rainmaker Digital Pictures in Vancouver. Rainmaker specializes in digital film opticals and visual effects. At Rainmaker, there are three primary contacts for *Highlander*: project coordinator, operations manager, and operations supervisor. These people coordinate telecine, editing, dubbing, shipping, and more.

Katie McFadden, operations manager, Gastown Post; Darryl Smith, operations supervisor, Gastown Post; and Joe Fisher, Rainmaker communications director, will guide us through the process. —M.R.

DARRYL BEGINS: The film is dropped off at the drop box at the lab downstairs. A scanner assistant picks up the processed film, and it's brought up here. The scanner assistant goes through all the paperwork and looks for the circled takes or good takes. They transpose all that information into what we call tape notes. Then the colorist takes the film and puts it on the telecine, the device that actually transfers film over to videotape and do what is called a best light transfer. They're making the film look very good, as well at matching it from take to take. We transfer that to digital Betacam, creating a dailies master. We're also synching the sound to picture because sound is recorded in the field on a quarter-inch Nagra.

KATIE CONTINUES: That digital Betacam dailies master then goes into the tape room and gets dubbed. Then the *Highlander* editors and assistant editors go to work doing what they do.

DARRYL: Next we gather up all the digital Betacam dailies, any other source tapes that are required for the online, and an edit decision list, or EDL, on a floppy disk. The online editor at Gastown takes all of this and loads it into our edit computers. We call this an autoassembly. It is a computer-driven assembly of the show. You're taking the digital Betacam dailies and laying that down on a new tape, generally taking about eight hours to online a forty-eight-minute show. What people might like to know is that this is not done in order. You're actually putting the show together in a checkerboard fashion. You use all the material from reel one, then you move on to reel two, and so on and so forth. So if you are watching the show in the room, you're only seeing little bits and pieces of a puzzle being put together.

KATIE: The next step would be a Digital Image Retouching, which we refer to as a DIRT— D-I-R-T—fix. And what they're doing there is going into the edit suite with a paintbox and removing objectionable pieces of dirt that are on the film. It's basically a quality control process. The show goes through two to three hours of the DIRT fix, and then we do the effects.

DARRYL: After effects [optical effects], we would move on to titling of the show and credits.

KATIE: Then we do a dub for Post Modern Sound, so they can continue with music. Meanwhile, the *Highlander* editors are doing all the work to cut it down to the domestic version. We then lay back the domestic cutdown of the master, which is from an edit decision list from the *Highlander* editors.

JOE: We call that the final stage version, and it's the most intellectually challenging part of the show because everyone is different; everyone's got their own particular little requirement.

DARRYL: Oftentimes, especially for the foreign deliveries, it seems that they're a little more lax in their nudity standards, and sometimes you'll have something a little more risqué, so sometimes in the domestic version that material is edited out or covered over with something a little less revealing.

KATIE: Remember when Ken had to paint out the nipples?

DARRYL: In the very first episode, Tessa was in the shower, and although the glass door was steamy and you couldn't really see a lot, you could see certain parts of her anatomy. So more steam was added to the door so you couldn't see the naughty bits.

KATIE: The next thing we would wait for is audio for the domestic layback, again, from Post Modern.

DARRYL: Which is from the laid-back foreign version so there are no audio changes; we simply version from the foreign master. And the length is all made up with the credits.

KATIE: And then we do the next show.

JOE: When post work is done on a series, all the processes that we just discussed are happening at the same time. The Effects guys are working on one show; the editor is working on another. The Post crew is juggling about eight shows at once, all at different stages. They have to be extremely well organized.

DARRYL: It's like a big chain of train cars; if one thing goes out of sequence, or if we run into a problem on either production end or post end, of course, everything just backs up.

Optical Effects

To lay the scene, imagine a room. It houses one of the most advanced effects editing systems in the world, a system that allows an editor to work simultaneously on eight layers at once. Imagine a man . . . sitting in front of a computer monitor, light pen in hand. Welcome to the world of optical effects. Digital compositors Tom "Sparky" Archer, Steven Pepper, and Ken Hayward will be our guides. —M.R.

Can you walk me through the process?

STEVEN: We start with the prepro [preproduction] meeting, which usually is where all the effects and the Quickening have been written out. We go through each transition and the Quickening and each effects shot. Then it's up to me and Tom to give a rough estimate as to exactly how long that effect will take, so from that, Tracy Hillman can then get an idea of the actual budget that's needed.

KEN: Don Paonessa has the creative mandate, and Tracy Hillman has the purse strings. They seldom walk apart. After Don and his editing team have completed the edit and locked the cut, and the producer and the director have signed off on it, that's when the first meeting with us takes place.

The *Highlander* opticals really exercise us on two entirely different levels, which is why we [currently] have two compositors on the show. To do lightning for the Quickening, you have to understand perspective, animation, and kinetics. The transitions require your whole mind-set to be in color and light and texture.

Tom, since they've nicknamed you Sparky, maybe you can tell me about the Quickening.

TOM: One of the reasons that I was hired here was because I can draw lightning. It's painted frame by frame; there's no lightning button to push. When Don and I have an episode, we'll sit down and we'll talk about what this Immortal is all about, the person that Duncan has killed. What kind of character was he? Was he an evil person? Then we'll discuss where we want to see the lightning come from. We work with a lot of perspective, coming out of frame, coming right towards you, and all sorts of fancy stuff.

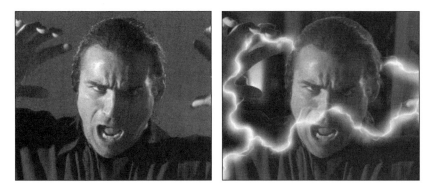

It's hand-painting, but it's nice that way. We can change the personality of the lightning in every show. We're always trying to think of something new to do—color, the shape of the bolt, the intensity of the bolt. Lightning can be very sensual. Sometimes it's kind of cruising around; other times it zaps him really hard. Again, it's how the character reacts to the Quickening.

Are there any Quickenings you really enjoyed?

TOM: The hundredth episode was a big show. The double Quickening was great. That was three full days, eight hours a day, of painting. I counted, and there were about two thousand bolts of lightning. It was huge. To compare, a small Quickening might be two hundred to three hundred bolts. And that submarine base is by far my favorite set; it was gorgeous. As soon as I saw it, I got so excited. That cool set, lots of pyrotechnics; it was great.

KEN: And just as an example, on any episode that requires a Quickening, there are at least seven hundred frames that have been hand-painted. Now just to get an idea of what that's like, take a pencil and a pad of paper, write your name in longhand, immediately write your name again, and do that seven hundred times . . .

TOM: . . . for a perfect twelve hours. And when I'm painting right on the frame, it's almost like painting right on the film, but we're painting on a video kind of digital frame. A bolt of lightning is a squiggly line with a nice glow. Lightning is a very difficult thing to do because it looks very easy to draw. When you first start drawing it, your line is very hard and it doesn't look natural. We have a touch-sensitive pen on the computer, so it's really different strokes and how hard you're pressing on the tablet. You

try for this nice little edge and different densities. Then you put a glow and you interact the glow when it hits and you try to make it look like real lightning. The *Highlander* Quickening lightning is white with a tinge of blue in it to give it that electricity.

Can you give me some examples of other optical effects?

KEN: There was the pioneer village of the 1800s, where one of the grips walked through and was wearing sunglasses and a walkie-talkie. What's wrong with this picture? Spot the flaw. We took him out.

STEVEN: In **"Little Tin God,"** we had to put in a temple. Also it was originally shot with two huts and that was it, but they needed a whole village. We did quite a bit of paint work, cutting out images and blending new images into that background. In a case like that, you are producing something that any normal viewer shouldn't be able to spot as not really existing.

KEN: Right. It may be Duncan on the crest of a hill and all of a sudden a thunderstorm comes up around him. We created the thunderstorm and put him in it. But it's not really a special effect since it could have happened. But we did it. Some of our best work, no one will ever know.

One of the more senior effects of the series was giving Joe legs in **"Armageddon."** That's an effect that required a very senior approach to it and very specific shooting. It also requires very meticulous compositing because what you are creating is something that has to be totally real, yet doesn't exist.

STEVEN: But it was pretty straightforward to do. You just have to make sure that you shoot all your elements correctly because, if they're not shot correctly, that's when the problems really occur. That's when you'll run into situations where the legs of the stand-in don't match up. The perspectives are wrong. The lighting is incorrect. When they shot it, Jim Byrnes was sitting on a bed and he would then move off. A stand-in actor would sit in the same position with his legs over the bed, the camera wouldn't move, and they wouldn't change any lighting. Basically, the scene would have to be the same as it was when Jim was in it.

KEN: They shot **"The Blitz"** right here in Vancouver on a rooftop. And then we had to re-create the entire experience of the actual Blitzkrieg. We worked three days on that one shot. But when the producers saw it, they said they believed it was the Blitz. You have to suspend your disbelief.

Then when you say, now we want to add magic and effects, it's an even deeper level of suspension of disbelief. So much of our work is spent making it look as if it actually did happen. Even though you and I both know it couldn't possibly have happened.

Audio Effects, or Scary BG

Post Modern Sound is a full digital audio postproduction facility. It occupies thirteen thousand square feet, including two dub studios, three acoustic recording stages (which combine an orchestra stage, iso-stage, Foley stage, and ADR stage), and eight offline editing suites.

The acoustic recording stage is a large modern room filled with audio equipment. The Foley studio is next door; it most closely resembles an old attic or a rummage sale. David Houle, president of Post Modern Sound; Vince Renaud, former sound supervisor and current mixer; and Tony Gronick, sound supervisor, will be our guides. Vince gives us a sound mark to begin. —M.R.

Can you walk me through the process?

DAVID: First, we take the field tapes, recorded on the set, and we load them into our computer. Then we do what is called a dialogue edit, where we go through essentially frame by frame and smooth out that track. When they're recording on the set, every time they change a camera angle, the actual timbre of the sound recorded will change. It will change with

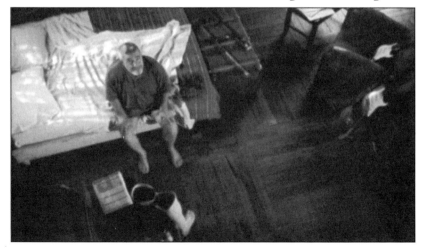

variations in the weather or with traffic or with airplanes passing over, etcetera. The job of the dialogue editor is to get the whole dialogue track as smooth as possible.

VINCE: The dialogue editors take it and spend a week with it. They try to clean it up and do some cross fades and change any words that they can't understand or change any words that have too much noise on them or mark it for whatever words that have to be recorded in the studio. That's called ADR, or automated dialogue replacement. So they mark all that have to be recorded for ADR. That's the dialogue end.

Next comes sound effects. We sit down with the producers, and they tell us what they want on the show and where. Then we generate a whole pile of notes about who's doing what. Then we spend a week cutting the effects, adding the Buzz sounds and the Quickening sounds, and coming up with all those goodies.

DAVID: Then, in conjunction with that, we will do the Foley recording and Foley edit. Foley is, of course, the inclusion of all the human sounds made in synch with the picture by the Foley artist. On *Highlander*, Foley tends to work closely with Sound Effects, so that those two groups can decide who will cover what, or, in some instances, that both will cover it. Or in other instances that certain sounds will have to be invented, but they're better invented by Foley artists.

Can you give me an example of a sound created by Foley artists?

DAVID: All the sword sounds were originally made by the Foley artists. We brought in fifty or sixty pieces of metal, pipe and steel rods. The Foley artists went on the stage and banged them all together to get a huge library of different sword sounds, not necessarily made with swords, although some were. There were some sounds that we found you just needed the sword blade in order to get the *whooshes* and the scrapes and things like that. But some of the real heavy sounds are made with big metal pipes banged against one another. They did a whole library of those, and now the sound effects editor can just cut them in.

VINCE: Then there's another person that cuts in all the background sounds, the traffic, the birds, the wind.

DAVID: For the background edit, we essentially look at each scene and do a texture edit. Whatever location they're in has an authentic kind of sound to it. Maybe the most interesting thing is that a lot of the European locations

have a different sound from North American locations. One that I recall was a long scene of a tour boat on the Seine. The whistles on the boats sound quite different than you might expect to find here in North America. A Paris market, a German castle, whatever it might be; the background sounds would be something different than, say, a cop show set in San Francisco.

Then there's the Walla recording. That is to say, all the people who are not main characters obviously make a noise. While the camera was pointed at them, and on the set, they may appear to be talking, but generally they're silent because you don't want all that extra noise. So, we'll be bringing in the group of Walla artists—W-A-L-L-A. Do you know where that comes from? They're not really supposed to say things, so that comes from mouthing "walla-walla-walla." Just like Foley is Mr. Foley from the radio days. So the Walla artists will do all the background sounds: background human sounds, people talking, screaming, and reacting.

VINCE: All that comes together finally on mix day, and we assemble forty or fifty elements down to two tracks of stereo or surround, depending on the show, and then it gets delivered off to the networks. That's it in a nutshell.

How many hours will Sound work on a show?

DAVID: Generally speaking, we are on a ten-day schedule. For ten days there might be six simultaneous shifts working on different things, like the dialogue editor, the effects editor, the Foley guys, etcetera. So the actual hours per show are two hundred to three hundred.

When do you decide what sound each show will have?

TONY: It's during the spot, which happens when we first see the picture, that Don Paonessa will give his ideas as far as what he wants in sound. A lot of the time, it will be described as "Put something weird here." We try and take his ideas and make them a reality. The Buzz for example . . . should we tell them? It's kind of undramatic.

VINCE: It's a trade secret.

TONY: I guess we can say. It's a metal grinder that's affected so it jumps from left to right and has reverb on it.

VINCE: And there's the *whoosh* sound that Mike Thomas has played around with. Mike was the previous sound effects editor. He's the sound mixer now. He's gone weird with the *whoosh*. Sometimes there are choirs underneath it.

Choirs?

TONY: Just getting a note of choir and then looping it, so it extends. Or we've taken the highs out of it and echoed it. Or one has an autopan on it, so we have it shifting from left to right. We've taken that one sound and done different things to it. It's so hard to describe sound without the actual sounds. If there were an audiotape, we could say, "Tony Gronick says, see cut seven."

VINCE: And some people are different sounds. The standard Buzz stays pretty much the same, then every once in a while they want something different for a Buzz, or different for a Quickening. Quickenings change a lot.

Quickenings have a sound?

TONY: The standard sound is lightning, but we've added electric zaps to give it a more electrical feel. Then there are explosions, which are all done on-screen, and then underneath that we add these spirit choir risings.

VINCE: And it depends on the show. For **"The Modern Prometheus"** we used a rock track underneath it. For **"The Innocent"** we used "Ode to Joy" and we went really weird, fed it through some bizarre processing in the harmonizer. I can't think of any other Quickenings like that one.

TONY: And it's not just the Buzz or the Quickening. There are other sound effects, sounds that are created. To give you an idea, in **"Avatar,"** we have a sound for Horton or the evil entity, this bubbling lava sound, camel growls slowed down . . .

CHESTER BIALOWAS, EFFECTS EDITOR, ENTERS AND FINISHES THE THOUGHT: . . . and scary BG [background].

TONY: Yeah, and some scary BG. We knew we wanted to make it scary, so we added these growls to it. The camel doesn't have the very harsh jagged sound that a lion growl might. The camel is more of a moaning growl, which won't stand out as much and can be blended in with the music in the background.

You can tell that you all enjoy your work on Highlander. Is it the creativity?

TONY: Very few shows let you get creative as far as sound. If you're doing a Western, there's not much room for that sort of stuff. But with *Highlander*, the weirder and the crazier we get, the more they seem to like it. Whether you can actually hear it on the television or not is a different story. And there can be problems when someone says, "Do something weird there" because your weird might be completely different from their weird.

CHESTER: Yeah, it's weird, but it's not the kind of weird that I like.

TONY: But the whole show isn't this way. If a car drives up and stops, a car drives up and stops.

CHESTER: It's always a fight between effects and music. To try and get these things to cut to the music is sometimes pretty tough. We do effects and music at the same time. Music is the more important element, if it's done right.

TONY: Yes, and if music is done right, they can identify that Effects can help them out. So if there's an explosion, they can actually write around an explosion.

CHESTER: Yeah; they'll leave room.

TONY: If they write the music and it goes over the top of that explosion, there's no room for us to get in our effects anymore.

CHESTER: And they'll always ask, "Can you make that explosion bigger?" And the usual answer is "Yeah, but we'll have to bring the music down."

TONY: We joke, "You should have heard that before it went to the mix; it was great." But it's amazing how you look at it. My background is mostly in effects, so I'm always looking at effects and sometimes thinking of music as the enemy. But then, when you look at it as a whole, music does make it jell together and work better.

*I have been told that I should ask you about the sound for "**Duende**."*

TONY: On "**Duende**" there were three scenes of flamenco dancing. The way something like that should be handled is that the music would be selected beforehand, then sent to the set so that they could play it and dance to it. Then when it came back, we would add the same music to it and it would be in synch and everything would work fine. But when the music for "**Duende**" got to set, they decided they didn't like it. They played new music on the set, but that music wasn't strong enough to be aired.

At that point, we had picture with people dancing extremely fast with no sound. So we thought about it for a while, cursed, swore, went for a beer, said, "Who cares; it's only television." I'm joking. But there were only two options. One, we could try and hope that the Foley people could replace every footstep. In flamenco, the dancers are hitting their heels and toes. We thought of Foley maybe holding the shoes in their hands and sort of drumming it. The other option was to bring in an actual dancer. We opted for the latter and we brought in the dancer who had actually taught Adrian.

She took one look at it and because it was picture edited, the picture had changed, it wasn't the proper timing of flamenco. So it didn't make any sense for her. "You wouldn't go from those footsteps to those footsteps," she said. But none of us could tell, and it worked rhythmically. So we had to go through shot for shot and try to get her to hit every footstep, which she did a very good job on. But then, at that point, when the new music was laid up, it wasn't in synch. So then we had to take what was done in Foley with her dancing and cut it like you would cut dialogue or effects, every single footstep, separately, and shake it around and try and make it work. We had to decide whether we wanted to go with the beat of the music and make it look a little loose in synch or vice versa.

Roger Bellon, Composer

On a rainy day in Los Angeles, while noshing on lentil soup, I learn about *Highlander*'s music from Roger Bellon. —M.R.

I am Roger Bellon. I am the composer since the beginning. The composer is the person who composes the music for the series. The music, theoret-

ically, is what can give the series or a film its color and, more importantly, its emotion.

Can you walk me through the process?

Every week we are sent a script. I read the script, just to give me an idea of what the story is about. When they have locked the picture, meaning that they have decided what the final edit is, they send me a video-cassette with time code and I watch it. Then Don Paonessa and I do a spotting session over the phone. The spotting session is where you decide to put the music. When does it start and when does it stop and what style it is and what it should be doing emotionally in the scene? That usually takes four hours for one forty-six-minute episode. In five seasons, there have been about fifty hours total of music for *Highlander*. That's probably thirty-five hundred pieces of music, which is a lot.

How long do you work on the music for a single episode?

I have about seven days to write the music, including recording and mixing. I usually take about two days to record and mix, so that's a little less than four days of actual composition. What usually happens is that I hole up in my studio in my home, compose the music, hire musicians, record it, mix it, and send it up.

Do you record with a full orchestra?

The drawback to recording *Highlander* with a large group is the time constraint. Because I am usually composing right up to the hour before I get to the recording session, it's hard to use large orchestras. If you have a larger formation, you need a lot of lead time for a copyist to copy out all the parts. So *Highlander* is done with computers and electronics and up to seven or eight musicians who come in and add on to it. It could be string players; it could be percussion; it could be guitar; it could be woodwinds; it could be voices; it could be anything. It depends on the needs of the show.

Sometimes what happens on *Highlander* is that Bill Panzer likes opera, as I do. It's a great idea to use opera when you can, because of its emotional implications and because it sounds big. But because of the time and budget constraints on *Highlander*, it is impossible for me to record with a hundred-piece symphony to create opera. So we will license music, which means you go to a special company and you may purchase, for a set amount of money, one play of an opera with a voice. And that has been done occasionally on *Highlander*, only because there's no other way to do it. But it's all original score; there's never been anything but original scores on these shows.

When the show is set in the past, do you try to be historically accurate?

Generally, if a show is set in, say, Europe in seventeen-whatever, we will be using instruments from that time. Sometimes you want to go against the grain. There was a show, **"The Modern Prometheus,"** which was set sort of during the time of Beethoven. So we decided to use Beethoven's "Moonlight Sonata." I took the "Moonlight Sonata" and performed it in the traditional way. But then to tie the rock-and-roll part of it together, it was also done in a seventies rock-and-roll, psychedelic way. So not only did you have the Beethoven part of it, which was the "Moonlight Sonata," but also on top of it you had a very modern orchestration. The music tied the past to the present, but also kept the historical accuracy.

Have you ever gotten a script and thought, now what do I do?

Yes, and it turned out to be great. **"Horseman"** and **"Revelation."** They were both really fun to do because the music had to be period in the sense that we were in the past, in the desert, Bronze Age. But what did that really mean? So I took some modern American Indian chanting, mixed it with some Asian chanting, mixed it with African drumbeats, and the whole together came up with a new sound. That was a lot of fun. When you went into the past it was very ethnically textured, but you had to make up the ethnicity, and, at the same time, it was very symphonic and operatic. Those were terrific shows. And they sounded very good; they were well mixed.

Do you have any favorite episodes?

There was a flapper show with Amanda where they go back to the twenties. They wanted a Stephane Grappelli violin thing. I called in Jerry Goodman, who's a virtuoso violin player and has been an idol of mine since my youth. He's an incredible player, and that piece turned out fabulous.

I've been able to bring in some wonderful musicians. There was a famous organist from the sixties British Beat movement, Brian Auger, of Brian Auger, Julie Driscoll & Trinity. I did a couple of shows in the fifth season where I was able to bring him in to do jazz R&B organ. That was nice.

I liked **"The Blitz"** a lot because texturally it was very interesting in terms of the score and the source pieces I wrote, plus the source pieces that were brought in. I also had to cover Vera Lynn's "We'll Meet Again," which was a big hit. I got to do my own version of that in a forties style.

I liked the first episode, **"The Gathering."** I thought that came out really cool. It was the first foray into the *Highlander* sound, and right off the bat it was nailed. It was right, exactly what it should have been.

In **"Brothers in Arms,"** I thought that Steven Geaghan did a fabulous job with the Vietnam War. And in that show I was able to do some quasi-Asian/Hendrix stuff, which was a lot of fun. There was a very rich musical palette on that one.

Highlander *doesn't have to have bagpipes?*

"Homeland" was the only show in all the shows that we hired and recorded a bagpipe player. We were going to Duncan's home; it had to be the bagpipes. The bagpipe player was Richard Cook, who played on *Braveheart*. He was outstanding. There have been other times when we have used a bagpipe sound, but it wasn't the main crux. In **"Homeland"** the bagpipe was one of the central motifs, and you had to hear it in all its splendor. I liked **"Homeland"**; it was very filmic. There's a lot of fantasy in it, and I was able to write a lot of interesting, nice music. I also did an arrangement of "Bonny Portmore," which is a Celtic tune. We got thousands of pieces of fan mail about that one.

CHAPTER SEVEN

The Last Day

"The family is breaking up. . . ."

November 28, 1997 . . . the last day of shooting for *Highlander: The Series*. Associate creative consultant Donna Lettow was one of the people on the set. —M.R.

Can you describe the last day of shooting?

Cold, wet, and rainy; welcome to Paris. We were filming in and around an old building, the Électricité de France, otherwise known as EDF, which, as far as we could tell, used to be possibly a generating station but is now just a lot of concrete with eerie metal scaffolding. It was actually colder inside the building than it was outside. I did not see most of the first scene being filmed because it was a drive-and-talk. Peter Wingfield was driving; Jim Byrnes was in the front seat; there was a camera attached to Peter's door and one on the hood. What you can't see is Dennis Berry, the director, and Bernard [Rochut], the sound man, crouched in the backseat. They drove around and around the complex for several hours filming the scene.

It was a seventeen-hour day. I rode in with Peter and Jim, and my call was at ten thirty A.M., and I got back to the hotel just at three A.M. It was a long, long day. I personally spent most of that time with F. Braun, who wanted to be rehearsing, but couldn't be, because he needed Peter, because the rest of the day was the final scene, the final sword fight and the Quickening.

The very last shot of the very last episode ever filmed was a Quickening, which was fitting. "Going out with a bang" we were calling it. In this case it was Methos getting the Quickening. We broke for dinner, first, about ten P.M., and in honor of the occasion, there was champagne in addition to wine at dinner. And Peter is sitting there looking around and saying, "These are the guys I'm trusting to blow me up?" So he had a glass, too, and felt better. The Quickening was the most incredible thing that I have ever witnessed. It takes place on a catwalk out in the middle of this complex. Dennis had cameras set up below it, parallel to it, and above it. So we had three cameras rolling. And there were fireworks, sparklers, smoke, and fire cannons. The cannons I had discovered earlier, when I was standing inside the building to stay out of the rain and all of a sudden there was this humongous explosion and a huge tongue of fire on the other side of the building. And Braun said, "Don't worry, that happens all the time; it's a fire cannon." They had two of those going off directly behind Peter. I had not previously seen a Quickening on-set, so they may all look this incredible; I don't know. But I do know that as it was going off, as the things were exploding and as the fire was shooting, members of the crew were gasping. Now since they sit through this every eight days, I'm thinking this one is bigger than usual. Certainly Peter thought so. Afterwards, he was saying he was traumatized. But the thing about a Quickening is that no matter what happens, you only get to do it once, and you have to keep going, no matter what happens. And, as a matter of fact, during this Quickening, Peter got hit in the face with a burning something, ember or whatever. So that afterwards, he had this red mark right on the point of his cheek. He said that he had looked up, one of those looking-up-while-throwing-his-arms-out moments, and something hit him right in the cheek. But he rolled with it, because he is the consummate professional.

After the Quickening subsided, the room was stunned quiet, and then Jim said, "Last shot for Peter," and everybody broke into tremendous applause. It has been a recent tradition that as one of the regulars finishes, they are given a round of applause by the crew. Jim's last scene had been five or six hours earlier, and when Jim finished filming the last take of his last scene, Dennis gave him a "Last shot for Jim." Tremendous applause; everybody loves Jim so much. They love Peter, as well, of course. Then it was Jim who led the applause for Peter at the end of the Quickening.

Bill Panzer had come prepared with the world's largest bottle of champagne, which we popped down by the Craft Services truck, and I swear it managed to supply the entire crew from this one bottle. And we all did a big toast to the show. Everyone was still stunned, and I don't think it was just the Quickening. I think that's when it really started setting in that "Thhhhat's all, folks," that we're not coming back and doing it again, tomorrow. The technicians and the crew could busy themselves packing up and doing the load-out and all of that. But the actors and the producers were just standing around, looking at each other, and realizing that the family is breaking up. It was very sad.

Can you tell me about the wrap party the next evening?

The wrap party was held in a very surreal location. It was a museum dedicated to carnivals. There was a big carousel in the middle, and there were antique carnival games, and the walls were decorated with sideshow posters. And it's all inside a two-hundred-year-old warehouse down on the docks by the Gare de Lyon. There was a live band that was managed by one of our drivers, Fethi. He was in **"Avatar"**; "I have some lovely white roses." Fethi's band played. The guy who played Benoit in **"Black Tower"** was there, performing on his Rollerblades. Had his stick and everything. And this space was so huge that there was room for him to have his own dance floor. People who had been in different episodes were all invited to come back. The whole crew was there, many with their families. There were a lot of kids playing the carnival games and a lot of the executives from Gaumont, as well. But it was very bittersweet. People were having a good time at the party, but there was always under it the knowledge of why we were having it, that it was sort of a wake in many ways.

CHAPTER EIGHT

Parting Words

"It was magic."

"*Our revels now are ended*" . . . final words from the *Highlander* family.

DAVID ABRAMOWITZ: I think the most remarkable thing about *Highlander* is that for the most part, everyone who works on it believes that they were involved in something special. And that we did more with less. I want to thank people for watching. And tell them that I know less than they think I know. And that for the most part I am winging it. And we have had the smallest writing staff in all of television. And the scripts haven't been terrible, so I think that everyone here has worked very hard. And I'm proud of them. And I would work with almost all of them, again and again and again. We will go on.

ROGER BELLON: The most important thing is that Davis-Panzer and Gaumont hired people and let them do what they do and gave them space. It's been a very enriching experience. I have grown not only creatively, musically, but also in terms of knowledge because there were so many things I had to deal with. And my music has gone out to the world. Peter Davis and Bill Panzer are great. They can be tough, but deep inside, they perceive you to be part of their family and you are treated that way. That's good. That's positive. And it is very unique.

DENNIS BERRY: Everyone is so happy to see that there is a memory of something that is a six-year journey, that was a big journey for us, a big part of our lives. It's a show that I really love. I grew. I became a better director during it. I learned a lot.

LAURA BRENNAN: The people on this show are incredible. The most amazing thing about them is their generosity of spirit. And even though I have not been part of *Highlander* for very long, I am so honored to have been part of it for even one season.

JIM BYRNES: What I have really appreciated is the opportunity to work. Solid work is solid work. The fact that the writers cared enough to ask me about my legs. Things like that. And I really want to thank the people who have taken the time to watch. I appreciate the thought that they put into it. And Ken Gord is the greatest. He's calm. He gets things done. And how well he gets it all done shows on the screen. He's also a great guy just to talk to. And Stan, Elizabeth, Peter, Adrian, they're all my friends. I love them. Sometimes you can take your friends for granted, but I want everyone to know how great these guys are. They're the best.

RICHARD COOK: *Highlander* was wonderful. It was a creative experience. And as an opportunity to be able to explore that incredible range of design in terms of period and geographical location, what a chance, it was a real challenge. Plus if there is one word that really applies to *Highlander*, it is the collaborative effort, truly. Not just from us guys who were producing the scenery and the set dressing, but also the camerawork, the lighting, very important. And the way they shot *Highlander* was so beautiful. And then the postproduction and Don Paonessa and his wonderful people. Everyone made a contribution.

ROGER DALTREY: I am just the luckiest bugger in the world at the moment. If only they paid us. I have really, really had fun. That's what makes it wonderful. It's like a family. I've only worked in France. The crew basically remains the same, and they do become like family, that's what's so great. It's almost like coming away for a vacation, except the hours are long, but you put up with that. The crew really helps. This crew really makes it easy. They are fabulous. It's great working with the French, especially on something like this. They're such anarchists, and that's what this show is, it's anarchy, but it gets done and that's the main thing.

STEVE GEAGHAN: If there's anything that can convey the spirit of *Highlander* it was the tremendous team effort to produce high-quality visual material on a limited budget. And it took a tremendous amount of energy and teamwork. And it was never looked at as a problem; it was looked at as a challenge, and this is what made *Highlander* excellent in its genre, maybe the best.

CHANTAL GIULIANI: *Highlander* is a marvelous subject for a production designer—many would like my position. It has allowed me to voyage through different civilizations, different countries, and different eras. It is a job that opens the mind and requires you to recognize what is essential with very little time to prepare.

KEN GORD: I would like our viewers to know that they were the smart ones, the ones that were tuned in while it was on the air. Because I predict that ten years from now or twenty years from now, *Highlander* will be *The*

Prisoner of whatever decade it is. Now we're still the best-kept secret on television.

ELIZABETH GRACEN: Jim Byrnes is great. He is a doll. He and I are really close. I adore him. We just did this *Highlander* Cruise in the Bahamas, and he and Peter Wingfield were there. He and I have always kept in touch, and it's really special to know that he will be my friend, forever. I think Adrian and Peter will be, too. I feel very blessed. Not all of it has been perfect, and work is work in the end, but I feel very blessed that I was involved in *Highlander*.

TRACY HILLMAN: The one thing that makes *Highlander* is that I have never worked for a greater group of people. Brent Clackson was great. I would work with him in a second. Bill Panzer, David Abramowitz, and Ken Gord are wonderful people. It's the sort of thing that makes the difference. And I honestly think that it shows. To tell you the truth, I would not be on this show without Bill, David, and Ken. I admire and adore each one of them. This is unlike any other show. I have had many, many jobs in this industry, but there has been no other show to work on like this. It has been the best people, the best experience. This show totally revitalized me.

GILLIAN HORVATH: I hope and I dream that we will all end up working together, again. I'd love to have this cast back. They're all hardworking and incredibly talented. And, in addition to being hardworking and talented, the kind of people who, after work, you can have dinner with. That's a lot to say. Steve Geaghan and Rex Raglan, our two Canadian production designers, the best; they did so much with no money. Same with Christina McQuarrie and all the costuming people. Our editors, I have seen them save footage and turn it into something you really wanted to watch. I am completely incapable of saying good-bye to *Highlander*. May it live forever.

PETER HUDSON: They were very good to me, and it was a good team. I loved being in Vancouver because you are treated so well, and everybody was competent and pleasant. What more could you ask for? Also, I suppose I would like people to know, apart from the people who worked on the show, who I think do know, that I'm really quite a nice guy. I can smile.

STAN KIRSCH: To the producers and the writers, I thank them for giving me the opportunity to play this character and to work with a great group of people. To my costars, I am indebted to them for showing up and learning their lines—kidding; they are a great group of people. You hear nightmare stories about other shows, but we really got along. I am going to miss those people, and I certainly hope my friendships with them will remain strong. I think they will. I don't know how often it will be that we all get together in one place at one time, but in the end I am very close to Peter and Jim and Elizabeth and Adrian. That's great. I thank them for being there and for being good people and for helping each other out through this whole thing.

DENIS LEROY: I would say that like the Highlander, who has traveled around the world, we have traveled to many countries. I hope the series opened the eyes of the viewers to the variety of history and people of our world. And as the production has been set up between people from different countries, I would like to remember the notion of communication between peoples and countries.

DONNA LETTOW: This is hitting me real hard right now because you got me on my last day of employment here at *Highlander*. And it's the knowledge that it is never going to be this good for me again. No matter where I go in this business or what I do, there is never going to be a family like this. There is never going to be a group of people who care so much about what they're doing. There's never going to be a venue to deal with the issues that we deal with. Some of these episodes, some of them that we've done this year, they're opera. There are not a lot of places that you can do this. It's sad to know that here, at the beginning of my television career, that I am at the pinnacle. And I am going to miss it.

CHARLES LYALL: All I know is that it was an absolutely wonderful show to work on. Ken Gord is a great guy to work with; he lets you do your job.

The crew had a synergy about them that was great. I've been on shows with ten times the budget, and *Highlander* taught me that less is more. That you can produce a tasteful, slick, good-looking show without all the bells and whistles. This show taught me how to make world-class television.

F. BRAUN McASH: One of the nice things is that the character of Duncan MacLeod has evolved from year to year, which gives you more to work with in the fights in terms of bringing out character aspects, the choices that you make. The historical flashbacks are great because I've gotten to work with every weapon right from the Bronze Age to the present. We've had a lot of really good directors: Adrian Paul, Dennis Berry, Richard Martin, Charles Wilkinson, Mario Azzopardi, Paolo Barzman. It's been a fun series to work on, because *Highlander* turns "Where are we?" into "When are we?" Which is a question you don't get to ask very often. I think one of the more valuable things that *Highlander* has given me is that I now know what I'm capable of. *Highlander* has been really good.

CHRISTINA McQUARRIE: It was wonderful. I think that *Highlander* was probably as much fun as I will ever have in this business, because I love period costume. It was like being a kid in a candy store. It was fantastic. It was very challenging and sometimes nightmarish. I'm very sad the show is over. It was a delight. I know people loved it. It was a good run.

STEIN MYHRSTAD: I think I'd really like a chance to be in a sword fight and appear as a bad Immortal. I really want my head cut off. I want to be responsible for someone else's Quickening. And I'm willing to go to a casting session. Thank you very much.

DON PAONESSA: The scripts have gotten better, the look has gotten better; we've elevated rather than declined, which is what many series do. I'm glad that people hooked into the show. I'm glad there is a following for it, because it has allowed me to stay employed for five years. For a series to run more than two years is a miracle. So, to the fans, thank you for the miracle.

ADRIAN PAUL: This may sound very cliché, but it has been like a family. I've made some great friends: Stan, Elizabeth, Jim, Peter. Roger Daltrey and all the guys and I are pretty close. It's really great, but it's also a little sad. This year I sat by a riverbank where they were shooting a Quickening and I thought, it's been a very large part of my life. I will always be thankful for it in many different ways because of the people I've met, because of the things that I've learned, and because of the experience that it's given me. It's a part of my life that I will never forget. I wouldn't trade it for the world.

Valentine Pelka: It's been such an interesting twelve months, and I think it was all started by *Highlander*; I mean, they really got me off on a roll. The people I've met have just been fantastic. I remember Peter Wingfield and I, we hadn't known each other very long and we were stuck in a caravan and we talked. I think we settled all the ills of the world in four hours. Great fun. *Highlander* is such a nice show. It is such a fantastic atmosphere.

Rex Raglan: *Highlander* was mad and crazy fun. I would say that the most fun for me is creating a reality outside of what you can go out the door and shoot, creating another reality that doesn't necessarily exist, or doesn't exist in our town.

Lisa Robison: Don't do it. Go to school; get a good education. Do whatever your parents tell you to do. Seriously, *Highlander* is fun. But we have a very quick turnaround, two weeks from first dailies to the online, so we have to move in and move on. [When pressed for more, Lisa replied, "I'm a shy Canadian."]

David Tynan: It's been a great team. It would be hard, I think, to find another one. I don't actually expect, unless they come back to *Highlander* in some other incarnation, to find a team like this that would be as much fun and as enjoyable to work with. And what was very moving about the show in some ways, about the people who worked for it, was that because *Highlander* shuts down in Canada and moves to France, a large number of the people who worked for it were suddenly out of work for a number of months. In this industry, that is not an easy thing to do. Yet, almost all of them would come back to *Highlander*, stop whatever they were doing, and return to *Highlander* year after year. That is a compliment to the show itself.

Peter Wingfield: The show belongs to us all. I am only just becoming aware of how good things are. And there's a sadness attached to that because, come December, it's finished. But there is also huge joy involved. I feel lucky to have played this. I find it extraordinary. I've done more episodes of *Highlander* than probably every other episode of every TV show that I have ever done in my life, and there is no part of me that wants it to stop.

Amy Zoll: I was very glad to be a very small part of *Highlander*. Everyone was fabulous to work with. *Highlander* opened my eyes to the world outside the ivory tower. It's been really good. And I am sorry to leave it.

Episode Guide

Season 1

"I am Duncan MacLeod, born four hundred years ago in the Highlands of Scotland. I am Immortal, and I am not alone. For centuries we have waited for the time of the Gathering, when the stroke of a sword and the fall of a head will release the power of the Quickening. In the end, there can be only one."

Adrian Paul as Duncan MacLeod; Alexandra Vandernoot as Tessa Noel; Stan Kirsch as Richie Ryan

#92102-1 **The Gathering**
Writer: Dan Gordon
Director: Thomas J. Wright
Christopher Lambert as Connor MacLeod; Richard Moll as Slan Quince; Wendell Wright as Sgt. Powell

March 13, 1872. Mac's Native American family is massacred by soldiers. From 1872 to 1882, Mac, in despair, retreats from the world to a cabin on holy ground. Mac's old friend, teacher, and clansman, Connor MacLeod, finds Duncan and tries to convince him to rejoin the Battle on the side of Good. In the present, street kid Richie Ryan tries to rob Mac's antique store. But the attempted burglary is interrupted by the evil Immortal Slan, who challenges Duncan. Roused from his peaceful life with his lover, Tessa, Duncan ultimately defeats Slan. In the end, Connor points out that Duncan has all the fun and all the good women.

#92106-2 **Family Tree**
Writer: Kevin Droney
Director: Jorge Montesi
J. E. Freeman as Joe Scanlon; Peter Deluise as Clinch; Tamsin Kelsey as Mrs. Gustavson; Matthew Walker as Ian MacLeod; Walter Marsh as Mr. Stubbs; Jessica Van der Veen as Secretary; Aurelio Di Nunzio as Security Guard; Mary McDonald as Old Peasant

Scottish Highlands; October 2, 1622. Mac is "killed" in battle and becomes Immortal. His adoptive father, Ian MacLeod, fearing supernatural inter-

vention, renounces Duncan. In the present, perennial foster kid Richie attempts to learn more about his natural parents. Instead, he falls prey to con man Joe Scanlon who, needing a place to hide and an easy mark, pretends to be Richie's long-lost father. In the end, Richie discovers the truth.

#92108-3 **The Road Not Taken**
Writer: Terry Nelson
Director: Thomas J. Wright
Soon-Teck Oh as Kiem Sun; Dustin Nguyen as Chu Lin; Christianne Hirt as Angie; Wendell Wright as Sgt. Powell; Kim Kondrashoff as Forks; Alan C. Peterson as Bartender; Paul Stafford as Officer No. 1; Lisa Bunting as Woman Hostage

China, 1780. Mac visits Kiem Sun on holy ground. The herbalist demonstrates a potion that he believes will cre-

ate the perfect warrior to protect him, but it has deadly side effects. In the present, a lethal drug kills a friend of Richie's. Mac suspects the source of the drug is Kiem Sun, who vowed to work on the potion for centuries, if need be, to perfect it. But it is a young disciple of Sun's, Chu Lin, who is selling the drug for his own gain. Mac and Kiem Sun track down Lin and stop him. But when it becomes clear to Mac that Sun will continue his experiments, Mac destroys the remaining sample of the drug.

#92103-4 **Innocent Man**
Writer: Dan Gordon
Director: Jorge Montesi
Vincent Schiavelli as Leo Atkins; John Novack as Sheriff Howard Crowley;

Victor Young as Lucas Desiree; Amanda Wyss as Randi McFarland; Wendell Wright as Sgt. Powell; Todd Duckworth as Deputy Struthers; Gary Chalk as Lemoyne; Colleen Winton as Gwenn; Jason Michas as Confederate Guard

Tennessee, 1863; during the Civil War. Mac is hanged as a prisoner of war, but is rescued by Immortal Confederate Captain Lucas Desiree. In the present, Desiree is killed in his isolated mountain retreat, where he, like Mac, had hoped to retreat from the Game for a while. A homeless veteran is charged with the crime. Mac clears the innocent man, unravels the mystery of who killed Desiree, and avenges his old friend by challenging and defeating the true killer, Sheriff Howard Crowley.

#92101-5 **Free Fall**
Writer: Philip John Taylor
Director: Thomas J. Wright
Joan Jett as Felicia Martins; Eli Gabay as Devereux; Jay Brazeau as Commissioner Comanski; Leslie Carlson as

Sam Thompson; Claudia Ferri as Devereux's Woman; Patricia Vonk as Female Executive; Ron Chartier as M.E. Assistant

It seems that a beautiful young woman attempts suicide by jumping off a building, only to awaken and discover she is Immortal. Mac agrees to become her mentor, and she becomes involved with Richie. But it is soon revealed that Felicia is a longtime Immortal, bent on tricking Mac and acquiring his Quickening. In 1880s France, we see Felicia murder the Immortal Devereux's wife and stepchild. Mac finally sees the truth and challenges Felicia. He defeats her, but spares her head at Richie's bidding.

#92107-6 **Bad Day in Building A**
Writer: Kevin Droney
Director: Jorge Montesi
Andrew Divoff as Bryan Slade; Amanda Wyss as Randi McFarland; Jay Brazeau as Commissioner Comanski; Duncan Fraser as SWAT Commander; Don MacKay as Stanley; Alf Humphreys as Janitor; Andrea Libman

as Belinda; Gary Jones as Klein; Bill Croft as Mancuso; Ken Kirzinger as Kirby; Vladmir Kulich as Pauling

While visiting the courthouse to clear up Tessa's traffic tickets, Mac, Tessa, and Richie are among those taken hostage by a group of men intent on freeing their leader, Slade, from prison. When Slade's demands are not met, he chooses a hostage to kill. Mac ensures he is that hostage. After being "killed," Mac returns from the "dead" to hunt down the gunmen, one by one. Eventually, all are killed, and the hostages are freed.

#92110-7 **Mountain Men**
Writer: Marie-Chantal Droney
Director: Thomas J. Wright
Marc Singer as Caleb; Wes Studi as Sheriff Benson; John Dennis Johnston as Carl the Hermit; Byron Lucas as Joshua Cole; Brent Stait as Eddie Doyle; Rick Poltaruk as Big John; Doug Abrahams as Benson's Deputy

In the 1860s in the Pacific Northwest, Mac learns tracking from Carl the Hermit. In the present, Mac's skills are put to use when Tessa is abducted by survivalists. Mac must track her down in the very same mountains in which he trained with the mountain man, Carl. The situation becomes more complex when the leader of the present-day mountain men, Caleb (revealed to be an Immortal), falls in love with Tessa. Mac ultimately rescues Tessa and challenges Caleb, whose head he takes.

#92111-8 **Deadly Medicine**
Writer: Robert L. McCullough
Director: Ray Austin
Joe Pantoliano as Doctor Wilder; Amanda Wyss as Randi McFarland; Beverley Hendry as Barbara Madison; Stephen E. Miller as Sgt. Herrald; Leslie Carlson as Sam Thompson; Catherine Lough as Carol; Stephen Fanning as Jack

Mac is hit by a speeding car and is "killed." When he revives in the emergency room, Mac attracts the attention of a deranged doctor, Wilder, who kidnaps Mac in order to learn the secret of his immortality. When Mac escapes, Wilder murders a potential witness, nurse Barbara Madison, and frames Mac for the killing. Ultimately, Wilder is killed and Mac is cleared.

#92112-9 **The Sea Witch**
Writer: David Tynan
Director: Thomas J. Wright
Stephen Macht as Alexei Voshin; Johannah Newmarch as Nikki; Phil Hayes as Marco; John Tench as Reese; Brooklyn Brown as Melinda; Scott McNeil as Dennis; Gina Brunton as Niva; Garry Davey as Soviet Major; Rob Morton as Owner; Adrian Holmes as Street Kid

Soviet Union, 1938. Mac tries to smuggle out Jewish refugees, but is betrayed by the captain of the *Sea Witch*, Immortal Alexei Voshin. In the present, Mac meets up with Voshin, who is now a drug dealer. Voshin and his henchmen are chasing an old girlfriend of Richie's, Nikki, who has stolen $50,000 in drug money in the hopes of making a better life for her small daughter, Melinda. Tessa, meanwhile, has become enamored of Melinda, and Mac must remind Tessa that as an Immortal he can never father a child. Finally, Mac and Voshin fight, and Voshin loses his head when he falls overboard and into the rotating propellers of the *Sea Witch II*.

#92109-10 **Revenge Is Sweet**
Writer: Loraine Despres
Director: Ray Austin
Vanity as Rebecca Lord; Christopher Ohrt as Walter Reinhardt; Christianne Hirt as Angie Burke; Tim Reid as Sgt. Bennett; Ken Kramer as Dr. Kramer; Kevin McNulty as Harry Dawes; Elizabeth Claridge as Molly Parker; Michael Cavers as Nobleman; Shirley Broderick as Noblewoman; Patrick Stevenson as Street Punk

London, Dover Road; 1728. Mac protects fellow coach passengers from Immortal Reinhardt's thieving. In Seacouver, on December 31, 1988, Mac fights Reinhardt, but Reinhardt goes overboard before the battle is done. Unbeknownst to Mac, Reinhardt's lover, Rebecca, believes Mac has killed Reinhardt. She vows revenge and, in the present, toys with Mac and Tessa before attempting to kill Mac with Reinhardt's sword. But she knows nothing of Immortals, and unknown to her, Reinhardt is alive and using her to get to Mac. In the end, Mac kills Reinhardt, and Rebecca discovers the truth and moves on with her life.

#92114-11 **See No Evil**
Writer: Brian Clemens
Director: Thomas J. Wright
John Hertzler as Marcus Korolus; Dee McCafferty as Michael "The Scalper"; Moira Walley as Natalie Ward; Amanda Wyss as Randi McFarland; Tim Reid as Sgt. Bennett; Fulvio Cecere as Tony Graffini; Kelli Fox as Police Woman; Raimund Stamm as Herbie; Wanda Wilkinson as Helen; Glynda Fitzgerald as Brunette Woman

Seacouver, 1925. Mac defeats Immortal serial killer Marcus. Marcus had been driven mad centuries before by the betrayal of the woman he loved. His true nature is revealed; he had been burned as a witch. In the present, a serial killer dubbed "The Scalper" is also attacking blond women and slaying them in the same locations as Marcus

did. Mac and Tessa become involved when The Scalper attacks Tessa's friend, Natalie. In the end, Tessa and Mac find the killer, and Tessa stops him.

#92115-12 **Eyewitness**
Writer: David Tynan
Director: Ray Austin
Tom Butler as Andrew Ballin; Amanda Wyss as Randi McFarland; Tim Reid as Sgt. Bennett; Sheila Paterson as Greta; Diana Barrington as Anne Wheeler; Christopher Gaze as Martin Sorrel; David Petersen as Detective Taylor

Tessa witnesses the murder of Anne Wheeler, but the police cannot find a body, so no one but Mac believes Tessa. As they investigate, Tessa and Mac eventually discover that Anne was killed by her Immortal ex-lover, who feared she would reveal the secret of his immortality. After Tessa is taken to a police safe house, Mac realizes that Anne's killer is Andrew Ballin, the Chief of Detectives. Mac rescues Tessa and Police Sergeant Bennett from Ballin's bomb. In the end, Mac takes Ballin's head and brings Anne's killer to justice.

#92118-13 **Band of Brothers**
Writer: Marie-Chantal Droney
Director: Rene Manzor
Werner Stocker as Darius; James Horan as Grayson; Earl Pastko as Victor Paulus; Amanda Wyss as Randi McFarland; Terry Howsan as Hoestler; Peter Diamond as Brigand

Waterloo; June 18, 1815. Mac meets the monk Darius on the battlefield. There Darius teaches Mac of the fragility of life and the fruitlessness of battle. Mac vows never again to wear a uniform. On January 29, 1816, in Paris, Mac leaves for America, unable to follow Darius' example. In the present, Darius warns Mac that his former protégé, Grayson, is now killing Darius' other students. Grayson is disillusioned that his former comrade-in-arms has become a man of peace, and he wants to draw Darius from the safety of the monastery and holy ground into combat. Mac protects Darius' mortal

student, peace activist Victor Paulus, and ultimately defeats Grayson. Later, Mac joins Tessa and Richie in Paris, where Tessa has taken a job as curator.

#92117-14 **For Evil's Sake**
Writers: David Abramowitz & Fabrice Zolkowski
Director: Ray Austin
Peter Howitt as Kuyler; Hugues LeForestier as Inspector LeBrun; Vernon Dobtcheff as Carlo Luchesi; Michel Voletti as Baron Deshields; Gerard Touroul as Inspector Sole; Jerome Keen as Anthony

France, 1783. Mac is bodyguard to the Baron Deshields, but, alas, Mac's formidable skills are not enough to protect the Baron from the Immortal assassin Kuyler. In the present, on a romantic note, Mac remembers Paris, 1980, when he escaped Kuyler and met Tessa by jumping into the Bateau Mouche, on which she was acting as a guide. But there is little time for romance, as Kuyler, "the greatest assassin in all of history," is again on the loose, still using his trademark disguise as a mime. Knowing Kuyler's taste for absinthe, Mac finds him, but the battle is postponed by Kuyler's threat to kill a group of children. Finally, Mac and Kuyler battle, and Mac takes Kuyler's head.

#92116-15 **For Tomorrow We Die**
Writer: Philip John Taylor
Director: Robin Davis
Roland Gift as Xavier St. Cloud; Werner Stocker as Darius; Hugues LeForestier as Inspector LeBrun; Mapi Galan as Renee de Tassigny; Jean Claude Deret as Dalon; Sandrine Caron as Nathalie; Tanguy Gouasdove as Stan; Francine Olivier as Madame Bertrand; Thierry de Carbonnieres as François Bertrand; Philippe Agael as Medical Examiner; Crystel Amsalem as Young Girl

France, 1917. Mac is a World War I Red Cross ambulance driver when he encounters Immortal Xavier St. Cloud on the battlefield. Xavier uses mustard gas to kill those in the immediate area so that he can rob a payroll truck. In the present, Mac realizes Xavier is in Paris when a jewelry store is robbed by someone using poison gas. Xavier confesses to Darius, but Darius cannot violate the sanctity of the confessional. Finally, Mac confronts Xavier and defeats him before he can kill and rob any more innocent people, but while the evil Immortal loses his hand to Mac, he keeps his head and escapes.

#92123-16 **The Beast Below**
Writer: Marie-Chantal Droney
Director: Daniel Vigne
Christian Van Acker as Ursa; Dee Dee Bridgewater as Carolyn; Werner Stocker as Darius; Fay Masterson as Jenny Harris; François Guetary as Detective; Joe Sheridan as Frank Wells

France, 1634. Mac rescues the Immortal Ursa from persecution and leads him to sanctuary in an abbey. In the present, the abbey has been destroyed, and Ursa now lives underground, beneath the Paris Opéra. The giant Immortal has become smitten with a fading diva, Carolyn, who tries to trick the innocent and simple Ursa into murdering a possible rival. Mac finally makes Ursa see the truth, and Carolyn is accidentally killed. Mac returns Ursa to sanctuary in an abbey.

#92120-17 **Saving Grace**
Writers: Elizabeth Baxter & Martin Broussellet
Director: Ray Austin
Julia Stemberger as Grace; Georges Corraface as Carlo Sendaro; Werner Stocker as Darius; Hugues LeForestier as Inspector LeBrun; Bruce Myers as Paul Warren

France, 1660. Mac meets the Immortal Grace, as she delivers a baby. Throughout the centuries, Grace has lived as a midwife, a doctor, and a scientist. Her one weakness is the handsome Immortal Carlo Sendaro. In Paris, in 1840, a worried Mac sees Grace off as she leaves for the Amazon with Sendaro. Grace ultimately learns Sendaro is not what he seemed, and she leaves him, but her former lover is obsessed with her. In the present, Sendaro returns to Paris and kills her current mortal lover, Paul, framing Grace for the murder in an attempt to force her to leave with him. It is up to Grace's old friend, Mac, to help clear her and stop Sendaro's deadly obsession. In the end, Mac and Sendaro battle, and Sendaro is beheaded by the Métro.

#92121-18 **The Lady and the Tiger**
Writer: Philip John Taylor
Director: Robin Davis
Elizabeth Gracen as Amanda; Jason Isaacs as Zachary Blaine; Fred Pearson as Pierre; Pierre Gerald as Henry Lamartine; Bertie Cortez as Ring Master; Michael Hofland as Bavarian Officer; David Lowe as Clown

Bavaria, 1804. Mac, living with Amanda, has just returned from Munich. Amanda leaves Mac, however, when she runs off with jewels stolen from the Baron Holstein. In the present, a day at the circus reunites Mac with his former lover, Amanda, who, of course, needs Mac's help. Her former partner, Blaine, has escaped from prison. Amanda has promised him Mac's head instead of hers. (But she swears to Mac she didn't really mean it.) Amanda decides the only way out is to steal a multimillion-dollar book. In the end, Amanda takes Blaine's head, and Mac gets back the book.

#92124-19 **Eye of the Beholder**
Writers: Christian Bouveron &
Lawrence Shore
Director: Dennis Berry
Nigel Terry as Gabriel Piton; Katia
Douvalian as Maya; Rachel Palmieri as
Cynthia Hampten; Thomas Kaufman
as Police Detective; Olivier Pierre as
Waiter; Edwin Gerard as Lawyer;
Manault Deva as Duchess

Paris, 1786. Mac and Immortal Gabriel
Piton, thief and womanizer, divert in a
whorehouse. When a marchioness
notices her missing pearls, Piton and
Mac duel with the authorities. In an
English palace, in 1803, Piton robs a
duchess who is a special friend of
Mac's. Mac and Piton duel, and Mac
spares Piton's life. In the present, Piton
is now a world-class fashion designer
with the talent of making women look
and feel beautiful. And he is still
obsessed with beautiful women and
beautiful objects, killing one of his
mortal lovers, Cynthia, when she discovers his thievery. Richie, meanwhile,
falls for the beautiful model Maya, but
Piton is now obsessed with her. Richie
is nearly killed by Piton, but escapes.
Mac intervenes, finally battles Piton,
and wins.

#92122-20 **Avenging Angel**
Writer: Fabrice Zolkowski
Director: Paolo Barzman
Martin Kemp as Alfred Cahill; Sandra
Nelson as Elaine; Patrick Floersheim
as Battini; Nathalie Presles as Clau-
dine; Yan Briand as Charles Bagnot

When a fatal stabbing doesn't kill him,
newborn Immortal Alfred Cahill
becomes convinced he is an avenging
angel, chosen to wage a war against
"perversion." He goes on a killing
spree, murdering prostitutes and
pimps. An old friend of Tessa's, Elaine,
now a call girl, is put in danger. Meanwhile, Mac tries to explain immortality,
the Rules, etc., to Cahill, but Cahill
cannot or will not understand. Mac is
finally forced to take his head and end
his murderous spree.

#92125-21 **Nowhere to Run**
Writer: David Abramowitz
Director: Dennis Berry
Peter Guinness as Colonel Everett
Bellian; Anthony Stewart Head as
Allan Rothwood; Jason Riddington as
Mark Rothwood; Marion Cotillard as
Lori Bellian

France, 1815. Mac is with a Highland
regiment. When a young man is erro-
neously executed, Mac is unable to
stop the firing squad. In the present,
Lori, the stepdaughter of Immortal
Colonel Everett Bellian, is raped by
Mark Rothwood. The colonel comes
after the rapist, laying siege to the family's house. The young man's father,
Allan, is an old friend of Tessa's. Mac, a
guest in the home of the accused,
intervenes. He urges the colonel to follow due process of the law, but the
Immortal wants immediate justice.
Mac and Bellian battle, and Mac wins,
but he will not take Bellian's head. Lori
finally kills Mark, when he has a gun
aimed at her father.

#92126-22 **The Hunters**
Writer: Kevin Droney
Director: Paolo Barzman
Roger Daltrey as Hugh Fitzcairn;
Werner Stocker as Darius; Peter Hudson
as Horton

Florence, Italy; 1639. Mac and Hugh
Fitzcairn are a duke's bodyguards. In
the present, Fitz arrives in Paris to warn
Mac that some of their Immortal friends
are vanishing under mysterious circumstances. Mac and Fitz find Darius dead
in his church, on holy ground. Fitz is
kidnapped. Mac realizes a group of
mortals are hunting Immortals. Mac
finds the Fifth Chronicle, a book that
Darius left hidden in his church, and
learns of a secret order that observes
Immortals. Mac finds the renegade
Watchers in time to save Fitz, but James
Horton, the renegade Watcher leader,
escapes. Mac, Fitz, Tessa, and Richie
bury Darius, scattering his ashes in the
Seine, so they can flow to the sea.

Season 2

"He is Immortal. Born in the Highlands of Scotland four hundred years ago. He is not alone. There are others like him. Some good, some evil. For centuries, he has battled the forces of darkness, with holy ground his only refuge. He cannot die unless you take his head, and with it, his power. In the end, there can be only one. He is Duncan MacLeod. The Highlander."

Adrian Paul as Duncan MacLeod; Alexandra Vandernoot as Tessa Noel; Stan Kirsch as Richie Ryan; Jim Byrnes as Joe Dawson; Philip Akin as Charlie DeSalvo; Michel Modo as Maurice

#93201 **The Watchers**

Writer: Marie-Chantal Droney
Director: Clay Borris
Peter Hudson as James Horton; Kehli O'Byrne as Lynn Horton; Cameron Bancroft as Robert; Douglas Arthurs as Joey; Brad Loree as Belson; Ajay Karah as Busboy

Determined to find Darius' killers and avenge his old friend's death, Mac returns to Seacouver. Tessa and Richie accompany him. There he meets Joe Dawson, a bookstore owner—or so he seems. It is soon revealed that Joe is a member of an ancient organization known as the Watchers. They observe and record the lives of Immortals, archiving and passing down the information through the ages. Unbeknownst to Joe, his brother-in-law, James Horton, has been recruiting renegade Watchers to kill Immortals. Horton even goes so far as to kill his own prospective son-in-law, Robert, to keep his secret. Joe finally discovers the truth and confronts Horton. Horton threatens to kill Joe. Mac and Horton

struggle, and after Horton shoots Mac, Mac runs Horton through with his katana. In the end, we know someone is watching.

#93202 **Studies in Light**
Writer: Naomi Janzen
Director: Peter Ellis
Joel Wyner as Gregor; Sheila Moore as Linda Plager; Gillian Carfra as Young Linda; Shane Kelly as Jonathan; Dwight McFee as Ray Holstrom; Patti Allan as Nurse; Mikal Dughi as Mother; Cayde Ritchie as Frightened Boy

American West, 1883. Mac helps his friend Gregor, a doctor, during a cholera epidemic. Gregor laments that no matter what he does, mortals still die. In the present, Gregor invites Mac to see his photographic exhibition. Mac is stunned to see the violent images in his old friend's work. Mac is further distressed to discover that the sensitive and caring Gregor has become a cynic. While at the exhibit, Mac sees his old love, photographer Linda Plager. Mac remembers Seacouver, 1938–39, when he met Linda and became her lover and mentor. The now seventy-three-year-old Linda is bewildered to see Mac looking as he did nearly fifty years earlier. Mac wants to tell the dying Linda the truth, but instead tells her he is Duncan MacLeod's grandson. Meanwhile, Gregor attempts to seduce the impetuous Richie into following his destructive lifestyle. It seems Gregor no longer feels alive, because he is Immortal. Gregor finally snaps, trashes the photographic exhibit, attacks Richie, and tries to attack Linda. Mac intervenes, and they battle. Only when Mac threatens to kill him does Gregor realize the truth; he can feel, and he does not want to die. Finally, Mac tells Linda that he is, in fact, "her" Duncan, and she dies in his arms.

#93203 **Turnabout**
Writer: David Tynan
Director: Clay Borris
Geraint Wyn Davies as Michael Moore; John Tierney as Old Father Morton; Alan Robertson as Judge Marvin Singer; Gaetana Korbin as Jeanette; Brittany Edgell as Nurse; Ian Alden as Young Father Morton

Seacouver, 1921. Mac's old friend Michael Moore is stalked by the evil Immortal Quenten Barnes. Barnes kills Michael's wife. In 1963 Barnes is finally caught and convicted of the murder of two young women; he is sentenced to death in the electric chair. In the present, Mac meets Charlie DeSalvo and buys his dojo. Joe returns and tells Mac that Barnes' tomb has been unearthed and he is free, killing the people responsible for his execution. Michael returns to town, asking Mac for help. Mac asks Joe for Barnes' Watcher file, but it's too sparse to be of use. As first Barnes' prosecutor, then his priest are killed, it becomes obvious that Michael is next on the hit list. Mac leaves Michael with Tessa and Richie for safety's sake, as he goes after Barnes. But when Mac finds the body of the Watcher that Joe sent with Barnes' file, Mac realizes, finally, that Barnes and Michael are one and the same. Mac must confront his old friend and, at Michael's plea, takes his head in order to stop Barnes.

#93204 **The Darkness**
Writers: Christian Bouveron & Lawrence Shore
Director: Paolo Barzman
Traci Lords as Greta; Andrew Jackson as Pallin Wolf; Frank C. Turner as Harry the Taxidermist; Lisa Vultaggio as Carmen; Richard Lautsch as Roman; Kendall Cross as Michelle; Adrian Hughes as James; Travis Mac-Donald as Kid

Gypsy camp, 1848. Carmen reads Mac's palm and tells him that he will never marry. In the present, Mac proposes to Tessa. She accepts, but a fortune-teller, Greta, they meet in a restaurant warns Tessa of danger. The prophecy proves true when Tessa is kidnapped by renegade Watcher Pallin Wolf. He has been killing Immortals by luring them into a sealed dark room, then gaining the advantage by wearing night goggles and taking their heads. Wolf intends the same for Mac, and Tessa is the "bait." With some help from Greta's visions, Mac finally finds Wolf's house. Richie tries to help, but is also taken. Mac is trapped in the darkness by Wolf, but he regains the advantage by striking a book of matches and momentarily blinding Wolf with the light. Mac kills Wolf. As Tessa and Richie, seemingly safe, walk to the car,

a young junkie accosts them and shoots, a senseless act of violence. Tessa is dead, but Richie is Immortal.

#93205 **An Eye for an Eye**
Writers: Elizabeth Baxter & Martin Broussellet
Director: Dennis Berry
Sheena Easton as Annie Devlin; Andrew A. Kavadas as Mick; Callum Keith Rennie as Neal; Eric Schneider as O'Hara; Kris Keeler as Tommy; Brian Furlong as Kerry; Terry Arrowsmith as Rawls

Ireland, 1919. Mac and Annie escape an ambush, but Annie's mortal lover, Kerry, is killed. Annie vows revenge. In the present, Mac and Richie witness an IRA terrorist attack. Richie, emboldened by his newfound Immortality, rushes in to save the Ambassador. One terrorist is killed and one captured, Annie. She vows revenge on Richie. Mac, meanwhile, becomes Richie's teacher, training him to fight. When Annie escapes, she and Mac, both having recently lost loved ones, find solace in each other. In the end, Richie and Annie do battle. Richie defeats her, but cannot bring himself to kill her. Mac convinces Annie to stop her quest for vengeance and agree to forgive.

#93206 **The Zone**
Writer: Peter Mohan
Director: Clay Borris
Santino Buda as Canaan; Sandra P. Grant as Asia; Alfonso Quijada as Tio; Leam Blackwood as Tom McGee; Ken

Camroux as Judd Collins; Tom Heaton as Old Man; Michael G. Shanks as Jesse Collins; Brian McGugan as Mark Wells; Lorena Gale as Woman

Pennsylvania mining town, 1920. Mac's friend, Jessie, the son of a mine owner, is killed during a confrontation in a mine strike. In the present, Joe comes to Mac for help. One of his Watchers has been killed in The Zone, an urban wasteland being taken over by the charismatic Canaan, who is urging his followers to rise up and take the material goods long denied them. Mac and Charlie (this is his old neighborhood) go to The Zone. Mac discovers that Canaan is not an Immortal, as Joe suspected, but once Mac sees the suffering in The Zone, he is determined to help ease it. Charlie introduces Mac to Asia, a nurse at the local clinic. Mac convinces Asia that it's time to fight back and arranges a neighborhood meeting. But, as it turns out, Asia is involved with Canaan. She is used as bait to lure Mac to his apparent death. When Mac returns from the "dead" and defeats Canaan in hand-to-hand combat in front of the people of The Zone, Canaan's evil hold is broken.

#93207 **The Return of Amanda**
Writer: Story by Guy Mullaly; teleplay by David Tynan
Director: Dennis Berry
Elizabeth Gracen as Amanda; Don S. Davis as Palance; Robert Wisden as Werner; Jano Frandsen as Rutger; Joe Maffei as Harry the Jeweler

Berlin, 1936. Mac smuggles a scientist out of Germany with Amanda's "help." In the present, Amanda returns, vowing that she's retired from her life of crime. Mac doubts her, especially since he's seen those two men watching her. Mac worries they might be Watchers, but they turn out to be FBI. Amanda has "liberated" some counterfeit money plates that were stolen in Germany before the war. Amanda is searching for an engraver to help her change the dates. She's concluded that if she has to give up her normal methods of gaining money, she'll have to print up some of her own. But it seems FBI agent Palance has the same idea. He frames Mac and Amanda for his partner's murder and demands that they hand over the plates. Mac and Amanda are forced to allow Palance to "kill" them, so they can videotape the execution and catch the thief.

#93208 **Revenge of the Sword**
Writer: Aubrey Solomon
Director: Clay Borris
Dustin Nguyen as Jimmy Sang;
Debbie Podowski as Lisa; Robert Ito as Johnny Leong

New York City, 1905. Mac's fruit-seller friend is killed by gangsters. In the present, a former student of Charlie's, Jimmy Sang, has become a martial arts movie star. His current movie is filming scenes in Charlie's dojo. When a stuntman is killed, Mac realizes that it was no accident and that Jimmy's life is in danger. We learn that the movie is based on Jimmy's youth, when he was an enforcer for a gang. Not wanting to have their secrets revealed, his former boss wants him dead. Mac finally saves the day.

#93209 **Run for Your Life**
Writer: Naomi Janzen
Director: Dennis Berry
Bruce A. Young as Carl Robinson;
Geza Kovacs as Carter; Roman Podhora as Kenny; Biski Gugushe as Ricky; Deejay Jackson as Officer Warren; Mark Acheson as Billy Ray; Bill Mackenzie as Sheriff; John Destry as Bobby; Susan McLennan as Betty; Adrian Holmes as Johnny; Mark Poyser as Ben

Louisiana, 1926. Mac rescues Immortal Carl Robinson from a KKK lynch mob. On May 17, 1954, Mac defends Carl in a segregated diner on the very day that the Supreme Court declares that segregation is unconstitutional. Carl is filled with hope. Now he can be whatever he wants to be—a major-league ball player, maybe even President. In the present, however, Carl has lost hope; he doesn't think anything can change or that he can make a difference. Carl

steals Charlie's car. Mac tries to rekindle Carl's belief in himself and in the world. Meanwhile, Carl is nearly killed by Carter, a white cop and a renegade Watcher. Carl thinks the man is racist, but Mac explains what's really happening: there are renegade Watchers searching out and killing Immortals. After a white cop, Kenny (Carter's partner), helps Carl and Mac stop Carter, Carl decides maybe there is hope.

#93210 **Epitaph for Tommy**
Writer: Philip John Taylor
Director: Clay Borris
Roddy Piper as Gallen; Andrea Roth as Suzanne Honniger; Ken Camroux as Honniger; Jan D'Arcy as Betty Bannen; Robert Collins as Johnson; Gabrielle Miller as Bess; Nicholas Harrison as Ned; Bill Dow as Harry; Paul McLean as Frank; Patricia Dahlquist as Mother; Jane Sowerby as Claire

Annapolis, Maryland; 1866. Mac's mortal lover, Bess, is accidentally killed by her fiancé, Ned, when Mac and Ned fight. In the present, Mac and the Immortal Gallen are fighting when Tommy, an innocent bystander, is killed. Mac is haunted by Tommy's death and strives to discover more about him. What Mac learns is that Tommy wasn't the innocent Mac believed. Gallen was planning to kill Tommy's boss, Honniger, so Honniger hired Tommy to kill Gallen. Instead, Gallen killed Tommy. In the end, Mac battles Gallen and takes his head. Mac also brings peace to Tommy's mother, who plans to return to the Highlands of Scotland.

#93211 **The Fighter**
Writer: Morrie Ruvinsky
Director: Peter Ellis
Bruce Weitz as Tommy Sullivan; Wren Robertz as George Belcher; Cali Timmins

as Iris Lange; Nicholas Lea as Rodney Lange; Tom McBeath as Coleman; Russell Roberts as Wilson; Charles Payne as Thunder Rodriguez; Topaze Hasfal-Schou as Marilyn; Ken Roberts as Wallace

San Francisco, 1891. Fast-talking Irishman and onetime boxer Tommy Sullivan talks Mac into fighting for money. Mac wins the fight, and Tommy gains $1,000, which he collects by killing the opposing fighter's manager. In the present, Tommy charms Mac into backing his current fighter, George, and Charlie into helping him woo a beautiful waitress, Iris. But when a rival manager, Coleman, who was trying to steal George away from Sullivan, turns up dead, Mac discovers the truth about his old friend. Coleman was blackmailing Iris with her brother's life, so Sullivan killed him. But when Sullivan kills George, Mac cannot look the other way. Mac and his old friend battle, and Sullivan loses his head.

#93212 **Under Color of Authority**
Writer: Peter Mohan
Director: Clay Borris
Jonathan Banks as Mako; Deanna Milligan as Laura Daniels; Lochlyn Munro as Tim Ramsey; Howard Storey as Sheriff; Gregory Smith as Kid

In the Pacific Northwest, in 1882, Mac is running the town newspaper when the Immortal bounty hunter and federal marshal, Mako, comes to town. Mac doesn't approve of his methods, but

Mako follows the letter of the law. In the present, Mako is after Laura Daniels, a young woman Richie has decided is innocent and in need of his protection. Mac is torn between helping Richie and seeing justice served. Mac learns that Laura murdered her husband and has been lying to Richie. Richie believes it was self-defense and goes on the run with Laura. Richie and Mako ultimately

fight after Laura is accidentally killed. Richie gets his first Quickening. Mac and Richie realize their relationship is no longer that of teacher and student. Richie must move on.

#93213 **Bless the Child**
Writers: Elizabeth Baxter & Martin Broussellet
Director: Clay Borris
Ed Lauter as Avery Hoskins; Michelle

Thrush as Sara Lightfoot; John Cuthbert as Billie Hoskins; Carolyn Dunn as Nora Fontaine; Doug Abrahams as Luke Hoskins; Dean Wray as J.J.; Johanna Wright as Margaret

Boston; December 31, 1923. At a New Year's Eve party, Mac celebrates with a friend. When their talk grows serious, Mac realizes he must break up with the girl. She wants children, and Mac knows that as an Immortal, he can never father a child. In the present, Mac and Charlie help Sara Lightfoot, a Native American woman who tells them she is running from a man, Avery Hoskins, who is trying to steal her baby. Hoskins and his brothers come after the foursome, and they flee. After a rugged flight through the mountains, Mac finally learns that the child is, in fact, Avery's son, stolen by Sara in ret-

ribution for the death of her daughter, killed by mercury poisoning from runoff from Hoskins' mines. Father and child are ultimately reunited.

#93214 **Unholy Alliance, Part I**
Writer: David Tynan
Director: Peter Ellis
Roland Gift as Xavier St. Cloud; Peter Hudson as James Horton; Stacey Travis as Special Agent Renee Delaney; Alexandra Stewart as Catherine Legris; Terry Barclay as Rick Davis; Roark Critchlow as Jason Talbott; Judith Maxie as Surgeon; J. B. Bivens as George; Philippe Agael as Anton Legris; Gerard Smurthwaite as Aurie; Franck Dubose as Michel; Steven Hilton as Barton; Beverley Elliott as Supervisor

Rural Scotland, 1670. Mac is tutor and weapons master to a chieftain's son. In the present, Xavier St. Cloud returns. This time, he has mortal mercenaries with him. They shoot his Immortal target and leave Xavier with an easy kill. Xavier and his men arrive at the dojo, but Mac and Charlie, warned by Joe, manage to escape death. Mac goes after Xavier, and Charlie goes with him. While Mac and Xavier battle, Mac spots Horton, the renegade Watcher who killed Darius. Mac, distracted, is shot and "killed," but manages to fall down an elevator shaft and out of sword range of Xavier. Xavier and Horton flee. Charlie is wounded. Mac goes to the cemetery to find Horton alive and well. "I'm the man you can't kill." Horton tells

Travis as Renee Delaney; Alexandra Stewart as Catherine Legris; Denis Fouqueray as Detective Malle; Pierre Lacan as Henri Martin; Manuel Bonnet as Cavalry Captain; France Anglade as Shop Owner; Jean François Pages as Luc Bergon; William Cagnard as Marc Cluny

French battlefield, 1814. Mac fights with a Highland regiment. Mac promises a dying French officer to pass on his signet ring to his son. In the present, as Charlie regains his strength, Joe attempts to help Mac and gives him an address. Mac follows the lead and finds Xavier. They battle. Horton intervenes with a high-powered weapon, and he and Xavier flee. Mac follows the evil duo to Paris. He is followed by Special Agent Delaney, who is searching for a killer. Ultimately, Horton almost escapes, but Joe shoots his brother-in-law. "It's finished, James." Mac and Joe make peace. Mac, with the help of his new neighbor, Maurice, finally finds Xavier and takes his head. It is over, or so it seems, until we see that Horton still lives.

Mac of the unholy alliance between himself and Xavier. Xavier will lead Horton to Mac, and Horton has promised Xavier he will be the last Immortal. Mac discovers that Joe saved Horton's life the first time around because Horton was Joe's brother-in-law, but Horton was cast out from the Watchers. Joe vows he knew nothing of Horton's evil plans, but Mac doesn't care.

#93215 Unholy Alliance, Part II
Writer: David Tynan
Director: Peter Ellis
Roland Gift as Xavier St. Cloud; Peter Hudson as James Horton; Stacey

#93216 The Vampire
Writer: J. P. Couture
Director: Dennis Berry
Jeremy Brudenell as Ward; Denis Lill as Baines; Trevor Peacock as Jacom; Tonya Kinziger as Juliette; Nathalie Presles as Helene; Jack Galloway as Peter Wells; Peter Vizard as William Stillwell; Claire Keim as Waitress; Michel Feller as Gentleman; Nigel

Nevinson as Doctor; Chrystelle LaBaude as Clerk

Paris, 1840. Immortal Nicholas Ward kills the owners of a business he wants. Feeding on popular frenzy and not blood, he covers his killings by making it appear that a vampire is terrorizing Paris. Mac prevents Ward from marrying (and then murdering) the murdered man's daughter and heir, but Ward escapes. In the present, Ward is back to his old evil tricks, now covering his motivated murders under the guise of serial killings. And, as before, he's earning his money the old-fashioned way, "he marries it." Mac and Joe team up to protect his next victim. In the end, Mac and Ward battle, and Ward loses his head.

#93217 **Warmonger**
Writers: Christian Bouveron & Lawrence Shore
Director: Bruno Gantillon
Peter Firth as Drakov; Angeline Ball as Beth; Tom Watson as Eli Jarmel; Alexandre Klimenko as Bartov; Andre Oumansky as President Chescu; Jerzy Rogulski as Vice President; Daniel Breton as Bodyguard; Frederic Witta as Nikov; Anna Miasedova as Katarina; Julie du Page as Nicole; Dominique Hulin as Ivan; Chinko Rafique as Cashier

Soviet Union, 1919. Mac saves the aristocratic and innocent Abernovs from the evil Immortal Drakov by promising not to fight him. In the present,

Drakov, now called Arthur Drake, remains an evil mastermind. Mac meets him, again, at the ballet, and stops Eli Jarmel from trying to shoot Drakov. Eli explains to Mac that his wife and two children were murdered by Drake. Eli tries again to "kill" Drakov and is shot in the attempt. On his deathbed, Eli begs Mac to kill Drakov. Mac finally explains the truth to Eli and tells of his promise. Eli urges Mac to recant and end the terror. "You think your word to Drake is honor? This is not about honor. This is about your pride, your vanity." Mac finally relents. "Eli, he won't kill again." "You promise?" "For whatever it's worth." "Good." And Eli dies. In the end, Mac fights Drakov and takes his head.

#93218 **Pharaoh's Daughter**
Writers: Elizabeth Baxter & Martin Broussellet
Director: Dennis Berry
Nia Peeples as Nefertiri; James Faulkner as Constantine; Jerry di Giacomo as Victor Benedetti; Diane Bellego as Angela Constantine

Mac senses an Immortal in an ancient sarcophagus and opens it to find Nefertiri, a handmaiden of Cleopatra's, buried two thousand years ago with her dead queen. Mac teaches her the ways of the modern world and becomes her lover. Nefertiri vows revenge when she finds Marcus Constantine, her former lover. The Egyptian Nefertiri blames the onetime Roman general for the death of her beloved mistress. Constantine is now a historian and museum curator who has turned his back on battle. He wishes only to preserve the past and remind people of history's lessons. But the newly revived Nefertiri sees only her recent past, not two thousand intervening years of history, and cannot let go. Nefertiri murders Constantine's wife, Angela. In the end, Mac must face her to save Constantine. She tries to kill him, and when she nearly succeeds, he takes her head. "Life always chooses life."

#93219 **Legacy**
Writer: David Tynan
Director: Paolo Barzman
Elizabeth Gracen as Amanda; Nadia Cameron as Rebecca; Emile Abossolo-

M'bo as Luther; James Smillie as John Bowers; Pierre Martot as Raynard; Roger Bret as Vender; Joseph Rezwin as Paul Millet; Louise Vincent as Alice Millet; Alan Brandon as Retailer; Bernard Herve as Hooded Leader; Gay Dhers as Hooded Man

Verona, Italy; September 11, 1635. Mac meets Amanda and her friend and teacher, Rebecca. When Amanda lifts Mac's purse, he retrieves it and offers to pay for their drinks. In the present, Rebecca is killed by another of her students, the Immortal Luther. Luther forces Rebecca to lay down her sword in exchange for her mortal husband, John's, life. Amanda vows revenge when she learns of Rebecca's death from John. Amanda comes to Mac for a last farewell, before her likely death at the hands of the formidable Luther. When Mac discovers her plan, he tries to take on her battle, believing he has a better chance of survival. We learn that Luther is hunting for pieces of an ancient crystal that Rebecca divided among her students. He believes that reuniting the pieces to create a whole crystal will make him invulnerable and ensure that he is the last Immortal. In the end, Mac and Amanda are left standing and Luther has fallen to Mac's blade.

#93220 **Prodigal Son**
Writers: Christian Bouveron & Lawrence Shore
Director: Dennis Berry
Michael Siberry as Hyde; Valerie Steffen

as Inspector Bardot; Nicolas Chagrin as Segur; Michelle Seeberger as Wife; Clement Harari as Scientist; Blake Dawson as Clerk; Xavier Jaillard as Attendant

Rural Scotland, 1630. Mac meets Martin Hyde, but Hyde has no interest in the newborn Immortal, Mac; Hyde wants Connor. In Paris, in 1700, Hyde kills Mac's friend and mentor, Segur, again not interested in the young Immortal Mac. In the present, Richie

returns; he needs Mac's help. An Immortal has been following him, refusing to fight him, but committing grisly murders wherever Richie goes. Richie is blamed for the homicides. Mac discovers that the man behind the killings is none other than his old

nemesis Hyde. But Hyde is not after the hatchling Richie; he is after the Quickening of an Immortal now worth taking, MacLeod. Richie is arrested for the murders. Mac tricks Hyde. The police shoot Hyde and take his sword. They find evidence to free Richie and implicate Hyde. In the end, Mac defeats Hyde. Later, Mac and Richie share a bottle of cognac, given to Mac by Segur, toasting old friends.

#93221 **Counterfeit, Part I**
Writer: Story by David Tynan; teleplay by Brad Wright
Director: Paolo Barzman
Martin Cummings as Pete; Meilani Paul as Lisa Halle; Peter Hudson as James Horton

England, 1730. Mac almost gets beheaded for poaching. In the present, Pete Wilder saves Richie from attack by men wearing Watcher tattoos. Richie is grateful to his new friend, but Mac is wary. When Mac's distrust gets Pete killed, Mac begins to doubt himself. Unknown to Mac, it is all part of James Horton's evil plan. Horton is secretly training escaped killer Lisa Halle to go after Mac when he's troubled and where he's most vulnerable, his heart. In the end, we see Lisa's new face, the work of a plastic surgeon. Lisa is now a dead ringer for Mac's mortal love, Tessa.

#93222 **Counterfeit, Part II**
Writer: David Tynan
Director: Dennis Berry

Alexandra Vandernoot as Lisa Halle/Milon; Peter Hudson as James Horton

Joe arrives in Paris to warn Mac that Horton may be alive and after Mac's head. But Mac has now met "Lisa Milon," and is thinking only of Tessa. Mac remembers Paris, 1983, when he tells Tessa about his immortality. Back in the present, Mac has an affair with Lisa, while Richie worries. Finally, Richie goes to Joe for help. As they search for the truth, Richie takes a bullet meant for Joe and saves his life. Then Lisa is kidnapped. His friends warn him that it's a trap, but Mac knows he cannot bury "Tessa" again. Only when Lisa tries to kill Mac does he see the truth. Lisa is killed, and Mac finally has a showdown with Horton. In the end, there is only one.

Season 3

"He is Immortal, born in the Highlands of Scotland four hundred years ago. He is not alone. There are others like him—some good, some evil. For centuries, he has battled the forces of darkness, with holy ground his only refuge. He cannot die unless you take his head, and with it, his power. In the end, there can be only one. He is Duncan MacLeod. The Highlander."

Adrian Paul as Duncan MacLeod; Stan Kirsch as Richie Ryan; Philip Akin as Charlie DeSalvo; Jim Byrnes as Joe Dawson; Lisa Howard as Anne Lindsey; Michel Modo as Maurice

#94301 **The Samurai**
Writer: Naomi Janzen
Director: Dennis Berry
Tamlyn Tomita as Midori/Maia; Robert Ito as Hideo; Stephen McHattie as Michael Kent

Japan, 1778. Mac is shipwrecked. He is befriended and aided by the samurai Hideo Koto. Before Hideo commits *seppuku* (ritual suicide) for the "crime" of harboring the barbarian MacLeod, Mac vows to Hideo that he will protect the Koto family for as long as he lives. In return, Hideo gives Mac the dragonhead katana that the Highlander uses to this day. In the present, Midori Koto witnesses the murder of her lover at the hand of her rich and powerful husband, Michael Kent. In response, she kills her husband. Midori goes to Mac for help, but we soon discover that Midori's husband is not dead; he is an Immortal. In order not to dishonor her family, Midori returns to her abusive husband and loveless marriage. Kent finally challenges MacLeod. Using the katana bequeathed him by Hideo, Mac takes Kent's head and frees Midori.

#94302 **Line of Fire**
Writer: David Tynan
Director: Clay Borris
Randall "Tex" Cobb as Kern; Chandra West as Donna

March 13, 1872; American Indian encampment. Mac's adopted Lakota family, Little Deer and her son, Kahani, are killed, and the people of their village are massacred by soldiers led by the Immortal scout, Kern. In the present, Donna, a former girlfriend of Richie's, returns with an eighteen-month-old child that she claims is Richie's son. Mac reminds Richie that Immortals cannot father children, but Richie wants the family he never had and might never be able to have again. When Donna finds Richie's sword, he is at a loss to explain. The older and wiser Mac tries to tell Richie it would be kinder and safer for his adopted family if he left them. When Kern threatens Donna and the baby, Charlie, Richie understands that Mac is right. Finally, Mac defeats the evil Kern and takes his head, while Richie lets go of the only family he will ever have.

#94303 **The Revolutionary**
Writer: Peter Mohan
Director: Dennis Berry
Miguel Fernandes as Karros; Liliana

Komorowska as Mara; Bernard Cuffling as Harry Wellfleet; John Novak as Mason; Andrew Kavadas as Anthony Dourcef; Lisa Vultaggio as Elda; Robert Iseman as Mike; L. Harvey Gold as Bourchek

Mexican Revolution; June 19, 1867. Mac and his fellow Immortal Paul Karros fight for Mexico and against Maximilian. Karros is a former Roman slave who once fought his way to freedom with Spartacus. In the present, Karros is leading a band of Balkan freedom fighters. Karros asks Mac to join the fight, but Mac refuses. However, Charlie is tempted by both the justice of the cause and by Karros' comrade-in-arms, the beautiful Mara. When a local negotiator for peace, Father Stefan, is nearly killed in an assassination attempt, Mac comes to realize that Karros is determined to fight at any cost, even to the point of trying to kill a trusted friend, murdering the hit man and sabotaging a possible peace agreement. When Mara discovers the truth, she threatens to expose Karros. He, in turn, attempts to kill her. Mac is forced to challenge Karros and defeat his old comrade. When Mara returns home, Charlie decides to accompany her and help her people rebuild their lives. Meanwhile, we meet emergency room doctor Anne Lindsey.

#94304 **The Cross of St. Antoine**
Writer: Morrie Ruvinsky
Director: Dennis Berry
Elizabeth Gracen as Amanda; Brion James as Armand Thorne/John Durgan; David Longworth as Father Peter; David Hauka as Martin Blinder; Jason Gray-Stanford as Jonah; Lloyd Berry as Billows; Gerry Rousseau as Rafe; Willow Johnson as Miss Welsley; Charles Andre as Bellam; J. B. Bivens as George

Fort Wolfe, Montana; 1817. The evil Immortal Durgan murders a priest and steals the Cross of St. Antoine. Mac vows to the dying priest that he will return the cross. In the present, Joe's new ladylove, art historian Lauren Gale, is murdered. Mac agrees to help Joe bring Lauren's killer to justice. Mac finds the Cross of St. Antoine on display in the Thorne Museum of Antiquities and discovers that wealthy, powerful, intellectual art collector Armand Thorne is really the formerly illiterate Durgan. He killed Lauren because she had discovered that many of his objets d'art were stolen. Mac persuades Amanda to come out of retirement and help him steal the cross and lure Durgan out of hiding in his protected fortress of a museum. Durgan kidnaps Joe and threatens to kill him; he wants to exchange Joe for the cross. In the end, with Amanda's help, Mac tricks Durgan into leaving holy ground. Mac challenges Durgan, takes his head, and fulfills his promise to return the Cross of St. Antoine.

#94305 **Rite of Passage**
Writer: Karen Harris
Director: Mario Azzopardi
Gabrielle Miller as Michelle Webster; Rob Stewart as Axel Whittaker; Alan Scarfe as Craig; Elizabeth Gracen as Amanda; Marie Stillin as Nancy Webster; Alexa Gilmour as Sharon; Robert Iseman as Mike; Lisha Snelgrove as Singer

Boston, 1896. Mac encounters the Immortal Axel Whittaker and his beautiful protégée. Mac soon discovers that Axel doesn't train his pupils, but keeps them dependent on him, and when they are of no more use to him, he takes their heads. In the present, Michelle Webster, the rebellious daughter of old friends of Mac's, is killed in a car accident. Anne tries to save her life, but it is too late. Or is it? As we soon learn, Mac has come to the hospital not only to comfort the grieving parents, but to sneak the newly born Immortal, Michelle, out of the morgue. Mac tries to be her teacher, but she has no use for the serious MacLeod. She wants to have fun, and when she meets Axel, he promises her just that. But Axel uses Michelle to lure Mac to his yacht. The challenge is met, and Mac takes his enemy's head. Michelle, witnessing her first Quickening, decides that Mac was right and agrees to be trained as an Immortal by Amanda.

#94306 **Courage**
Writer: Nancy Heiken
Director: Charles Wilkinson
John Pyper Ferguson as Brian Cullen; Stefan Arngrim as Harry; Jonathan Scarfe as Alan Kelly; Jennifer Copping as Katherine; Mark Acheson as Laszlo; Catherine Lough as Marcia; Peter Bryant as Orderly; Colleen Rennison as Robin; Marc Baur as Mike Barrett

Switzerland, 1810. Mac and renowned swordsman Immortal Brian Cullen are traveling when Cullen is challenged by a mortal. In San Francisco, in 1854, Mac finds Cullen in an opium den, scared and trying to forget the challengers waiting for him. In the present, Cullen is still addicted to drugs and alcohol. He runs into Richie at Joe's and decides to go after him. During a high-speed game of Chicken with Richie, Cullen crashes into a bus full of

passengers. Many are killed. Mac tries to convince the once-great Cullen to stop abusing drugs and alcohol, but Cullen believes Mac is simply trying to take away his courage and make him helpless. Meanwhile, Mac begins dating Anne. Cullen attacks Mac, and Richie points out that he's no longer the best; he's simply a junkie. Mac tries to defend Cullen: "I think who you are can depend on who you meet. Who would I be if Connor MacLeod had never found me? If I had never met Fitzcairn, Tessa, or you?" Mac believes he can still help Cullen, but it is too late. Cullen tricks Mac into meeting him, then runs him down before trying to take his head. Mac is nearly killed, and in the end, he must defeat his old friend.

#94307 The Lamb

Writer: J. P. Couture
Director: Dennis Berry
Myles Ferguson as Kenny; Eric Keenleyside as Dallman Ross; Alf Humphreys as Frank Brody; Linden Banks as Commander; Jesse Moss as Sean; Christina Jastrzembska as Catherine

Virginia, 1862. Mac helps slaves escape to freedom on the Underground Railroad. During battle, he meets the young drummer boy Sean, an Immortal. Sean asks for Mac's protection, but Mac must help the runaway slaves. He leaves Sean in what he believes to be a safe place, but to no avail. Mac returns to find the boy dead. In the present, Mac and Richie meet the Immortal Kenny, who had his first death at the age of ten. Seemingly innocent "young" Kenny asks "older" Immortals for paternal protection, then, as we later learn, surprises them and takes their heads. Kenny attempts to get Mac, but is thwarted by Anne. Kenny tries to get Anne out of the way, permanently, by running her down. Mac, after talking to Richie and Joe, finally realizes the truth and arrives in time to rescue Anne. Mac goes after Kenny to stop him from killing again and they battle, but Kenny escapes Mac's blade by getting on a school bus filled with young children.

#94308 Obsession

Writer: Lawrence Shore
Director: Paul Ziller

Cameron Bancroft as David Keogh; Nancy Sorel as Jill Pelentay; Sherry Miller as Sarah Carter; Duncan Fraser as Mr. Renquist; Laura Harris as Julia Renquist; Kim Kondrashoff as Henry Carter; Nancy Sivak as Ginny; John R. Taylor as Jake

Philadelphia, 1825. Mac acts as Immortal David Keogh's second, when the former indentured servant asks Julia's father for her hand in marriage. Julia rejects Keogh. In the Pacific Northwest, in 1882, Mac is in love with the beautiful Sarah and plans to marry her, but, unknown to Mac, she is already married. When her husband arrives in town, Mac tries to get Sarah to run away with him, but she refuses. When her husband shoots him and Mac revives, Sarah rejects Mac, and he finally leaves. In the present, Keogh wants to marry the mortal Jill, but she wants nothing to do with the Immortal Keogh. Jill goes to Mac for help, hoping he can convince Keogh to leave her in peace. Mac tries to get Keogh to face the truth. When Jill is accidentally killed while trying to get away from Keogh, Keogh blames Mac. They battle, but Mac cannot take his old friend's head.

#94309 Shadows

Writer: David Tynan
Director: Charles Wilkinson
Garwin Sanford as John Garrick; Frank C. Turner as Official; Margaret Barton as Hag; Catherine Lough as Marcia; Dorian Joe Clark as Cop One;

Jonathan Palis as Sheriff; James Timmins as Merchant; Amy Adamson as Margaret of Devon; James Rogers as Cory

English village, 1665. Mac finds his old friend Immortal stonecutter Garrick, about to be burned at the stake as a witch. Mac tries to defend his friend, but then he, too, is accused. Mac escapes, believing that Garrick has as well. But unbeknownst to Mac, Garrick is recaptured and burned. In the present, Mac is tormented by dark visions of his own death. Anne tries to convince him to seek professional help, but Mac refuses. Instead, he seeks out his old friend, Garrick, who convinces Mac that this specter is merely a racial

memory that haunts all Immortals and that the only way for Mac to defeat the dreamlike hooded figure is to lay down his sword and accept it. When Mac, exhausted, sees the figure for the last time, and puts down his sword, we see that it is no longer a trick of the mind. It is Garrick, seeking revenge for what he views as Mac's abandoning him to the flames, to be burned alive, centuries earlier. At the last moment, Mac realizes it is Garrick and no mere shadow. Mac saves his own life and takes Garrick's head. Anne, frustrated that Mac has secrets he cannot or will not share, leaves him.

#94310 **Blackmail**
Writer: Morrie Ruvinsky
Director: Paolo Barzman
Bruce Dinsmore as Robert Waverly; Anthony De Longis as Lyman Kurlow; Barbara Tyson as Barbara Waverly; Kelly Fiddick as Johnny Sondringham; Bill Croft as Peter Matlin; Vincent Gale as Will Lattimore; Justine Priestley as Lisa Crane; P. Adrien Dorval as Jailer; Gordon Tipple as Hangman

English town, 1805. Immortals Peter Matlin and Lyman Kurlow kill a young gentleman, Lattimore, for his money. They then frame Mac's friend Johnny for the murder. Mac confesses and is hanged to save his friend. Mac challenges Kurlow, but Kurlow escapes. In the present, lawyer Robert Waverly is leaving his mistress's apartment when he sees Mac and Matlin in combat. Waverly gets the fight, the Quickening, everything, on tape. He then tries to blackmail MacLeod; if Mac kills Waverly's wife, Barbara, then Waverly will not turn Mac in to the police. Mac refuses. However, when Matlin's partner, Kurlow, comes after Mac, Waverly proposes another deal to Mac. Waverly will kill Kurlow, Mac will kill Barbara, and the police will never suspect a connection. Waverly shoots Kurlow, who revives and strangles the lawyer. Mac knows he will be accused of the killing and realizes he will have to leave town and start anew. Joe and Mac go to see Barbara, to try to tell her what really happened. They arrive to find Kurlow holding Barbara and waiting for MacLeod. Mac rescues Barbara and takes Kurlow's head. Barbara exonerates Mac with the police, thanks him for saving her life, and promises she knows nothing about what she saw on the videotape.

#94311 **Vendetta**

Writer: Alan Swayze
Director: George Mendeluk
Tony Rosato as Benny Carbassa; Ken Pogue as Simon Lang; Stella Stevens as Margaret Lang; Tamara Gorski as Peggy McCall; Michael Sunczyk as Sid; Edgar Davis Jr. as Joey; Aurelio Di Nunzio as Sal; Ernie Prentice as Gray-haired Man

Seacouver, 1938. Mac meets petty gangster Immortal Benny Carbassa and falls under the spell of singer Peggy McCall at the Coconut Lounge. Benny tries to warn Mac that Joey and Sid Lankovski own the club and Peggy is Joey's girl. But Peggy dances with Mac to make Joey jealous. As it turns out, Sid wants Peggy. He shoots and "kills" MacLeod and then his own brother. He tells Peggy they shot each other. In the present, Benny turns Mac over to aging mobster Simon Lang, aka Sid Lankovski, who wants Mac dead. He thinks that Mac is actually Mac's grandson and that the Mac of the 1930s told his grandson everything. When Mac confronts Simon, Peggy learns the truth. She kills Simon for murdering his brother and her true love in 1938. Meanwhile, Anne returns, determined to give their relationship another try and to not push Mac to reveal his secrets.

#94312 **They Also Serve**

Writer: Lawrence Shore
Director: Paolo Barzman
Mary Woronov as Rita Luce; Michael Anderson Jr. as Ian Bancroft; Barry Pepper as Michael Christian; Vivian Wu as May-Ling Shen; Marc Baur as Mike Barrett; Oliver Becker as Justin Russell; Lorraine Landry as Maureen Russell; Mina E. Mina as Kahn

Outer Mongolia, 1780. Mac trains under Master May-Ling Shen. Eventually, Duncan and May-Ling become lovers. In the present, Immortal Michael Christian has been taking heads from unarmed and vulnerable opponents, including May-Ling. How is Christian having such success? It seems his Watcher, Rita Luce, is doing more than simply observing; she is interfering, providing Christian with information about his fellow Immortals. Darius' and May-Ling's former Watcher, Ian Bancroft, confronts Rita, and she kills him. MacLeod, unaware of Rita and Christian, decides to go to the Island on a vision quest. Richie goes to Joe and tells him that Mac is alone on the Island without his sword. Rita overhears and tips Christian. Joe

Jr. as Carlos; Celine Lockhart as Nun; Ravinder Toor as Cop; Robert Iseman as Mike; F. Braun McAsh as Derelict

Spanish Civil War, 1937. Mac and the Immortal Kage are journalists covering the war. But Kage betrays Mac and has his friends shot so that he will be on the profitable "winning" side. In Cambodia in 1975, Kage is dealing heroin

finally realizes what is going on and warns Richie. Richie goes to the Island with Mac's katana, but Mac has managed to take Christian's head with his own sword. When Mac returns to Joe's, Rita knows Christian is dead.

#94313 **Blind Faith**
Writer: Jim Makichuk
Director: Gerry Ciccoritti
Richard Lynch as Kage/John Kirin; Conrad Dunn as Matthew; Dave Cameron as Todd Milchan; Nick Vrataric as Tim Parriot; Alfonso Quijada

and refuses to help Mac rescue refugee children, who are then killed by the Khmer Rouge. In the present, Kage is called John Kirin, and he has become a religious leader. When he "dies" in Anne's emergency room and then returns from the "dead," his followers believe it's a miracle. When a tabloid reporter covering the "miracle" turns up dead, Mac is certain that Kirin is guilty. Mac confronts Kirin, who vows to Mac that he's changed, the deaths of those innocent Cambodian children forever transforming him into a man of peace. As it turns out, the real killer is a follower of Kirin's who believed that he was protecting Kirin. In the end, Mac and Kirin have made their peace, and Kirin leaves, hoping to do good.

#94314 **Song of the Executioner**
Writer: David Tynan
Director: Paolo Barzman
David Robb as Kalas; Eugene Lipinski as Paul; John Tench as Max Jupe; Demetri Goritsas as Timon; Vince Metcalfe as Dan Tarendash; Lynda Boyd as Karen; Katherine Lough as Marcia; Paul Bittante as Detective; Allixandria East as Nurse

European monastery, 1658. Mac takes sanctuary with the immortal Paul in the monastery that he founded to provide refuge for solitude, peace, and healing of the spirit. Mac meets Kalas, an Immortal with a heavenly singing voice. Alas, his spirit does not match his voice and Mac discovers that Kalas has been taking the heads of Immortals as they leave holy ground. Mac has Paul banish Kalas from his beloved monastery world. Kalas vows revenge. In the present, Paul and his monastery choir are touring. Kalas has now gotten Paul off holy ground and takes his head. Meanwhile, Anne is blamed for negligence in the deaths of two patients, and drugs are found at Joe's Bar. Mac realizes that Kalas is out to destroy all he holds dear. Mac challenges Kalas and soon discovers that Kalas is as skilled as he is, maybe better. To save his head, Mac falls from the concert hall catwalk, landing, seemingly dead, at Anne's feet. Kalas escapes, and Mac goes to France, allowing Anne to think he's dead, but it is far from over.

#94315 **Star-Crossed**
Writer: Jim Makichuk
Director: Paolo Barzman
Roger Daltrey as Hugh Fitzcairn; David Robb as Kalas; Frederic Witta

as Patrick; Valerie Zarrouk as Naomi; Gian-Franco Salemi as Prince; Elodie Frenck as Arianna; Guillaume Barriere as Scribe; Gerard Touratier as Watch; Fabrice Bagni as Manservant; Virginie Peignien as Inspector

Verona, Italy, 1637. Mac meets Immortal Hugh Fitzcairn. Mac works for the prince, protecting his beautiful and supposedly virtuous daughter, Arianna. But it seems Mac's martial skills are no match for Fitz's amorous skills. The

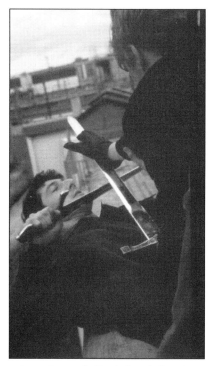

prince demands Fitz's head, but Mac demands his right to retribution and "kills" Fitz with his sword, thus saving his life. The two become friends for life. In the present, Fitz picks up his old friend Mac at the airport. Fitz has

found true love with the beautiful Naomi, and he's teaching at the Cordon Bleu. But when Naomi's jealous ex-lover Patrick is found dead next to a computer displaying Fitz's falsified credentials, the innocent Fitz goes on the run. Mac realizes it's happening again; Kalas is now in Paris, and he's trying to destroy Mac's oldest and dearest friend. Kalas finds Fitz under the bridge at the Bastille, and Fitz challenges him. As a horrified Mac watches, bound not to interfere, Kalas takes Fitz's head. Mac challenges Kalas, but he escapes. Mac mourns Fitz.

#94316 **Methos**
Writer: J. P. Couture
Director: Dennis Berry
Peter Wingfield as Methos; David Robb as Kalas; Carmen Chaplin as Maria Campolo; Patrice Valota as Marc Saracen; Olivier Marchal as Philippe; Jean François Pages as Basil Dornin; Ken Samuels as Roger; George Birt as Don Salzer; Charles Maquignon as Bartender; Denis Sylvain as Inspector; Debbie Davis as Danielle

Paris, 1920. Mac encounters Kalas, now known as opera virtuoso Antonio Neri. When Kalas attempts to kill a young woman under Mac's protection, Mac challenges Kalas, and they fight. Kalas escapes, but not before Mac inflicts a near-beheading wound to the throat, destroying the singer's vocal cords and the angelic voice that has been his life for centuries. In the present, Richie joins a top-level motorcycle racing team. Meanwhile, Watcher Don Salzer is killed by Kalas. Joe realizes that Kalas is looking for Methos, the legendary, and possibly mythological, oldest living Immortal. Kalas believes that with Methos' Quickening he will be invincible. Joe advises Mac to go visit Methos scholar Adam Pierson at the University. Mac and Adam meet. "Duncan MacLeod of the Clan MacLeod, have a beer. Mi casa es su casa." Mac sees the truth: "Methos." Meanwhile, Kalas discovers his secret and challenges Methos, who nearly loses. Methos realizes that he will not be able to defeat Kalas and offers Mac his head, believing that the two of them can defeat Kalas in this way. Mac refuses and challenges Kalas, but Methos and the police arrive to arrest Kalas for Salzer's murder, and the battle is not finished. Methos admonishes, "Remember, Highlander: live, grow stronger; fight another day."

#94317 **Take Back the Night**
Writer: Alan Swayze
Director: Paolo Barzman
Kim Johnston Ulrich as Ceirdwyn; Benjamin Pullen as Bonnie Prince Charlie; Marc Edouard Leon as Paolo; Peter Semler as Callum; Jean François Pages as Basil Dornin; Ariane Le Roux as Neva; David Gregg as Steven; Frank Messin as Gaston; Terence Leroy-Beaulieu as Mario; Jonathan Zaccai as Louis; Antony Miceli as Raoul; Olivier Siou as Laurent; Thierry Bois as Blond Man; John Charles Maratier as Angus

Scotland, 1746. After Culloden, Mac and Ceirdwyn aid Bonnie Prince Charlie in his escape from Scotland. But Mac will not leave with his prince; he wants the English to pay. Later, Ceirdwyn finally convinces Mac that revenge is not the answer, not even in the aftermath of the bloody battle of Culloden. In the present, when Ceirdwyn and her mortal husband are killed by a street gang, she uses her skills as an ancient Celtic warrior to hunt them down and exact revenge. Ultimately, Mac reminds Ceirdwyn of the lesson she taught him: revenge solves nothing. In return, Ceirdwyn reminds Mac that although loving a mortal can be dangerous for the mortal, it is up to the mortal to make the choice. Mac decides to call Anne and tell her the truth. Richie, meanwhile, "dies" in a crash that claims the life of the champion motorcycle racer Basil.

#94318 **Testimony**
Writer: David Tynan
Director: Dennis Berry
Alexis Daniel as Kristov; Selina Giles as Tasha; Xavier Schliwanski as Alexei; Georges Keyl as Bohdan; Bertrand Lacy as Doctor Chandon; Lawrence Shore as Man at Airport

Russian Steppes, 1750. Mac shares the fire and food with Kristov's band of Cossacks. But when the Cossacks slaughter innocent farmers who are living on the czar's land and burn their village, MacLeod intervenes. In the present, Mac tells Anne the truth about his immortality, and she flies to Paris. At the airport, Anne saves the life of a young woman, Tasha, who is smuggling drugs for Kristov. Mac tells Anne everything about who he was and what he is. Meanwhile, Mac vows to stop Kristov, but Kristov kidnaps Richie. Kristov offers Mac a deal: kill Tasha and stop her from testifying against him, or Kristov will take Richie's head. Mac arrives to save Richie, but Richie gets free, faces Kristov, and takes his head. Richie leaves Paris.

#94319 **Mortal Sins**
Writer: Lawrence Shore
Director: Mario Azzopardi
Roger Bret as Father Bernard; Andrew Woodall as Ernst Daimler; Claude Berthy as Father Guillaume; Jean-Claude Deret as Georges Dalou; Thierry Gary as Iggy; Georges Janin as Young Bernard; Laurent Deutsch as Young George; Lyes Salem as Aram; Pierre Rousselle as Jean

France, 1943. Mac is with the French Resistance when he meets the young boy Bernard. Bernard sees Mac "die" and then revive. Mac swears him to secrecy, but Bernard has his own wartime secret; he accidentally killed a Nazi major, Ernst Daimler, and tossed him in the Seine. In the present, Daimler appears at Bernard's, now Father Bernard's, church. Father Bernard realizes that Daimler is like Mac and asks Mac for help. Daimler is again training brownshirts, and he needs to be stopped. Meanwhile, Anne tells Mac

that she is pregnant by an old friend who comforted her after Mac's "death." Daimler kills Mac's old friend and fellow Resistance fighter, Georges. When Daimler kills Father Bernard and nearly kills Anne, Mac must take Daimler's head. Anne witnesses it all and realizes what being part of an Immortal's life really is. As a doctor and a mother-to-be, Anne cannot deal with the part of herself that wanted Mac to kill Daimler. Anne decides to leave Mac.

#94320 **Reasonable Doubt**
Writer: Elizabeth Baxter
Director: Dennis Berry
Paudge Behan as Lucas Kagan; Geraldine Cotte as Simone Tomas; Richard

Lintern as Tarsis; Delores Chaplin as Clarise; Robert Cavanah as Franklin Waterman; Jacques Ciron as Head Clerk; Didier Terron as Claude; Rebecca Potok as Madame Camille; Laurence Mercier as Woman; Olivier Kandel as Young Kagan; Pierre Alexis Hollenbeck as Rudy; Azzedine Melliti as Rene

Paris, 1930. Immortals Kagan and Tarsis rob a bank where Mac is transacting business. When innocents are shot by Tarsis during the getaway, Mac finds the robbers and kills Tarsis, but does not challenge Kagan because he was not a murderer. In the present, a Leonardo da Vinci sketch is stolen, and two guards are killed. Mac offers to act as a go-between to ransom the drawing. Mac soon discovers that it was stolen by Kagan. Meanwhile, Mac's neighbor, Maurice, asks Mac to speak to his troubled niece, Simone. Mac

learns the worst when he discovers that not only is Simone a prostitute, she's Kagan's accomplice. Mac goes after Kagan, but Kagan protests his innocence and vows to change his ways if Mac will spare him. When Mac and Maurice find Simone, the only remaining witness to the killing of the guards, dead, Mac knows that Kagan will never change. Mac challenges Kagan and takes his head.

#94321 **Finale, Part I**
Writer: David Tynan
Director: Mario Azzopardi
Elizabeth Gracen as Amanda; David Robb as Kalas; Peter Wingfield as Methos; Roland Gift as Xavier St. Cloud; Sian Weber as Christine Salzer; John Suda as Hamza; Debbie Davis as Danielle; Emmanuel Karsen as Nino; Patrick Albenque as Genet; Charles Maquignon as Gerard; Mykhael Georges-Schar as Businessman

Algiers, 1653. Xavier confronts Mac's friend and mentor, Hamza. Mac tries to intervene, but Xavier is not interested in the young MacLeod. Mac is surprised when Hamza decides to flee rather than fight. Mac refuses to leave, and Hamza is killed by Xavier. In the present, Amanda accidentally helps Kalas escape from prison. (She was trying to break him out, so she could challenge him and take his head.) Kalas kidnaps Amanda to use her as bait, but she escapes. Meanwhile, Christine Salzer, widow of the Watcher killed by Kalas (in **"Methos"**), decides to get revenge on both Immortals and Watchers by turning over the Watcher Chronicles to the media. Dawson and Methos, as mild-mannered Watcher Adam Pierson, try to convince Christine not to do it. Dawson, desperate to stop her, tries to kill her outside the newspaper office, but Mac and Methos stop him. As Christine enters the building, they all know their lives will never be the same.

#94322 **Finale, Part II**
Writer: David Tynan
Director: Dennis Berry
Elizabeth Gracen as Amanda; David Robb as Kalas; Peter Wingfield as Methos; Sian Weber as Christine Salzer; George Harris as Vemas; David

Gilliam as Jeremy Clancy; Matthew Geczy as Martin; Emmanuel Karsen as Nino; Karim Salah as Sultan; Albert Pariente as Guard

Constantinople, 1753. Amanda is masquerading as a dancing girl for the Sultan, but is arrested as a thief when she steals his jewels. Mac rescues her before the sentence can be carried out. In the present, Mac and Amanda finally declare their love for each other. Meanwhile, Christine is telling all to newspaper publisher Clancy, but before the story can be printed, Kalas kills Christine and Clancy, and steals the disk. Kalas then offers Mac a deal: Mac's head for the disk. Joe and the Watchers try to find Kalas, but to no avail and at the cost of more dead Watchers. Methos, Amanda, and Joe try to talk Mac out of facing Kalas, but soon realize there is no other choice. Mac agrees to meet Kalas on top of the Eiffel Tower. Mac finally defeats Kalas and takes his head. The resulting Quickening, amplified by the Tower, causes a power surge that disrupts all the computers in Paris, including Kalas'. The information on the disk is destroyed, and anonymity for the Watchers and the Immortals seems ensured. Mac, Amanda, Joe, and Methos share a champagne toast: "To old friends and new ones."

Season 4

"He is Duncan MacLeod, the High-lander. Born in 1592 in the Highlands of Scotland, he is still alive. He is Immortal. For four hundred years he's been a warrior, a lover, a wanderer, con-stantly facing other Immortals in com-bat to the death. The winner takes his enemy's head and with it, his power.

"I am a Watcher, part of a secret society of men and women who observe and record, but never interfere. We know the truth about Immortals. In the end, there can be only one. May it be Duncan MacLeod. The High-lander."

Adrian Paul as Duncan MacLeod; Stan Kirsch as Richie Ryan; Jim Byrnes as Joe Dawson

#95401 **Homeland**
Writer: David Tynan
Director: Adrian Paul
Carsten Norgaard as Kanwulf; Kristin Minter as Rachel MacLeod; Laurie Holden as Debra Campbell; Matthew Walker as Ian MacLeod; Scott McNeil as Robert MacLeod; Anna Hagan as Mary MacLeod; Ewan Clark as George Lalonde (Sudsy); John Tierney as Angus; William Samples as Bruce; Gerard Plunkett as James Bailey; Robert Moloney as Kevin McSwain; Billy Mitchell as Brian McSwain; Forbes Angus as Constable; Andrew MacGregor as Donal

Glenfinnan, Scotland, on the shores of Loch Shiel; 1618. MacLeod, before he became an Immortal, is in love with the beautiful Debra, but she is betrothed to his cousin, Robert. The cousins are forced to battle when Robert, learning Debra loves Mac, challenges Mac. Against his will, Mac kills Robert. But the lovers are not to be; there is only further tragedy when Debra accidental-ly falls to her death. In Glenfinnan, Scotland, in 1624, Mac, now Immor-tal, returns home because he has learned that his village has been attacked and his father gravely wound-ed. Mac claims his father's sword and goes after the Viking marauder Kan-wulf. They meet and do battle, and Mac believes he has killed the Immor-tal Kanwulf. Alas, Mac is too newly Immortal—he has not yet met his teacher, Connor—to know that an Immortal must take his enemy's head. In the present, Mac buys a Celtic heir-loom at an antiquities sale; it is the bracelet he gave Debra in 1618. When she died, he buried it with her. Duncan decides to return home for the first time in over 250 years and restore the bracelet to its rightful resting place. Back in the Highlands, he meets a kinswoman, Rachel MacLeod, who tells him of a centuries-old legend: "He came back from the dead to claim his father's sword, he killed the Viking, and stopped the slaughter." When two locals are killed, Mac is reminded of Kanwulf. When he meets the village "minister," Father Laird, Mac knows his fears are well founded; it is Kanwulf, returned to find the mystical axe that Mac took from him in 1624. Mac and Kanwulf battle, and Mac takes the Viking's head. Once more, Duncan MacLeod of the Clan MacLeod has returned to save his village.

#95402 **Brothers in Arms**
Writer: Morrie Ruvinsky
Director: Charles Wilkinson
Wolfgang Bodison as Andrew Cord; Philip Akin as Charlie DeSalvo; Liliana Komorowska as Mara; Chris Bradford as Young Joe Dawson; Jeffrey Renn as Young Ian Bancroft; Garrison Chrisjohn as Dr. Weldon; Mercedes Tang as Vietnamese Woman

Joe Dawson meets an old friend, Andrew Cord. Cord is the marine sergeant who saved Joe's life back in 1968, after the mine explosion in Vietnam that took his legs. While recovering in the hospital, Joe met Ian Bancroft, who explained to Joe that Cord was an Immortal. Ian recruited Joe to become a Watcher. When Charlie DeSalvo returns and tries to assassinate Cord, we learn that Cord is not the man Joe believes him to be. While they were in the Balkans, Cord killed Charlie's love, Mara, and tried to kill Charlie. Mac wants to fight Cord to save Charlie, but Joe begs Mac not to battle Cord. Cord, however, goes after Charlie and kills him. Charlie dies in

Mac's arms, but not before Mac reveals the truth to Charlie, that both he and Cord are Immortals; Charlie could never have killed Cord. Mac challenges and defeats Cord but, blaming himself for Charlie's death, ends his friendship with Joe.

#95403 **The Innocent**
Writer: Alan Swayze
Director: Dennis Berry
Pruitt Taylor Vince as Mikey; Callum Keith Rennie as Tyler King; Philip Hayes as Alan Wells; Chilton Crane as Helen Wells; Dwight McFee as Jack Spice; Darryl Shackelly as Chaske;

Hagan Beggs as Doc Hobbs; Patrick Stevenson as Lockport; George Austin as Anderson; Craig Brunanski as Sheriff; Bobby Stewart as Officer Winston; Terry Howson as Water Delivery Man

McKewansville, Dakota Territory; 1868. Mac saves the Native American Chaske from Spice, a slaver. When Mac takes him into town for medical treatment, Chaske kills Spice and is, in turn, killed. In the present, Richie meets the Immortal Mikey, a large man of limited mental development who is fascinated with trains. Mikey is alone because Alan, the Immortal who had been taking care of him, is killed by the Immortal Tyler King and also because Mikey has accidentally killed Alan's wife, Helen, while trying to keep her quiet during the battle. Richie brings home Mikey to Mac, but Mac warns Richie of the difficulties of trying to take care of Mikey. King comes for Mikey, but Mac will not allow it and ultimately takes King's head. When the police try to arrest Mikey for Helen's and Alan's murders, Mikey kills one of the policemen. Mac and Richie now both realize that Mikey is a danger not only to himself, but to those around him. Richie takes responsibility for Mikey, but Mikey seems to realize the truth and lays his head down on the train tracks. Meanwhile, Mac buys an old house that he begins to renovate.

#95404 **Leader of the Pack**
Writer: Lawrence Shore
Director: Mario Azzopardi

Justin Louis as Peter Kanis; Travis MacDonald as Mark Roszca; Venus Terzo as the Duchess; Rachel Hayward as Valerie Meech; Jenafor Ryane as Alicia; Kim Restell as Julie; Yee Jee Tso as Gerard; Greg Rogers as Detective Sheridan; Veena Sood as Shandra Devane; Christopher Gaze as Sheriff; Michael Dobson as Cop; Christopher Lovick as Shepherd

England, 1785. Mac is consort to a duchess. There he meets the Immortal Kanis and his dogs. Kanis is the leader of a pack of dogs. The dogs run down and exhaust Kanis' prey, and Kanis then moves in for the kill. In the present, Kanis and his dogs are back and tracking Mac, who is now teaching at the university. In the end, Mac finally defeats Kanis with a bit of help from a friend. Richie, meanwhile, has seen Mark Roszca, the young junkie who killed Tessa and Richie ("**The Darkness**"). The police do not believe Richie, who can hardly tell them the real reason he knows Mark is Tessa's killer. Richie vows revenge. When Mac learns that Mark is now clean and sober and has a pregnant fiancée, he moves on. How can he do to her what Mark did to him when he killed Tessa? But Richie wants blood. However, in the end, Richie finally allows Mark and his budding family to go free.

#95405 **Double Eagle**
Writer: David Tynan
Director: Mario Azzopardi
Elizabeth Gracen as Amanda; Nicholas

Campbell as Kit O'Brady; Tim Henry as Jim Rainey; Garvin Cross as Ray; Tony Marr as Laundry Worker; Mario Azzopardi as the Count

San Francisco, 1888. Amanda wins the Double Eagle saloon from Immortal Kit O'Brady in a poker game. Kit is furious not only that she won his beloved casino, but also that she threw his good-luck Double Eagle coin into the sewer. In the present, Kit is in town, looking for a change of luck and a partner with money who can help him buy a racehorse. Kit still blames Amanda for a century of bad luck. When Amanda arrives, Mac tries his best to keep them apart, but to no avail. Amanda and Kit threaten to kill each other, but Mac has

a better idea. He's bought the racehorse, named Double Eagle, for Amanda and Kit, making them partners. When the horse wins the big race, Amanda and Kit decide making money is more fun than making war. In the end, Amanda allows Kit to win her share of the horse in a game of draw.

#95406 **Reunion**
Writer: Elizabeth Baxter
Director: Dennis Berry
Elizabeth Gracen as Amanda; Lisa Howard as Anne Lindsey; Myles Ferguson as Kenny; Mike Preston as Terence Kincaid; Ryan Michael as Sheriff; Luc Corbeil as Merriman; Joel Wirkkunen as McPhee; Lisa Butler as Kenny's Mother

South Pacific, 1778. Mac is ship's pilot on Captain Kincaid's mutinying ship. Mac saves Kincaid from a beheading, leaving him marooned on a deserted island, knowing it won't be his true death. But two centuries later, Kincaid is not thanking Mac for saving his head in return for a century of endless deaths. In the present, Kincaid enters the scene chasing Kenny, the child Immortal. Kenny runs to Anne for help. Mac agrees to hide Kenny for one night. At Mac's, Amanda and Kenny reunite. It seems that Amanda was Kenny's teacher; she found him after his first death in 1182 and trained him to survive by both his wits and his sword. Kenny decides that what he wants most, now, is Mac's head, so he tries to hand it straight to Kincaid.

When Mac defeats Kincaid, Kenny tries for Mac's head, but Amanda stops him, and Kenny escapes once again.

#95407 **The Colonel**
Writer: Durnford King
Director: Dennis Berry
Elizabeth Gracen as Amanda; Sean Allan as Simon Killian; Lisa Butler as Melissa; Dave "Squatch" Ward as Cisco; Antony Holland as The General; Sean Campbell as Sergeant Merton; Christine Upright-Letain as Andrea Henson

French battlefield; Armistice Day, 1918. Red Cross worker MacLeod witnesses Colonel Simon Killian sending his troops into bloody battle after he knows World War I has officially ended. At the colonel's court-martial, Mac testifies not only to the massacre but to Killian's mental instability, ensuring that the Immortal will be locked up for "life" rather than be shot. In the present, Killian is back for revenge. Meanwhile, Amanda befriends a mortal, Melissa, who wants so much to be like Amanda that she copies her clothes and hairstyle. Killian kidnaps Melissa, thinking she is Mac's girl-friend. Melissa is seriously hurt. When Mac goes after him, Killian locks Mac up in a subterranean vault, wanting Mac to suffer the seventy years of captivity that he did. Amanda, refusing to believe that Duncan is dead, convinces Joe to break the rules and help her find Mac. Amanda and Joe free Mac. Now free, Mac defeats Killian in combat. In the end, Amanda decides to leave town, upset at the harm she caused to Melissa, but before she goes, she asks Mac to make peace with Joe, because life is too short. Mac goes to see Joe, and the two men share a drink.

#95408 **Reluctant Heroes**
Writer: Scott Peters
Director: Neill Fearnley
Peter Outerbridge as Paul Kinman; Kevin McNulty as David Markum; Jill Teed as Kaayla Brooks; Nicola Cavendish as Queen Anne; Tony Scanling as Lord Dennis Keating; Fred Henderson as Desantis; Stephen Dimopoulos as Vince Petrovic; Kevin Lesmister as Earl of Welsley; Eileen Barrett as Alice Markum; Peter Bryant as Cop

England, the court of Queen Anne; 1712. Immortal Paul Kinman kills Mac's friend Lord Dennis Keating in a duel after he had promised Mac he would not do so. Mac wants revenge, but promises Queen Anne he will not fight while she reigns. In the present, when coming home from the movies, Mac and Richie witness a murder attempt on grocer David Markum and his wife. Mac saves David, but his wife, Alice, is killed. Mac and Richie go after the killer and discover it is Mac's old enemy Kinman, now a hired assassin. Kinman and Mac begin a battle, but the police arrive to arrest Kinman. FBI agent Kaayla Brooks asks Mac and Richie to testify against Kinman, but they refuse. Mac cannot take Kinman's

head if Kinman is in jail. David begs Mac to testify, and Mac finally relents. Meanwhile, we learn that Agent Brooks is Kinman's lover. She kills her own partner to break Kinman out of jail. Kinman then kills her. Mac finally faces Kinman and avenges the deaths of Dennis Keating and Alice Markum.

#95409 **The Wrath of Kali**
Writer: David Tynan
Director: Duane Clark
Kabir Bedi as Kamir; Veena Sood as Shandra Devane; Sue Mathew as Vashti; Brent Stait as Colonel Nigel Ramsey; Molly Parker as Alice Ramsey; Alec Willows as Martin Millay

India, 1764. Mac is liaison for the British Colonel Ramsey. At court, Mac meets the Immortal Kamir, who is a priest of the goddess Kali. While out riding one day, Mac comes upon a funeral and "rescues" the newly widowed Vashti before she can join her husband on his funeral pyre. Vashti and Mac become lovers, but she ultimately does what duty requires, and joins her husband in death. In the present, an ancient statue of the Hindu goddess Kali is purchased by the university at which Mac teaches. Kamir comes to town, determined to return the Kali to her ancestral Bengali homeland. Not everyone agrees. After the dealer who sold the Kali to the university is found murdered, Mac realizes that Kamir is up to his old ways. Mac tries to stop the killing by returning the Kali to Kamir. But when Kamir goes after Mac's friend Professor Shandra Devane, Mac decides the only way to finally stop Kamir is to challenge him. Kamir is defeated, but Mac understands and respects his beliefs. In the end, Mac sends home the Kali.

#95410 **Chivalry**
Writers: Michael O'Mahony & Sacha Reins
Director: Paolo Barzman
Peter Wingfield as Methos; Ann Turkel as Kristin; Emmanuelle Vaugier as Maria Alcobar; Beverley Hendry as Louise Barton

Normandy, 1659–1660. After rescuing her from bandits, Mac becomes the Immortal Kristin's protégé and lover as she teaches him to become a gentleman. However, when she commissions his portrait, Mac falls in love with the painter, the lovely Louise. When Mac tries to leave Kristin, she kills Louise and tries to take Mac's head. In the present, Kristin seduces another young Immortal, to whom she believes she has much to teach: Richie. Methos arrives in town in the guise of mild-mannered Watcher Adam Pierson to tell Mac that Kristin is in town and seeing Richie. Mac tries to warn Richie about Kristin, but Richie will not listen. When Kristin

#95411 **Timeless**
Writer: Karen Harris
Director: Duane Clark
Peter Wingfield as Methos; Ron Halder as Walter Graham; Rae Dawn Chong as Claudia Jardine; Ocean Hellman as Alexa Bond; Brent Fidler as Jeremy Beaufort; David MacKay as Gremio

Rural England, 1663. Mac is in Walter Graham's traveling Shakespeare troupe. In the present, Walter, who has shepherded the careers of mortals for centuries, sees his golden opportunity when he meets the world-renowned pianist Claudia Jardine. Walter kills

tries to take his head, Richie realizes Mac is right. Mac and Methos go to Kristin and arrive in time to save Richie's friend, Maria, from drowning. Mac battles Kristin, but cannot kill a woman he has held in his arms. Methos, born centuries before the age of chivalry, has no such compunction, and takes Kristin's head.

Claudia at what he considers the pinnacle of her genius and beauty. She becomes Immortal. Walter is elated. Claudia is stunned, then stricken, when she realizes her musical genius has vanished with her mortality. Claudia comes to understand that it was her fear of her own death that created her musical spark. She refuses to pick up a sword or learn to defend herself, so she can regain that fear and her music. Meanwhile, Methos, in the guise of Adam Pierson, falls in love with Alexa, a waitress at Joe's. Alexa initially rebuffs his advances, but finally relents. And then Joe reveals the truth: Alexa is terminally ill. Methos gives her a choice: to spend her remaining time dying or spend it living, with him. Alexa chooses life, and she and Methos leave to travel the world in her remaining time.

#95412 **The Blitz**
Writer: Morrie Ruvinsky
Director: Paolo Barzman
Lisa Howard as Anne Lindsey; Duncan Fraser as Captain; Alison Moir as Diane Terrin; Beverley Elliott as Karen; Robert Iseman as Mike Lundy; Tim Dixon as Harry; Tracy Olson as Lord Sewell; David Adams as Emcee; Brent J. D. Sheppard as Rescuer; George Gordon as French Officer; Byron Lawson as Second Rescuer

London, October 1940. Mac is trapped in the Underground during the Blitz with the woman he loves, reporter Diane Terrin. Ultimately, they run out of air, and Diane dies in his arms. Mac, of course, survives. In the present, Dr. Anne Lindsey and paramedic Mike Lundy respond to a call for help when an explosion devastates a subway station. A further explosion kills Mike and traps the pregnant Anne and another woman, Karen. Mac desperately tries to reach Anne, before he loses her like he lost Diane. Mac finally reaches Anne, and Mac and Karen help

deliver the baby. Anne's daughter is named Mary, after Mac's mother. After they are rescued, Mac presents Anne and Mary with the house that he has been renovating.

#95413 **Something Wicked**
Writer: David Tynan
Director: Dennis Berry
Byron Chief-Moon as Jim Coltec; Benjamin Ratner as Bryce Korland; Darcy Laurie as Harry Kant; Carla Temple as Denise; Dan Muldoon as Captain; Michael Gall as Tall Beatnik; Colin Foo as Clerk; Carl Chase as Robert Davis

American West, 1872. Mac's Sioux family and the people of their village are all killed. Mac is filled with hate and a need for revenge. Later that year, Mac meets the Immortal Coltec, who "heals" him. Coltec is a Hayoka, a Native American holy man who takes evil into himself to protect his people and bring peace. In Greenwich Village, New York, in 1958, Coltec beheads Beat poet Korland, an evil Immortal Mac has been tracking. In the present, Coltec's people are now all dead, so he feels responsible for taking on the evil of the world. However, Coltec is growing weaker, unable to handle so much darkness. When he kills the evil Immortal Kant, it is too much, and the evil finally takes over. Mac realizes Coltec is in trouble and tries to help his old friend, but it is too late. Mac must take Coltec's head, and with it the Dark Quickening. Mac is changed. He stops by Joe's Bar and hits Joe. He then returns to the dojo and tries to take Richie's head, but is stopped by Joe Dawson, who shoots him. Joe contemplates taking Mac's head and ending the cycle of evil, but cannot. Joe releases Mac, who flees town and boards a ship.

#95414 **Deliverance**
Writer: David Tynan
Director: Dennis Berry
Peter Wingfield as Methos; Michael J. Jackson as Sean Burns; Carl Chase as Robert Davis; Valeria Cavalli as Dominique Davis; Kristin Minter as Rachel MacLeod; Geoffroy Boutan as Claude Massanet; Morgan Cooke as Antoine; Patrick Burgel as Albert; Julien Bizot as Driver

France, 1917. Mac transports a shell-shocked soldier to Sean Burns' hospital. Sean is a psychoanalyst dedicated to healing the mind. In the present, the evil MacLeod arrives in Le Havre. After a contretemps, Mac is rescued on the brink of death by Methos, who soon discovers how evil Mac has become. Mac threatens to take Methos' head on holy ground. Mac steals a car, tries to run down Methos, and goes to visit his

old friend Sean Burns. But instead of asking for help, Mac takes Sean's head as Methos helplessly watches. Methos realizes the only way to stop Mac might be to kill him, but Mac escapes, again, and heads to Paris. He finally ends up in Darius' church, begging God to help him or stop him. Methos tracks him down and convinces Mac to go to a holy spring. When Mac enters the spring, carrying his father's sword (brought to Paris by Rachel MacLeod, at Methos' request), he is confronted by his evil self, and they fight. In the end, Duncan MacLeod of the Clan MacLeod triumphs over the evil.

#95415 **Promises**
Writer: Lawrence Shore
Director: Paolo Barzman
Kristin Minter as Rachel MacLeod; Ricco Ross as Kassim; Ben Feitelson as Nasir Al Deneb; Vernon Dobtcheff as Hamad; Tomer Sisley as Reza; Peta Wilson as Inspector; Karim Salah as Boadin Al Deneb; Soumaya Akaaboune as Aliya; Dine Souli as Official

North Africa, 1755. Mac's young friend Reza is to be executed. Mac makes a deal with Kassim, the Immortal prefect of the land: if Reza is allowed to escape, Mac promises Kassim he will owe him a favor for a favor, a life for a life. In 1460, Kassim promises his dying lord, Boadin Al Deneb, that one day the house of Al Deneb will again rule the land. In the present, Kassim demands that Mac fulfill his centuries-old promise and assassinate Hamad, the tyrannical dictator of a small Middle Eastern country, in order to put a good man, Nasir Al Deneb, on the throne. Mac's inability to do so gets Kassim "killed" and makes it impossible for him to serve the Al Deneb family as he has for centuries. Mac tries to help by asking Hamad to promise a life for a life. Mac saved Hamad; now Hamad must spare Nasir. Hamad promises Mac he will do it, but instead kills Nasir. Meanwhile, Kassim sets fire to the barge and kidnaps Rachel MacLeod to force Mac to fight. Mac defeats Kassim, but does not take his head. Rachel returns home to the Highlands of Scotland. In the end, Mac goes to Hamad and reminds him that he did not fulfill his promise to spare Nasir, but Mac will now keep his word: he throws Hamad from the window. "A life for a life."

#95416 **Methuselah's Gift**
Writers: Michael O'Mahony & Sacha Reins
Director: Adrian Paul
Elizabeth Gracen as Amanda; Peter Wingfield as Methos; Anthony Hyde as Nathan Stern; Jamie Harris as Daniel Geiger; Nadia Cameron as Rebecca; Patrick Serraf as Man; Guy Amram as Kelly

Masked thugs try to take Amanda's head while she sleeps and steal the crystal given to her centuries ago by her teacher, Rebecca. It seems Amanda's crystal is part of the Methuselah Stone, a mystic talisman said to bring eternal life and invulnerability to the wearer.

When Amanda breaks into the Watcher Gallery to steal the remaining crystals and finds Methos already there, she becomes convinced that Methos was the one who tried to kill her, in order to complete the stone. In truth, Methos is trying to complete the stone, but not for himself. He hopes to save Alexa, who is dying in Geneva. Together Amanda and Methos decide to steal the crystals, but are caught by the head of the Watchers, Stern. Amanda escapes with the crystals, but Methos is shot. Stern then offers Amanda a trade, Methos' life for the crystals. Despite a double cross, Amanda and Mac rescue Methos, but in the process the stone comes apart, the pieces of the crystal lost in the river.

#95417 **The Immortal Cimoli**
Writers: Story by Sophie Decroisette; teleplay by Scott Peters
Director: Yves Lafaye
Elizabeth Gracen as Amanda; Crispin Bonham Carter as Danny Cimoli; Simon Kunz as Damon Case; Louise Vincent as Lina Cimoli; Roger Lumont as Marco Mastina; Patrick Mille as Jean-Philippe de Lefaye III; Stephane Boucher as Edward Bellamy; Veronique Baylaucq as Annie; T. C. Holmes as Immortal
English countryside, 1795. Mac's student Jean-Philippe is killed by Damon Case, who believes that Immortals' ritual combat is his purpose for being, ordained by God. In the present, magician Danny Cimoli is hit by a truck and "killed." When he awakens he realizes

he is the Immortal Cimoli. Amanda and Mac find him at the circus, taking bullets to the heart to the delight of the crowds, who think it's all an act. Mac and Amanda try to tell Danny about the Game and other Immortals, but Danny is mainly interested in becoming a magician better known than Harry Houdini. When Case arrives to claim Danny's head, Mac realizes it is too late for Danny to train. Mac challenges Case and defeats him. Danny finally heads to Vegas. When another Immortal finds Danny, he has achieved his fifteen minutes of fame. Meanwhile, Mac and Amanda go to Moscow with the circus.

#95418 Through a Glass Darkly

Writer: Alan Swayze
Director: Dennis Berry
Peter Wingfield as Methos; Dougray Scott as Warren Cochrane; Struan Rodger as Bonnie Prince Charlie; Gresby Nash as Andrew Donnelly; Laura Marine as Nancy Goddard; Luc Bernard as Inspector Deon; F. Braun McAsh as Innkeeper; Shannon Finnegan as Sarah; George Salmon as James

Eriskay Island, Scotland; 1745. Mac and Warren Cochrane fight to free Scotland from English oppression and put Bonnie Prince Charlie on the throne. In 1746, Cochrane is "killed" just prior to Culloden. Mac goes on alone, but the Scots suffer a brutal defeat at the hands of the English at the battle of Culloden. In Normandy, in 1786, Mac and

Cochrane meet with the aging Prince Charlie, who is now a drunkard, clearly unfit to lead men or to rule, but Cochrane sees only his beloved Bonnie Prince Charlie. In the present, Methos has returned to France, and Alexa has passed on. While at the cemetery, Mac encounters his old friend and comrade, Cochrane. But Cochrane cannot remember who or what he was. As he and Mac try to put the pieces back together, Mac, with a little help from Methos, finally discovers the awful truth. Cochrane has become delusional about Prince Charlie and in a rage killed his own student, Andrew Donnelly, for daring to say something against the prince. Cochrane finally remembers what he has done and challenges Mac so that Mac will fight and kill him. Mac defeats him, but will not take his head. As Mac leaves, Cochrane again sees only his beloved Prince Charlie.

#95419 Double Jeopardy

Writer: David Tynan
Director: Charles Wilkinson
Stacey Travis as Renee Delaney; Marc Warren as Morgan D'Estaing; Roland Gift as Xavier St. Cloud; Jean-Paul Muel as Inspector Dufay; David Gabison as Manager; Hester Wilcox as Angela; Richard Lukas as Detective; Philippe Bouclet as Philippe D'Estaing; Stan Reitz as Bernard D'Estaing; Pascal Laurent as Hastings

France, 1806. Lieutenant MacLeod leads British troops taking over the

D'Estaing estate. In the present, CID Agent Renee Delaney ("**Unholy Alliance**") returns to ask for Mac's help in finding a killer. It seems someone robbed a diamond store by using poison gas. All the evidence points to Xavier, but Mac knows St. Cloud is dead; he took his head. It is soon revealed that the culprit is Xavier's student Morgan D'Estaing. Morgan poisons a police inspector and nearly kills Renee, but Mac saves her. Morgan is then arrested, but fakes suicide in jail and escapes. Morgan and Mac finally battle, and although Morgan cheats and uses a poisoned dagger, Mac is victorious and takes his enemy's head.

[Note: In the United States, "**Double Jeopardy**" did not air as part of the fourth season. It was aired as part of the Paris section of season five.]

#95420 **Till Death**
Writers: Story by Beatrice Mathouret; teleplay by Michael O'Mahony & Sacha Reins

Director: Dennis Berry
Peter Wingfield as Methos; Roger Daltrey as Hugh Fitzcairn; Jeremy Brudenell as Robert de Valicourt; Cecile Pallas as Gina de Valicourt; Michael J. Jackson as Sean Burns; Michel Feller as Footman

Château de Valicourt, 1696. Mac and Fitz vie for the hand of the beautiful Gina. To test her suitors, she enlists their help in recovering stolen gold from Robert, Baron de Valicourt. Instead of recovering the gold, however, Gina loses her heart to the daring Baron de Valicourt, and they are married; every century the lovers renew their vows before their friends and fellow Immortals. In the present, however, the Valicourt marriage is on the rocks. Gina wants out, but Robert wants his marriage to survive. Mac agrees to play Cupid and attempts to reunite the couple. His plan? Enlist Methos' help in staging a fight with Robert. Methos and Robert "battle," and Gina does realize she loves her

husband. Gina and Robert are reunited. One problem: Gina is now determined to take the head of the man who tried to "kill" her husband. Gina finds Methos at the barge, but it all works out in the end, and Gina asks Mac to again give away the bride.

#95421 **Judgment Day**
Writer: David Tynan
Director: Gerard Hameline
Peter Wingfield as Methos; Stephen Tremblay as Jacob Galati; Jesse Joe Walsh as Jack Shapiro; Graham McTavish as Charlie; Benjamin Boyer as David Shapiro; Danielle Durou as Realtor; Nicolas Bonnefous as Gate Guard; Christine Rivere as Nadia

Joe is called to Paris with the news that Mac is dead. When he arrives at Mac's barge, however, he sees Mac. Before they have a chance to speak, Joe is kidnapped. Methos arrives, and Mac tells him about Joe. With a bit of prodding, Methos agrees to see what "Adam" can find out. As it turns out, Joe has been taken by the Watchers and put on trial for treason by the Watcher Tribunal. It seems Watcher-related deaths have risen dramatically since Joe told Mac about the Watchers. The Watcher Tribunal is determined to stop the killings and punish Joe. Mac tries to help his friend, and argues his case before the Tribunal. Methos arrives as Adam and also pleads for Joe. But when the son of Tribune Shapiro is killed, there is no hope. Joe is found guilty and condemned to death at dawn. Mac escapes, but Joe will not

leave; he believes he is guilty of breaking his Watcher oath. As the execution is about to take place, all hell breaks loose, as Immortal Jacob Galati mows down everyone with a machine gun. Mac arrives to save Joe, but what he finds is a lot of dead Watchers.

#95422 **One Minute to Midnight**
Writer: David Tynan
Director: Dennis Berry
Peter Wingfield as Methos; Stephen Tremblay as Jacob Galati; Jesse Joe Walsh as Jack Shapiro; Romina Mondello as Irena Galati; Peter Hudson as James Horton; Michel Feller as Mikel; Yan Epstein as Jean Dumar; Xavier Jaillard as Magistrate; Zoltan Csala as Guard; Manuel Guillot as Emile; Oliver Vitrant as Watcher

Central Europe, Gypsy camp; 1847. Mac is traveling with Immortal Gypsies Jacob and Irena Galati. Irena is raped, and Jacob kills her attacker. In the present, a wounded Joe has been saved by Methos and is hiding in his wine cellar. As Mac investigates, he discovers the person who has been killing Watchers is Jacob. In 1992, Horton and his renegade Watchers found Jacob and Irena and took her head. Jacob, nearby, took her Quickening. Jacob escaped, vowing to destroy any mortal tattooed with the Watcher symbol. Mac tries to convince him that not all Watchers are killers, but is hard-pressed to prove it when the Watchers begin hunting Jacob as they have been hunting MacLeod. Methos helps Joe get to Shapiro with news of the real killer, likely saving MacLeod, but condemning Jacob. The Watchers capture Jacob with Joe's help, and Shapiro beheads him, as the nearby Mac receives his old friend's Quickening. Mac threatens to kill Shapiro in retaliation and to let all-out war begin. But Mac shows leniency so that it will be over and there will be peace. Shapiro is removed from office. Joe's death sentence is rescinded, and he is allowed back into the Watchers. Adam Pierson is never seen again, as Methos makes the choice of who he is.

[Note: In the United States, **"One Minute to Midnight"** aired as the opener of season five.]

Season 5

"He is Duncan MacLeod, the Highlander. Born in 1592 in the Highlands of Scotland, he is still alive. He is Immortal. For four hundred years he's been a warrior, a lover, a wanderer, constantly facing other Immortals in combat to the death. The winner takes his enemy's head and with it, his power.

"I am a Watcher, part of a secret society of men and women who observe and record, but never interfere. We know the truth about Immortals. In the end, there can be only one. May it be Duncan MacLeod. The Highlander."

Adrian Paul as Duncan MacLeod; Stan Kirsch as Richie Ryan; Jim Byrnes as Joe Dawson

#96501 **Prophecy**
Writer: David Tynan
Director: Dennis Berry
Tracy Scoggins as Cassandra; Gerard
Plunkett as Roland Kantos; Jeremy
Beck as Young Duncan MacLeod;
Matthew Walker as Ian MacLeod;
Anna Hagan as Mary MacLeod; Allan
Clow as Neil MacGregor; Deryl Hayes
as Andrew Beckmann; Tom Heaton as
Old Tom; Ernie Pitts as Cop; Cluny
MacPherson as Robert MacLeod;
Kaspar Michaels as Partner

Glenfinnan, Scotland; 1606. Young
Duncan MacLeod had heard of the
Witch of Donan Woods, but he
thought she was a fairy tale old men told
to scare young boys. That is, until the
day the "witch," Cassandra, saved him
from a wolf. Or did she? In the present,
Mac returns to Seacouver to find Cassandra waiting for him. She tells
MacLeod of a prophecy of a Highland
child born on the Winter Solstice who
has seen both darkness and light and
who can stop an evil one, Kantos. Cassandra warns Mac that he must be prepared; Kantos knows magic or the
power of suggestion, whatever it might
be called, and he can convince his
opponents of anything. Mac is nearly
defeated, but Cassandra saves him.
Kantos then uses his power to get the
police to kidnap Mac and bring him to
Kantos. With a little help from Cassandra, Mac and his younger self meet.
Mac doubts he will be able to defeat
Kantos, but the boy knows: "You'll win
because you're good and Good always
wins over Evil. Did you not know
that?" And the boy tells him how to
defeat Kantos' voice of darkness: don't
listen.

#96502 **The End of Innocence**
Writer: Morrie Ruvinsky
Director: Gerard Hameline
Real Andrews as Haresh Clay; Chris
Humphreys as Graham Ashe; Chris
Martin as Carter Wellan; Rachel
Hayward as Delila; Gerry Rousseau as
Raymond Fairchild; Gary Jones as
Hotel Guest

Europe, 1657. Immortals Wellan and Clay find Mac's mentor Graham Ashe and Mac. Clay challenges Ashe, who sends Mac to holy ground. They battle and Clay wins, but Ashe begs for his life. Clay takes his head. In the present, the last time Richie saw Mac ("**Something Wicked**"), Mac tried to take his head. While they've been apart, Richie has been making a name for himself. Mac tries to talk to Richie, but the lesson Richie has learned is that "There can be only one," and to get them before they get you. While at a bar, Richie meets Wellan, picks a fight, and takes his head. Now Clay is out to avenge his friend's death. Clay tracks Richie and, as they battle, breaks Richie's sword. Richie escapes, and Joe tells Mac what is going on. Richie tries to steal a sword and is arrested, thus saving him from Clay. Mac bails him out and gives Richie Ashe's sword. Richie and Mac both go after Clay, and Mac finally tells Richie the truth. Clay shamed Mac after Ashe was killed, and Mac did nothing. Richie allows Mac his revenge, and he takes Clay's head. In the end, Mac tells Joe, "For thousands of years Immortals have fought and Watchers have observed them. One day, there'll only be one of us left, and someday maybe none at all. Somebody has to record that we've lived. Somebody has to record the history we've seen and the lessons we've learned. I know what I said, but our lives, our story, has to be recorded not by some petty clerk, but by someone who feels, someone who does, someone who has honor, like you."

#96503 **Manhunt**
Writer: David Tynan
Director: Peter Ellis
Bruce A. Young as Carl Robinson; Eric McCormack as Matthew McCormick; Eric Keenleyside as Trey Franks; Stephen Dimopoulos as Seth Hobart; Aaron Pearl as Corman; Jim Leard as Detective Frayne; Rhys Williams as Talbot; Kevin Hansen as Clayton Hobart; Jo Bates as Glenda

Mac's old friend, Carl Robinson ("**Run for Your Life**"), has turned his life around and is now a major-league baseball superstar. Carl is challenged by the Immortal Corman after a game, and witnesses find him standing over the decapitated body. Carl is accused of murder and is forced to go on the run. Things go from bad to worse for Carl when Special Agent Matthew McCormick, an Immortal lawman who specializes in serial killings, takes on the case. We learn that McCormick and Carl share a past. In Louisiana, in 1854, McCormick was the son-in-law of slave owner Seth Hobart, the man who first "killed" Carl. McCormick became Carl's friend and teacher. However, McCormick believes Carl betrayed a promise by killing McCormick's in-laws, Hobart and his son, Clayton. McCormick is determined to make Carl pay for the murders by bringing him in now. However, when Trey Franks, the trainer for Carl's team, confesses to the killing, McCormick's chance is lost. McCormick, Carl, and Mac know that Trey is innocent, but Trey believes that it is better that he go to jail rather than Carl. Mac finally convinces McCormick and Carl to make peace, and together they fake Carl's death in a police shoot-out so that Trey can go free and Carl can teach him that everyone is worth something.

#96504 **Glory Days**
Writer: Nancy Heiken
Director: Gerard Hameline
Ian Tracey as Johnny Kelly; Marcia Strassman as Betsy Fields; Jim Crescenzo as Mr. Luca; Robin Mossley as Jimmy The Weasel; Aurelio Di Nunzio as Guard; Mike Kopsa as Tommy; Bob Dawson as O'Grady; Bob Wilde as Dominic Delio; Philip Heinrich as Bobby; Larry Morrison as Roadie; Mario Battista as Big Gino

New York City, 1929. Johnny K, a petty criminal, is killed by the mob and becomes Immortal. Mac tries to teach him, but he ignores Mac and goes off on his own. In the present, Johnny is now a cold-blooded assassin out for Mac's head, and he doesn't play by the Rules because he never had a teacher. Johnny attempts to "kill" Mac, so that he can then take his head. Mac finally forces Johnny out into the open by taking away his one advantage, secrecy. Mac plasters Johnny's face on seemingly every billboard and milk carton in town. Johnny finally comes out of hiding, they battle, and Mac takes his head. Meanwhile, Joe's old high school flame, Betsy, walks into Joe's Bar. She seems interested in Joe, but Joe seems unwilling. Joe eventually admits to Mac

that it is because he never told Betsy about the loss of his legs. In high school, they were the football hero and the prom queen. Now, thirty years later, Joe finally tells her the truth, and it doesn't matter to her. Old passions are renewed. However, when she tells him she is leaving town, Joe is convinced it is because of his legs. However, Betsy finally tells him the truth; she's married.

#96505 **Dramatic License**
Writers: Michael O'Mahony & Sacha Reins
Director: Peter Ellis
Elizabeth Gracen as Amanda; Sandra Bernhard as Carolyn Marsh; Alistair Duncan as Terence Coventry; April Telek as Roxanne; Keith Holmgren as Gerald; Stephen Sisk as Tim; Sheila Tyson as Assistant

England, 1786. Mac fights Immortal Terence Coventry, then teams up with him against a thieving barmaid. In the present, romance novelist Carolyn Marsh's latest best-seller, *Blade of the MacLeods*, features a dark-eyed sexy Scots hero named Duncan MacLeod and a boorish Englishman named Terence Coventry as his enemy. As Mac tries to find out how this seeming stranger knows so much about him, it is revealed that she is Conventry's estranged wife, determined to get revenge on her husband by blackening his name in her books and making Mac seem larger than life. It is Amanda who finally discovers the real truth. Carolyn still loves her husband, but is convinced she cannot compete with the heroines that Conventry has known during his long life. When Coventry learns this, he is stunned, for he madly loves his wife; the couple is reunited. Mac and Amanda create a little romance of their own as Duncan sweeps her off her feet.

#96506 **Money No Object**
Writer: James Thorpe
Director: Rafel Zielinski
Elizabeth Gracen as Amanda; Nicholas Lea as Cory Raines; Tim Henry as Sam Grinkhov; Tom McBeath as Detective Dennis Tynan; Alex Bruhanski as Reynaldo; John Moore as Farmer

Missouri, 1926. Mac and Amanda leave the circus and on the road meet smooth-talking Immortal Cory Raines as he robs an armored car, then gives a part of the money to a poor family.

Cory asks Amanda to join him, and they go on a five-state crime spree, robbing, faking death to get away, then having Mac, under protest, dig up Cory. In the present, Amanda is reunited with the charming Cory when he robs a check-cashing stand. Cory asks Amanda to help him rob the Federal Reserve and rejoin him in his carefree life of crime. Amanda is tempted by the adventure, which she misses. When Mac won't ask her to stay with him, she goes with Cory. When Cory's scheme goes astray and Amanda gets arrested, Mac finds Cory, stops the heist, and rescues a marching band, but gets blown up for his efforts. Then Mac, Richie, and Cory discover that Amanda has not been arrested, but kidnapped for real by Sam Grinkhov, the owner of the check-cashing stand, who wants his $1.4 million back. He calls Mac and offers to trade Amanda for the money, but Cory has already given away the

money. Mac, Richie, and Cory have a plan and work together to get back Amanda. When Amanda is safe, Mac finally has his revenge on Cory and blows him up. Amanda leaves, but tells Mac she will see him in Paris.

#96507 **Haunted**

Writer: Scott Peters
Director: James Bruce
Kathy Evison as Jennifer Hill; Kevin John Conway as Alec Hill; John Novak as Gerard Kragen; Lisa Butler as Genevieve Hill; Larke Miller as Woman

San Francisco, 1886. Immortal Alec's mortal wife, Genevieve, is killed by the Immortal Gerard Kragen, her former lover. Alec vows revenge on Kragen and makes Mac swear he will kill Kragen if Alec dies before he can. In San Francisco, in 1888, Mac tries to convince Alec to get on with his life. Alec will not listen; he believes in the eternity of the soul and is waiting for Genevieve. In the present, Alec's last wife, Jennifer, believes she is haunted by her husband's spirit. She goes to his old friend Mac for help. She believes Alec's spirit won't rest until the man who took his head is killed. She believes it is Kragen. Richie finds himself strangely attracted to the widow and she to him. Joe's not surprised. As he has to tell Richie, Richie is the one who took her husband's head. Mac, meanwhile, is hunting for Kragen, believing him to be Alec's killer. Mac takes Kragen's head. Mac returns to find out that not only

has he killed the wrong man, but that Richie has slept with Jennifer. When Richie finally tells Jennifer the truth, she asks Mac to take Richie's head to appease Alec. Mac refuses. Jennifer shoots Richie, and just before she is ready to take his head, MacLeod stops her, with the help of Alec's spirit.

#96508 **Little Tin God**

Writer: Richard Gilbert Hill
Director: Rafel Zielinski
Andrew Divoff as Gavriel Larca; Roger R. Cross as Derek Worth; Nathaniel DeVeaux as Reverend Thomas Bell; Steve Bacic as Luke; Terry Barclay as Paco; Christopher J. P. Racasa as Enrique; Kira Clavell as Coyatu

Peru, 1830. MacLeod meets Immortal Gavriel Larca. Larca is living with the Moche, an aboriginal Peruvian people who worship "The Decapitator," a god who takes the heads of his enemies. Larca has allowed the Moche to believe he is a god. Larca sacrifices Mac's guide, but this ritual blood sacrifice exposes the Moche to a fever, and the entire village dies. Larca will never forgive MacLeod for destroying his life and turning his people against him. In the present, Larca is again living as a god. He convinces unknowing newborn Immortals that he is God and has granted them the gift of eternal life. When he finds MacLeod, Larca enlists his disciples to kill Mac, by convincing them that Mac is Satan. Larca's followers do not understand their true nature, nor do they know the Rules of the

Game, even attacking Mac on holy ground. Larca is finally defeated when MacLeod enlists the help of a true man of God, Reverend Bell, who convinces one of Larca's newest pupils, Derek, to hear the truth.

#96509 **The Messenger**
Writer: David Tynan
Director: James Bruce
Peter Wingfield as Methos; Ron Perlman as the Messenger; Robert Wisden as William Culbraith; Awaovieyi Agie as Jeffrey; Patrick T. Gorman as Sergeant Hickson; Mitch Davies as Captain Greenwell; Lloyd Berry as Harry the Boat Guy

Andersonville, Georgia; 1864. Mac is imprisoned in the hellish Southern POW camp run by Colonel William Everett Culbraith. When Culbraith refuses to allow a surgeon to help the wounded Jeffrey, a runaway slave friend of Mac's, and Mac is forced to end his friend's suffering, Mac vows revenge. Unknown to Mac, Culbraith has just received news of the death of his wife and her children. In the present, Mac again meets Culbraith and wants to take his head. However, there is a new Immortal in town, a Messenger who preaches the word of peace. He believes all Immortals can lay down their swords and live as brothers. His name? Methos. Mac is convinced that this Methos is a false prophet and that if Richie, who has become a follower, puts down his sword in the name of peace, he will lose his head. The real Methos, however, is rather amused; he figures that anyone looking for Methos will go after the impostor, who's telling everyone who and where he is. Meanwhile, the Messenger tries to convert Culbraith and Mac to the way of peace.

Culbraith seems to be moved, and the battle is stopped, but later, he goes to the Messenger's house and takes his head. When the unarmed Richie arrives, Culbraith goes after him. Mac arrives with Richie's sword and, now armed, Richie takes Culbraith's head.

#96510 **The Valkyrie**
Writer: James Thorpe
Director: Richard Martin
Peter Wingfield as Methos; Musetta Vander as Ingrid Henning; Jan Triska as Nicolae Breslaw; Fulvio Cecere as Alan Wilkinson; Martin Evans as Colonel Stauffenburg; L. Harvey Gold as Igor Stefanovich; Peter Hanlon as Karl Brandt; Patrick Keating as Adolf Hitler; Dean Balkwill as David; Lim Leard as Detective Robert Frayne; Noah Heney as Brownshirt #1; Raoul Ganeev as Guard

Berlin, 1935. British Intelligence agent Mac discusses Hitler with Immortal Ingrid Henning. When two brownshirts beat David, a young Jewish friend of Mac and Ingrid's, Mac fights the brownshirts, but Ingrid reminds Mac that he has accomplished nothing; there are always more. In Berlin, in 1944, Mac, Ingrid, and Colonel Stauffenburg discuss Operation Valkyrie, a German plot to assassinate Hitler. Ingrid wonders whether she can go through with it; she has never before killed a mortal. In Rastenburg, East Prussia, on July 20, 1944, Mac plants a bomb in Hitler's bunker, but it does not kill the dictator. As Hitler staggers from the wreckage, Ingrid has a chance to shoot him, but she hesitates at pulling the trigger on an unarmed man, and the chance is lost. In the present, Ingrid has been making up for that mistake by becoming a one-woman crusade against dictators and tyrants, both real and possible. She vows there will never be another like Hitler. Interpol inspector Breslaw is on her trail. While he understands her motives, he believes she needs to be stopped. When she tries to kill Wilkinson, a neo-Nazi running for the Senate, Mac foils the attempt. When she kills a cop, Mac stops defending her. Then the police think they have killed her, but Mac knows she has not really been stopped. When Ingrid makes a second attempt on Wilkinson, planting a bomb that would kill hundreds of mortals, Mac confronts her and takes her head.

#96511 **Comes a Horseman**
Writer: David Tynan
Director: Gerard Hameline
Peter Wingfield as Methos; Tracy Scoggins as Cassandra; Valentine Pelka as Kronos/Koren; Richard Ridings as Silas; Marcus Testory as Caspian; Greg Michaels as Tippet; David Longworth as Paxton; Sotigui Kouyate as Hijad

Agua Dulce, Texas; 1867. Mac and the Texas Rangers chase Koren and his Comancheros. Mac almost takes Koren's head, but Koren escapes. In the present, Cassandra (**"Prophecy"**) returns. She knew Koren as Kronos, the leader of the Four Horsemen. In the Bronze Age they destroyed Cassandra's village. She vowed revenge, and has been hunting the Horsemen across the millennia. Kronos, it seems, has also come to town in search of a Horseman. It is Methos. Kronos gives Methos a choice: lose his head or join Kronos. Methos chooses survival. Cassandra tells Mac that Methos was one of the Four Horsemen and that after he murdered the people of her village, he took her as his slave. Mac does not want to believe her, but Methos ultimately confirms the story. "I killed ten thousand and I was good at it. And it wasn't for vengeance, it wasn't for greed; it was because I liked it. I was Death. Death on a horse." MacLeod is devastated. Cassandra goes after Kronos, but Methos saves her. Mac, meanwhile, in search of Cassandra, confronts Kronos, and they fight. Methos interrupts the battle. Mac promises Cassandra that

they will find Kronos and Methos. Methos, meanwhile, must face Kronos, who wants to know why Methos saved MacLeod. Methos tells Kronos that Caspian and Silas are alive and that he saved Kronos so that the Four Horsemen could ride again.

#96512 **Revelation 6:8**
Writer: Tony DiFranco
Director: Adrian Paul
Peter Wingfield as Methos; Tracy Scoggins as Cassandra; Valentine Pelka as Kronos; Richard Ridings as Silas; Marcus Testory as Caspian; Bertie Cortez as Dr. Cernaveda; Betrand Milliot as Inmate; Nathalie Gray as Nurse

One by one, Methos and Kronos are reuniting the Horsemen. Silas is living in the Ukrainian forest. Caspian is imprisoned in a Romanian asylum for the criminally insane. Mac and Cassandra track the Horsemen to Romania, where Methos leaves behind a clue. Or does he? Cassandra believes it is a trap; nonetheless, Mac and Cassandra follow Methos and company to Bordeaux. The Horsemen have a new plan for world domination. They no longer need horses and swords to strike terror in the hearts of men; they have a new weapon: a lethal virus. Methos arranges a meeting with MacLeod, warning Mac of Kronos' plan. Mac wants to know why Methos didn't tell him. "What I've done, you can't forgive. It's not in your nature." Meanwhile, Kronos takes the opportunity to kidnap Cassandra. Was

Methos really trying to warn Mac, or was it a diversion so Kronos could get to Cassandra? Caspian and Silas are sent to kill MacLeod, but Mac takes Caspian's head and escapes Silas. Mac then tracks the Horsemen to their lair in an abandoned submarine base. Cassandra is imprisoned, but alive. While Kronos goes to battle MacLeod, he tells Methos to instruct Silas to kill Cassandra. Instead, Methos joins the battle, challenging Silas. As Mac takes Kronos' head, Methos takes Silas'. After the double Quickening, Cassandra wants to take Methos' head, but Mac stops her.

#96513 **The Ransom of Richard Redstone**
Writer: David Tynan
Director: Gerard Hameline
Sonia Codhant as Marina LeMartin; Tom Russell as Edward Cervain; Gary Hetherington as Carlo Capodimonte; Frank Middlemass as Baron LeMartin; Astrid Veillon as Desiree; Sylvain Rougerie as James Foulard; Matthew Thompson as James; George Gay as Parking Attendant

France, 1978. Mac and his girlfriend, Desiree, win big at Baron LeMartin's casino. However, they are robbed before they can enjoy the fruits of their winnings. In the present, Richard Redstone, aka Richie Ryan, is wearing a rented tux, driving a "borrowed" Ferrari, and is playing at the high-stakes tables at the casino, now owned by Carlo Capodimonte. Richie flirts with the beautiful Marina LeMartin, but soon finds himself under the influence of a horse tranquilizer and awakens in a strange bed, tied to the bedposts. No, it's not what you think. The Château LeMartin has been in Marina's family for generations, but now Carlo is threatening to foreclose on an old loan and take the Château. Marina has kidnapped Richie, thinking he is a rich American. Richie, who has fallen for Marina, asks Mac for help in saving the Château. Mac realizes that Carlo is the man who robbed him in 1978. Mac and Richie confront Carlo, and Carlo "kills" Mac. Richie then blackmails Carlo into returning the Château to LeMartin. In the end, Mac discovers an old cache of expensive wines in the cellar. The LeMartins will have no more money problems.

#96514 **Duende**
Writer: Jan Hartman
Director: Richard Martin
Anthony De Longis as Otavio Consone;

Carmen DuSautoy as Anna Hidalgo; Deborah Epstein as Luisa Hidalgo; Dolores Chaplin as Theresa del Gloria; Claudie Arif as Duenna; Marie Vernalde as Young Anna; Arturo Venegas as Don Diego del Gloria; Monique Messine as Housekeeper; Felipe Calvarro as Rafael; Elisa Tonati as Gilda; Elsa Franco as Isabella

Madrid, Spain; 1851. Immortal Otavio Consone is a master of the sword. While he and Mac are friends in the art of the sword, they become rivals in the art of love. They both vie for the hand of the beautiful Theresa, but her father chooses the aristocratic Consone as the better match. Consone and Mac fight a duel, and Consone bests MacLeod, but Theresa intervenes and agrees to marry Consone if he will spare MacLeod. Mac objects, but Consone agrees. Mac leaves. In Madrid, in 1853, Mac returns to Theresa and discovers that Consone has killed her. In the present, Mac finds that he must protect Anna Hidalgo and her daughter, Luisa, from Consone. Twenty-five years earlier, master flamenco dancer Anna had refused to marry Consone. In response he killed her lover. Later, he ran her down, permanently disabling her. Now Luisa is the dancer, but Consone has seduced and married her, much to Anna's horror. It is up to Mac to force Luisa to hear the truth about her new husband. Once she does, she leaves Consone. Consone and Mac do battle in the Magic Circle, and Mac takes Consone's head.

#96515 **The Stone of Scone**
Writers: Michael O'Mahony & Sacha Reins
Director: Richard Martin
Elizabeth Gracen as Amanda; Roger Daltrey as Hugh Fitzcairn; Michael Culkin as Bernie Crimmins; David Barrass as Harry; Harry Jones as Andrew; Neville Phillips as Butler; Paul Barrett as Bobby; Colin Reese as Uriah; Barnaby Apps as Patrick; Valerie Ann Wyss as Barmaid

London, 1720. Mac is trying to steal the legendary royal throne of Scotland, the Stone of Scone, from Westminster Abbey for the Scots, at the same time that Fitz is trying to blow up the Abbey and King George, for the Catholics. Fitz and Mac debate who has the more valid case and finally decide to fight a duel on the field of honor, a golf course, to see whose plan they will attempt together. Unknown to Mac, Fitz cheats. In 1950, Mac finally discovers Fitz's chicanery. Amanda, believing the Stone to be a priceless gem, convinces Mac to try once again to steal the Stone. She wants to fence the Stone and pay off her gambling debts. Fitz wants to make up for his past deceit to MacLeod, and Mac wants the Stone returned to the Scots. The trio breaks into the Abbey on Christmas and successfully steals the Stone. Amanda is more than a little distressed to discover that they've stolen a hunk of worthless rock. Amanda is arrested by Scotland Yard for treason and makes a deal, turning over Fitz. Fitz is arrested. Mac manages to finagle a pardon from Sir Winston Churchill, and returns a stone to the Abbey. In the end, Mac, Amanda, and Fitz return to the golf course, and we see that Mac has, indeed, returned the Stone to the Scots . . . at the Royal Highlands Golf Club.

#96516 **Forgive Us Our Trespasses**
Writer: Dom Tordjmann
Director: Paolo Barzman
Elizabeth Gracen as Amanda; Peter Wingfield as Methos; Chris Larkin as Steven Keane; Michael J. Jackson as Sean Burns; Barbara Keogh as Grandmother; Geoffrey Bateman as Richard Dunbar; Marine Jolivet as Inspector Begue

England, 1746. After the battle of Culloden, MacLeod goes on a killing spree against the English. Among his victims is Richard Dunbar, the Earl of Rosemont, the English officer who ordered the destruction of the Scots. Mac kills the earl in front of his own son and the Immortal Steven Keane. Keane vows revenge and hunts for MacLeod, but he is stopped by their mutual friend, Sean Burns. Sean convinces Keane that MacLeod is a good man and that it was a time of war and madness. In the present, Keane is back. Keane knows that MacLeod killed not only the earl, but also Sean Burns (**"Deliverance"**). Now Keane wants justice. How can MacLeod explain the murder of an old friend with talk of an evil Quickening? Amanda urges Mac to take Keane's head and be done with it. Mac will not. Amanda goes to Methos for help; she knows that MacLeod's heart is not in the battle, and she fears he will be killed. Methos and Amanda both try a variety of ways to stop a confrontation, but despite his friends' best efforts Mac finally faces Keane and wins the battle in what he considers a trial by combat. But Mac allows Keane to walk away.

#96517 **The Modern Prometheus**
Writer: James Thorpe
Director: Adrian Paul

Peter Wingfield as Methos; Jonathan Firth as Lord Byron; Jeffrey Ribier as Mike Paladini; Tracy Keating as Mary Shelley; Michel Modo as Maurice; Katie Carr as Claire Clairmont; Christopher Staines as Percy Shelley; F. Braun McAsh as Hans Kershner; Don Foran as Jerry

1816. Doctor Adams aka Methos is part of Romantic poet Lord Byron's decadent circle of friends. They rely on laudanum and morphine to inspire them. One night, as they tell ghost stories, a cuckolded husband, Hans, challenges Byron. Methos and Mary Shelley witness Byron's first Quickening. When Byron is "killed" by Hans' sword and then "revived" by the lightning, Methos explains to Mary that both he and Byron are Immortal. Thus inspired, Mary, of whom Methos is enamored, writes *Frankenstein; or The*

Modern Prometheus. In the present, Byron is a rock star, but he has grown weary of his Immortal life and his muse has fled him. He lives a debauched and destructive life, filled with alcohol and drugs. The only way he can "create" new poetry and music is to steal it from others. Byron lures Mike Paladini, a promising young blues guitarist and friend of Joe's, into his dark lifestyle. Mike is not strong enough to match the Immortal Byron, and he overdoses. Blaming Byron for Mike's death, Mac decides to take Byron's head. Methos tries to get Byron to leave town; Byron refuses. Methos tries to stop Mac, lamenting the loss of Byron's music and poetry to future generations. Mac will not be swayed; he believes the cost is not worth the price; he takes Byron's head. In the end, Mac and Methos share a drink, while Joe plays the blues.

#96518 **Archangel**
Writer: David Tynan
Director: Dennis Berry
Peter Wingfield as Methos;
Valentine Pelka as Kronos; Edward Jewesbury as Jason Landry; Emily Raymond as Allison Landry; Peter Hudson as James Horton; Reinhild Steger as Medical Officer; Patrick Gordon as Hermit; Richard Temple as Foster; Michel Scourneau as Cemetery Official; Pierre Rousselle as Detective; Bruno Grimaud as Customs Man

Scottish Highlands, 1625. Mac meets a hermit who foretells Connor MacLeod's arrival and Duncan's destiny. The hermit explains that at the start of the current millennium he had defeated a great evil that comes into the world every thousand years. He prophesies that Mac will be the Champion for the next millennium. He then takes his own head with Mac's sword, so that Mac will receive his first Quickening and grow strong to defeat the evil. In the present, Mac and Richie are accosted by archaeologist Jason Landry, who is raving about the millennium. Before they are able to learn more, Mac spots his old dead nemesis James Horton. Mac goes after Horton, and Richie follows. When they return, they find Landry dead, strangled. Mac refuses to believe that Horton is dead and accuses Joe of hiding something. More dead people appear to Mac. This time it's Kronos. Methos arrives and gets more than a little worried when Mac tells him that he's seen Kronos. According to his granddaughter, Alli-son, Landry was obsessed with the Zoroastrian demon, Ahriman, and a cycle of evil that comes to the earth every one thousand years. Landry believed that the next Immortal Champion is MacLeod. Allison is killed in a mysterious fire, and the police believe that Mac set it. Methos and Joe try to talk to Mac and offer help. Richie, meanwhile, spots Horton holding a gun to Joe. He calls Mac to tell him what's going on, but the real Joe is standing in the barge with Mac. Not listening to Mac, Richie goes to "Joe"'s rescue. Mac goes to help Richie, but neither understands who or what he is facing. Ahriman confronts Mac in the form of Horton, Kronos, and Richie, individually and separately. As Mac fights for his life against these multiple incarnations of evil, he takes the demon's head, but then he realizes it's a trick. He has, in fact, killed his student and friend, Richie.

Season 6

"He is Duncan MacLeod, the Highlander. Born in 1592 in the Highlands of Scotland, he is still alive. He is Immortal. For four hundred years he's been a warrior, a lover, a wanderer, constantly facing other Immortals in combat to the death. The winner takes his enemy's head and with it, his power.

"I am a Watcher, part of a secret society of men and women who observe and record, but never interfere. We know the truth about Immortals. In the end, there can be only one. May it be Duncan MacLeod. The Highlander."

Adrian Paul as Duncan MacLeod; Elizabeth Gracen as Amanda; Peter Wingfield as Methos; Jim Byrnes as Joe Dawson

#97601 **Avatar**

Writer: David Tynan
Director: Dennis Berry
Peter Hudson as Ahriman/Horton;
Rachel Shelley as Sophie Baines;
Danny Dyer as Andrew Baines; Odile
Cohen as Anna Tremaine; Fethi
Zouaoui as Flower Vendor; Leonard
Guillain as Mover; Nathalie Gray as
Morgue Attendant

A year has passed since MacLeod took
Richie's head. He has been in seclusion
in Kampak Monastery, mourning
Richie and readying himself for battle.
Mac returns to Paris and finds Joe at
the cemetery where he has buried
Richie. Mac reminds Joe of the Zoroastrian legend of a thousand-year cycle of
evil and that he, MacLeod, is the

Avatar, a champion sent to fight the
evil. Mac asks Joe and the Watchers for
help in his battle. Joe agrees. Mac,
meanwhile, rescues Sophie Baines from
drowning in the Seine. Or does he?
Sophie is the late Jason Landry's assistant. And as Mac and Sophie finally
discover, Sophie is no longer truly
among the land of the living. The
demon continues to visit Mac and
offer temptations; Mac will not be
swayed. Ahriman next tempts Sophie.
If she kills MacLeod, Ahriman will give
her back her life and spare her brother,
Andrew. Sophie tells Mac what Ahriman wants, but she cannot kill Mac;
she realizes he is the champion. She
warns him that each champion must
find his own way to defeat the evil.
When her brother, Andrew, tries to kill
Mac, she knows what she must do; she
returns to her watery grave in the river.
Mac and Joe continue to investigate
how to defeat Ahriman.

#97602 **Armageddon**

Writer: Tony DiFranco
Director: Richard Martin
Valentine Pelka as Ahriman/Kronos;
Peter Hudson as Ahriman/Horton;
Dudley Sutton as Father Robert
Beaufort; Terence Beesley as Jackie
Beaufort; Jean-Yves Thual as Ahriman

Mac goes to his old friend Father Robert
Beaufort for help and finds him mourning the loss of his brother, Jackie, who
has committed suicide. Ahriman/Hor-
ton goes to see Joe and tries to get him
to stop helping MacLeod. He tells Joe

that Watchers do not interfere, and if they do, they die. Four Watchers are killed, and Joe blames himself. He stops having the Watchers help, but Joe will not desert MacLeod. Ahriman again visits Joe and asks him to abandon Mac; he tempts Joe with the restoration of his legs. Joe will not fail Mac. Ahriman/Kronos tempts Robert to doubt his church and his faith, and to commit suicide, but Mac saves Robert. Mac finds clues to the destruction of Ahriman from an ancient German mystic, cave paintings, and a Tibetan singing bowl. Mac finally realizes that the more he hates the demon, the more he is lost. The true answer to the destruction of evil is peace. Mac finally defeats the demon by rejecting all provocation to violence. As Joe explains, "You have avenged Richie's death. Mac, you have defeated Ahriman. You are still Duncan MacLeod of the Clan MacLeod."

#97603 **Sins of the Father**

Writer: James Thorpe
Director: Dennis Berry
Dara Tomanovich as Alex Raven; Charles Daish as Grant Thomas; John Scarborough as George Thomas; Joe Scarby as Gerard LeBlanc; Ian Richardson as Max Leiner; Aaron Swartz as David Leiner; Dean Cook as Young Max Leiner; Jay Simon as Cameron

After Mac plays bocci with his old friend George Thomas, they go to their cars, where Mac senses another Immortal. George's car blows up. Mac asks George's grandson, Grant, who could have done this. Grant says he has no idea. Mac encounters Immortal Alex Raven; he believes that she has something to do with George's death. Mac finally learns the truth when he meets Max Leiner. In 1942, in the Warsaw

Ghetto, Nazis killed Max's father, David, and left Alex for dead. Alex vowed to protect the young boy and has done so to the present day. Max and Alex are trying to restore millions of dollars stolen from the Jews by the Nazis and funneled into foreign banks. The truth is finally revealed when Grant tries to kill Mac and Alex. Grant confesses to murdering his grandfather because George was going to give back the money. Grant tries to kill Max, but Mac and Alex arrive, and Grant accidentally falls to his death. In the end, Mac and Alex find George's confession, and Max is grateful that the blood money will finally be returned.

#97604 **Diplomatic Immunity**
Writer: James Thorpe
Director: Richard Martin
Jasper Britton as Willie Kingsley; Anita Dobson as Molly Kingsley; Ed Bishop as Edward Banner; Alexis Denisof as Steve Banner; Paula Jane Ulrich as Young Molly Ivers; Paul Bandey as Swinson; Malcolm Rennie as Smythe; Edward Hamilton-Clarke as U.S. Investigative Service Guard; Martin Jaubert as Butler

London, 1836. Mac witnesses a duel between Immortal Willie Kingsley and his former partner Smythe. Much to his own joy, Willie is shot. It was all part of a plan. Willie had embezzled £100,000. Now "dead," he could head for the Americas with his money and his freedom. In the present, Mac encounters Willie and his mortal love,

Molly. Willie is up to his old tricks; he gets hit by a car, Molly loudly mourns over her "dead" husband, and the frantic drivers write her a check rather than face the authorities. However, they try the scam one too many times, and as Willie lies "dead," a driver kills Molly. Willie asks Mac for help; he got a partial license plate number. It seems the car belongs to the American Embassy. Mac goes to his old friend Edward Banner for help; it's his car. Willie believes Edward is the killer and assassinates him. As it turns out, the driver and real murderer is Edward's son, Steve. Steve is an addict and had gone out looking for drugs. Willie vows to kill Steve, and Mac vows to stop him. Willie and Mac battle and Mac wins, but gives Willie his life only as long as Steve lives.

#97605 **Patient Number 7**
Writer: David Tynan
Director: Dennis Berry
Alice Evans as Kyra; Michael Halsey as Milos Vladic; Mark Leadbetter as Gaston; Donald Standen as Richard Albright; Steve Lyon as Zep; Stephane Petit as Lazlo; Emile Ambossolo M'bo as Jocko; Nabil Massad as Vendor; Antonia Corrigan as Little Girl; Michael Morris as Businessman; Robert Bradford as Hospital Guard

France, 1640. Mac meets the Immortal Kyra when as Queen Anne's protector, she battles some of Cardinal Richelieu's guards. Mac and Kyra end up sharing a room, a bed, and a heated discussion on the merits of a Scotsman's weapon. In the present, Mac meets his old friend Kyra on the streets of Paris, but she runs away. Mac follows, and it becomes clear that Kyra has no memory of who or what she is. When the police arrive, Mac and Kyra flee. Kyra remembers only snippets of her immediate past when she was patient number seven in the psychiatric ward and two men armed with guns came after her. Mac tells her who she really is, and they try to discover what she cannot remember and why. Meanwhile, Immortal General Milos Vladic and his men are out to kill her. Kyra ultimately remembers what happened: Vladic was a general who committed genocide and was put on international trial, but the chief judge, Richard Albright, was murdered by Vladic. Kyra was Richard's bodyguard and his lover. Her memory restored, Kyra takes Vladic's head and avenges Richard's death.

#97606 **Black Tower**
Writer: Morrie Ruvinsky
Director: Richard Martin
Andrew Bicknell as Devon Marek; Rochelle Redfield as Margo; Alexi K. Campbell as Dice; Luke D'Silva as Abel Montoya; Julius D'Silva as Ruben Montoya; Adam Henderson as William Robert Shemp; Alain Creff aka G.Z.U. as Benoit

Scotland, 1634. Mac meets Devon Marek, son of a duke, as he lies fatally wounded. Marek "dies" and is reborn Immortal. However, the gentleman

Marek is not interested in learning anything from the "lowly" MacLeod and is furious at losing his dukedom. In the present, Mac and the lovely Margo begin what looks like a beautiful evening, but Margo is kidnapped and Mac must save her. Mac follows the bait to a toy company and finds Marek, who has hired four bounty hunters to kill Mac. The game proposed? Mac must save Margo and defeat the bounty hunters. And it is a game, at least to computer whiz Dice. Marek has led him to believe that what is all too real to MacLeod is a live-action simulation of a virtual reality game. Dice finally realizes it's not a game when Marek kills a policeman. Mac defeats the bounty hunters and rescues the girl, but then discovers that Margo is part of the plan. She shoots Mac, but Marek

shoots her. Finally, with a little help from Dice, Mac and Marek meet, and Mac takes his enemy's head.

#97607 **Unusual Suspects**
Writer: Morrie Ruvinsky
Director: Dennis Berry
Roger Daltrey as Hugh Fitzcairn; Cleo Rocos as Juliette Fitzcairn; Hugh Simon as Tynebridge; Nicholas Clay as Loxley; Malcolm Rennie as Drimble; Claire Keim as Marie; Christophe Guybet as Pierre

England, October 1929. Mac arrives at Fitzcairn Manor, North Tidworth, to attend Fitz's funeral. As he stands with the mourners, he realizes that the dearly departed is hiding in the greenhouse, witnessing his own funeral. Fitz tells Mac that he "died" of a heart attack, but Immortals don't die of heart attacks, unless, of course, they're induced. Yes, it's clear; Fitz was murdered, and bad timing, too. The now rich Fitz had everything he owned funneled into American stocks for his return-from-the-dead fund, but he's a bit behind in his paperwork, so he's got no new name to inherit the money; he's broke. Fitz asks Mac a favor: find the killer and protect his grieving widow, Juliette, from the murderer. Mac and Fitz hatch a plan. The plot thickens, and there are more murders. It is finally revealed that the widow Fitzcairn is the killer. The police cart off Juliette. But it's not all a happy ending; the stock market has crashed, and Fitz is bankrupt.

#97608 **Justice**
Writers: Michael O'Mahony & Sacha Reins
Director: Richard Martin
Justina Vail as Katya; Grant Russell as Armando Baptista; Diane Bellego as Elena Moreno; Mathew Radford as William of Godfrey; Godfrey James as Frederick of Godfrey; Rita Ghosn as Mia Baptista; Tobias Raineri as Ramon Castillo; Bernard Chabin as Jose; Franck Boclet as P.I.

Mac meets mortal fencing master Armando Baptista and soon discovers that the Immortal Katya is trying to kill Baptista. Mac intervenes, saves Armando from Katya's arrow, and warns him. Mac and Katya battle, and Mac finally hears her story. Baptista killed Katya's adopted daughter, Elena, but as a man of influence, he was not convicted. Mac asks Baptista what happened. Baptista explains that he and Elena had been married for ten years when he discovered that she had been having an affair with his young protégé, Ramon. Baptista returned home to find them in bed and, in a jealous rage, shot them. In the end, Katya challenges Armando, but as she has the sword to his throat, Elena's daughter, Katya's "granddaughter," Mia, enters. Katya realizes that Mia loves her father. Katya walks away.

#97609 **Deadly Exposure**
Writer: James Thorpe
Director: Dennis Berry
Sandra Hess as Reagan Cole; Bob Cryer as Brian Murphy; Christian

Erickson as Jack Kendall; Dave Hill as Rowan Mitchell; Sam Douglas as Baxter; Brian Protheroe as Bannock; Bogdan Marian-Stanoevitch as Sears; Gunilla Karlzen as Celine; Michel Albertini as Raphael Vega; Doug Rand as Comic; Valerie Anne Wyss as Journalist

London, 1833. MacLeod meets Immortal bounty hunter Reagan Cole when she first catches him, then frees him when she realizes his "crime" was dallying with a duke's wife. In the present, Reagan decides to take a vacation in Paris after her most recent captive is killed. While at a sidewalk café, she witnesses the murder of a journalist who is taking pictures of underwear model Brian Murphy. Reagan ends up rescuing Murphy from thugs, and the two are soon embroiled with the police and Interpol. Reagan goes to her old friend MacLeod for help. They discover that there are pictures of assassin/terrorist Jack Kendall on the murdered journalist's film. Reagan deduces that the terrorist is in Paris to stop a summit on European unity. Murphy is murdered. Reagan coerces Interpol into working with her; she knows what Kendall looks like. At the summit, she discovers a bomb, which is safely removed. She then discovers Kendall, but he is wired with explosives. She puts a bullet through his brain and saves the day. In the end, Reagan and MacLeod renew their acquaintance.

#97610 **Two of Hearts**
Writer: James Thorpe
Director: Richard Martin

Claudia Christian as Katherine; Steven O'Shea as Nick; Jack Ellis as Bartholomew; Patrick Rameau as Bertrand; Olivier Picasso as Checco; Mark Sarne as Baron; Boris Anderssen as Mr. Faith; Veronique Baylaucq as Secretary; Rowena Cooper as Berta Symes; Norman Chancer as Caruso

Northern England, 1270. Immortal Katherine is a healer when Immortal Bartholomew arrives in her village, asking for people to follow him on a crusade to Jerusalem. When Katherine questions his levying of a baronial tithe, she challenges him, but she is shot in the back before the battle is done. While Katherine is lying "dead" in a mass grave, Bartholomew advises that an example be made of her village. All are killed. In the present, Katherine finally finds Bartholomew in Paris, still lining

his pockets with money gathered in the name of one of his so-called holy missions. She again challenges him, and he again calls on mortal and armed backup. Katherine's mortal love, Nick, rescues her, and they devise a plan to find proof of Bartholomew's evildoing so that the money can go to the orphans for whom it was intended. In the end, Katherine and Bartholomew have a fair fight, one-on-one, with swords, and she takes her enemy's head.

#97611 **Indiscretions**

Writer: James Thorpe
Director: Dennis Berry
Louise Taylor as Amy; Benedick Blythe as Morgan Walker; Paulette Williams as Charlotte; David Saracino as Beck; Kenan Raven as Stein; Paris Jefferson as Toni; Deborah Steele as Marisa; Marc Andreoni as Sailor

New Orleans, 1808. Methos in his guise as Doctor Benjamin Adams becomes lover to Charlotte. Unfortunately for them, Immortal Captain Morgan Walker, Charlotte's "owner," makes an unexpected and early return. Methos escapes, but Morgan realizes there was another Immortal in his bed; Morgan kills Charlotte. Morgan then challenges Methos, who will not fight. In the present, Watcher Amy has a rough first assignment; she's watching Morgan and witnesses not only Morgan tricking women into slavery, but also a murder. When she questions Joe about how a Watcher tenth in her class, straight out of the Academy, gets a

plum field assignment, the truth comes out: Joe is Amy's biological father. Meanwhile, Methos is back in town and checking the Watcher Chronicles. He's looking for Walker because he's just had a run-in with him and wants to avoid another. Meanwhile, Amy is captured by Walker, and Joe goes to Methos for help. Walker's thugs attack Joe and Methos; the duo goes on the run. Joe finally tells Methos the truth about Amy. Walker calls Joe and proposes a trade: Methos for Amy. They all meet at an abandoned power station, where Walker releases Amy. Methos and Walker battle, and Methos wins. "Just because I don't like to fight doesn't mean that I can't." In the end, Amy leaves town.

#97612 **To Be**

Writer: David Tynan
Director: Richard Martin
Roger Daltrey as Hugh Fitzcairn; Martin McDougall as Liam O'Rourke; Peter Hudson as James Horton; Thierry Langerak as Allan; Alexandre Zambeaux as Terry Rafferty; Kathleen McGoldrick as Tara; Olivier Vitran as Tom

London, 1946. Irish terrorists Immortal Liam O'Rourke and his mortal lover, Tara, plant a bomb in a pub that kills innocents. Mac stops them from escaping, and they are arrested, convicted, and sentenced to life. O'Rourke stays in jail until Tara dies. In the present, Amanda stops by to visit MacLeod on her way to Cairo, but her plans quickly change when O'Rourke kidnaps her. Joe is the next victim, and Mac soon realizes that the Irishman has both Joe and Amanda. Mac vows that he will not let anyone else he cares about die because of him. Mac finds O'Rourke and bests him, but O'Rourke tells Mac that he will have both Amanda and Joe killed if Mac does not willingly surrender. Mac agrees—his life for theirs. However, Methos has a plan and arrives in a blaze of gunfire. O'Rourke guns down Mac. He awakens to find Fitz, but Fitz was killed by Kalas (**"Star-Crossed"**); Mac is confused. Fitz tells Mac that he's an angel and that he's there to help MacLeod. It seemed to everyone upstairs that Mac was about to give up his life. Fitz takes Mac on a tour, to show him a world where there never has been, never will be a Duncan MacLeod. They first visit Amanda. She is a black widow who murders her husbands for their money. Mac tries to stop her from murdering her current husband, but instead Amanda shoots him and is then killed as a group of renegade Watchers attack and take her head. Next stop: Joe Dawson. In this world, Joe is an alcoholic in a wheelchair, playing his guitar on the streets for pocket change. Fitz explains that the Watchers stopped watching and started killing. Joe was outgunned and outnumbered by Horton and the renegade Watchers, so he gave up. While standing near Sacré-Coeur, Mac spots Tessa.

#97613 **Not To Be**

Writer: David Tynan
Director: Dennis Berry

Roger Daltrey as Hugh Fitzcairn; Alexandra Vandernoot as Tessa Noel; Stan Kirsch as Richie Ryan; Valentine Pelka as Kronos; Martin McDougall as Liam O'Rourke; Peter Hudson as James Horton; David Hoskin

as Andres Seguy; Lisa Butler as Jillian O'Hara; Olivier Vitran as Tom; Eva Gord as Customer

Fitz continues to show Mac a world where there has never been a Duncan MacLeod. Here, Mac is overjoyed to see Tessa alive and with two children. Fitz must remind him that this Tessa never met Mac. Mac goes to see her in the gallery where she works and finds that she no longer sculpts. He also discovers that she is married to businessman Andres Seguy. Fitz warns Mac that he is playing with fire, but Duncan cannot stay away from Tessa. They share a night of passion, but this Tessa has only regrets. Mac also learns that in this world, Fitz has been dead for 280 years, some business about blowing up King George going horribly wrong without the interference of a certain lummoxing Scotsman. Next up, Mac meets Methos, but this Methos is wearing black leather and sporting a serious attitude. Fitz and Mac take a jump back in time to 1995. Methos in his Watcher guise of Adam Pierson is in love with fellow Watcher Jillian. In an effort to stop the renegade Watchers and prove to Horton that not all Immortals are abominations, she reveals Methos' true identity to Horton. Horton kills her and shoots Methos, but Kronos arrives and saves Methos. Methos becomes bitter and filled with hate, and the Horsemen ride again. It seems Methos had not

changed enough without Mac's influence. And what of Richie? That's another sad tale. Richie is a petty thief who is shot and killed, but arises as an Immortal without a teacher until Methos finds him. Methos and Kronos teach Richie more than how to use a sword. As a final test, they ask Richie to kill Joe Dawson, the man they consider responsible for the deaths of Silas and Caspian, but Richie cannot kill Joe. Kronos and Methos teach him the last lesson, the reckoning of a weak link. Methos takes Richie's head. Back in the alternate present, Joe has lost the Watchers, and Methos and Kronos have taken him hostage, determined to find Horton. Instead, Methos finds Mac. They fight, and Duncan takes his head. Or does he? Fitz appears and tells Mac that it's time to go home; there are friends who need him. Mac awakens to find Methos; they concoct a plan and rescue Joe and Amanda. Mac battles O'Rourke and takes his head. In the end, the friends share a toast. Mac: "You know, I don't know who or what you are, Methos, and I know you don't want to hear this, but you did teach me something. You taught me that life's about change, about learning to accept who you are, good or bad. And I thank you for that." Joe: "I can't imagine my life without you, Mac. Fact is, I don't want to." Mac to Amanda: "I love you. I do. You make my heart glad. You always have."

Key to Photographs

Highlander Online

The Official *Highlander* Web site:
http://www.highlander-official.com

The Adrian Paul Fan Club Web site:
http://members.aol.com/peaceapfc/
index.html

The Jim Byrnes Fan Club Web site:
http://diversions.simplenet.com/jbfc/

The Peter Wingfield Fan Club Web site:
http://www.lightlink.com/hilinda/pwfc/

The Valentine Pelka Fan Club Web site:
http://www.geocities.com/Hollywood/
Hills/5573/pelka.html

The Anthony De Longis Web site:
http://www.delongis.com/

The Stan Kirsch Web site:
http://www.stankirsch.com

The Gathering: The Official *Highlander*
Fan Club Web site:
http://www.dwarflander.com/fanclub.htm

Roger Bellon and The Music from
Highlander: The Series Web site:
http://www.bellchant.com/

The Rysher *Highlander* Web site:
http://www.rysher.com/highlander/

USA Network *Highlander* Web site:
http://www.usanetwork.com/content/
tv/highlander.html

The Gaumont Web site:
http://www.gaumont.fr

Highlander and *Highlander*-related Fan Clubs

PEACE—The Adrian Paul Fan Club
P.O. Box 4593
North Hollywood, CA 91617

Jim Byrnes Fan Club
2588 El Camino Real D-357
Carlsbad, CA 92008-1290

Peter Wingfield Fan Club
PWFC
P.O. Box 4472
Ithaca, NY 14852-4472

Valentine Pelka Fan Club
VPFC
P.O. Box 16181
Lubbock, TX 79490-6181

Anthony De Longis Fan Club
ADLFC
P.O. Box 323
Burbank, CA 91503-0323

The Gathering
The Official *Highlander* Fan Club
P.O. Box 123
Aurora, CO 80040-0123

Roger Bellon
The Music from *Highlander: The Series*
Bellchant Records
c/o Bellchant Music, Inc.
P.O. Box 46-2030
Los Angeles, CA 90046-2030